DONNY'S
Inferno

Also by P. W. Catanese

The Donny's Inferno Series
Down in Flames

The Books of Umber Trilogy
Happenstance Found
Dragon Games
The End of Time

The Further Tales Adventures Series
The Thief and the Beanstalk
The Brave Apprentice
The Eye of the Warlock
The Mirror's Tale
The Riddle of the Gnome

DONNY'S Inferno

· 1 ·

P. W. CATANESE

ALADDIN

NEW YORK LONDON TORONTO SYDNEY NEW DELHI

ALADDIN

An imprint of Simon & Schuster Children's Publishing Division
1230 Avenue of the Americas, New York, New York 10020
First Aladdin paperback edition April 2017
Text copyright © 2016 by P. W. Catanese
Cover illustration copyright © 2016 by Jeff Nentrup
Also available in an Aladdin hardcover edition.
All rights reserved, including the right of reproduction
in whole or in part in any form.
ALADDIN and related logo are registered trademarks of Simon & Schuster, Inc.
For information about special discounts for bulk purchases,
please contact Simon & Schuster Special Sales at 1-866-506-1949
or business@simonandschuster.com.
The Simon & Schuster Speakers Bureau can bring authors to your live event.
For more information or to book an event contact the Simon & Schuster Speakers
Bureau at 1-866-248-3049 or visit our website at www.simonspeakers.com.
Art direction by Jessica Handelman
Cover designed by Karin Paprocki and Steve Scott
Interior designed by Mike Rosamilia
The text of this book was set in Perpetua.
Manufactured in the United States of America 0317 OFF
2 4 6 8 10 9 7 5 3 1
The Library of Congress has cataloged the hardcover edition as follows:
Catanese, P. W.
Donny's inferno / by P. W. Catanese. — First Aladdin hardcover edition.
pages cm
Summary: In a moment of desperation, Donny Taylor accepts an offer
from a demon who will save his life if he works for her, and soon he finds himself
in Hell but a new, kinder, gentler Hell where not everyone is happy about the
changes and some will do anything to bring back traditional ways.
ISBN 978-1-4814-3800-1 (hc) — ISBN 978-1-4814-3802-5 (eBook)
[1. Hell—Fiction. 2. Future life—Fiction. 3. Demonology—Fiction.
4. Fathers and sons—Fiction.] I. Title.
PZ7.C268783Don 2016
[Fic]—dc23
2015004461
ISBN 978-1-4814-3801-8 (pbk)

FOR LISA.
ONCE AGAIN BUT REALLY ALWAYS.

CHAPTER 1

When it began, there was light. A red flickering light. And a hint of smoke that stung his nose.

Donny coughed and tried to rub the irritation from his eyes. His brain was still half asleep, but he knew there were at least three things wrong. One was the smoke. Another was that strange glow. *Something's on fire,* he thought. The third was somehow worse. When he'd finally fallen asleep the night before, curled up in a corner of the top floor of this abandoned building, all he wanted was to wake up and find out that everything that had happened late yesterday was just a terrible dream. He wanted to open his eyes and see his room and his bed, and laugh about the crazy nightmare.

No such luck. It happened, all right. His life was now a disaster zone.

He sat up, put his chin on top of his knees, and shook his head as he remembered. His father had been speaking to some man who Donny couldn't see. His father didn't know Donny was home, standing just inside the front door. As Donny listened, he thought his dad was joking at first, talking like a gangster from some movie. But after a while the truth had become clear: his father, Benny Taylor, was a criminal. A violent, dangerous one. Somehow he'd hidden that from his son for all these years.

Then things happened so fast. Getting caught eavesdropping. Running with his father at his heels, screaming for him to stop.

It was crazy, picking this place to hide. But that was just the way it had worked out. His first instinct was to race to Kevin's house. But his father was chasing him, and his best friend's house was the first place Donny would be expected to run. So he kept on running, weaving between buildings and across the streets of Brooklyn. He finally managed to outrun his father after he darted through somebody's backyard and hopped a fence. Suddenly the old empty brewery on Franklin Avenue was right in front of him. He knew the place. Kevin had brought him there a few weeks before and showed him how to get inside. *Urban exploration,* Kevin called it. He always wanted to go into abandoned places, boarded-up buildings, the creepier the better. They leaned a wooden palette against the brick wall and used it as a ladder to reach a broken window. The old brewery had been scary that day, with its cavernous first floor and dim, dusty upper stories. But it was scarier now because he had no home to go back to.

It was still dark outside. Donny looked out a broken window. The skyscrapers of New York twinkled in the distance, always beautiful. The reddish light came from outside, reflected from the walls of the building across the street. As he watched, a tongue of flame rose up and licked the windowsill.

"Oh no. Oh no, no, no." He scrambled up and ran to the door that led to the stairs. When he pushed it open, smoke and heat gushed from the stairwell. He backed away, coughing and spitting. A pair of squealing rats shot through the opening and brushed past his legs.

The stupid building has to be seventy years old, and it picks tonight to burn down! Think, he told himself. And then: *Fire escape.* There had to be one, even in a building this old. *Where?* He whirled, staring out every window of the wide-open floor, and finally spotted a rusty black railing. There was a door right beside it. He ran to it, yanked it open, and stepped onto the fire-escape landing. Just four stories to the street and he'd be out of trouble. But before he was down a single flight, fire billowed from the floors below, sifting through the grating and reaching for him. As he retreated from the blistering heat, he shouted for anyone to hear, "Help! I'm up here! Send help!"

The room he'd left had filled with smoke. *Idiot,* he told himself. *Should have closed the door to the stairs.* The only option left was to climb all the way to the roof and look for another way down. The top of the fire escape ended in a wobbly, corroded ladder, bolted to the brick, which took him over the edge of the roof.

Smoke flooded up every side of the building. He ran to each side and searched for any escape route. The drainpipes were long gone, and there was nothing to shinny down. The buildings next door weren't close enough to let him jump. And it was a fatal distance to the ground. There were no options.

He heard a roar somewhere below as the fire gorged on air. Flames lapped over the roof's edge and forced him to back away. *Of all the places to hide,* he thought. A sensation he'd never known came to him: the certainty that he had only moments to live. He put his hands around his mouth and shouted again, "Help!"

Suddenly he heard a voice close behind him. "Well. Someone sounds nervous."

He spun around. A girl—or a woman?—was standing on the roof. She looked like a little of both. It was hard to tell, as the sting of smoke forced him to squeeze his eyes almost shut. She stood there, a slim figure, her arms folded and, insanely enough, a sly grin on her pale pretty face.

"We have to get out of here!" he shouted. It was a mistake to talk—the smoke sandpapered his throat, and he

4

started to cough. He pulled the front of his hoodie over his mouth.

"We certainly do," she said. "Lucky for you, I'm willing to take you with me. As long as you'll make me a promise."

"A promise?" he said through the sweatshirt. *Great,* he thought. *Now there's a fire and a crazy person.*

She stepped closer. "That's right. But it's a significant promise. You should think it over, but don't take too long." She stomped the roof with the heel of one of her boots. "This'll burn through any second now." As if she had prompted it, part of the roof nearby sagged and collapsed, and flames shot through the gap from the howling inferno below.

"I promise!" Donny shouted. His eyes were closed for good now—the smoke was too intense.

She seized him by the collar and drew his ear to her mouth. If she was afraid of the fire that was about to take the whole building down, there was no hint of it in her voice. "You don't even know what I'm asking yet. Here it is: You work for me. And you do what I ask. For as long as I want. Promise me that, and I'll save your life."

"But" was all Donny could say, and then he just went on coughing. The heat came closer. He felt it on his skin, and even through his jeans.

"Oh, don't worry. I won't make you do anything illegal. For the most part. And I don't see what choice you have, honestly," she said.

He heard sirens growing louder. When he forced his eyes open for a moment, he saw bright pulsing lights in the smoke. The fire trucks, finally. But it was too late for him. More of the roof caved in, dangerously close.

"Shake my hand," she said. "That will do."

A powerful blast of hot air struck him like a wave of boiling water. He fell to his knees and put his elbows across his head. Pain was everywhere. He could feel it coming: his hair about to burst into flames, his skin about to fry.

"I can't tell if you're demented or stubborn!" he heard her shout over the din of the fire. "I mean, you have seconds to live at this point, and it's not a pretty way to go. I'm leaving now. Are you joining me? I'll even accept a thumbs-up."

Donny felt his mind going dim. *No air,* he thought. The roof under his knees groaned and tilted, pitching him sideways. He thrust a hand out, and another hand was there in an instant, gripping his. Powerful arms lifted him easily. *Someone else is here,* he thought. It couldn't be her—she couldn't be so strong. He heard her voice again, whispering something he could not understand in some bizarre tongue. The fire built to a crescendo of heat, light, and howling wind, and then it was gone, switched off like a radio. Heels clacked on a hard surface, and then the strong arms set him down on a cool smooth floor.

CHAPTER 2

You know something?" the girl asked. "That was a terrible time to be indecisive. I'll never get the smell of smoke out of these clothes."

Donny tried to respond, but it only triggered another coughing fit. He curled sideways on the stone floor with his arms across his stomach. His eyes and lungs still burned. He blinked and tried to focus, but saw everything through a blur of tears. All he knew was that they'd ended up in a corridor, away from the smoke. Only one other person was with him: the girl.

She kneeled beside him. "Jeepers. You're all singed," she said. He could smell it: the stench of burnt hair. His nose wrinkled.

It took a few minutes, but he was finally able to breathe deep without coughing. "How did we get here?" he asked quietly. "Is this the basement?"

She laughed. "Not the basement." Her hand gripped his arm, helping him sit up. "Can you see a little better now?"

He blinked some more, then rubbed his eyes and looked again. The corridor came into focus at last. He saw smooth rock walls all around and an arched doorway ahead. Behind them, the corridor curved out of sight, but he saw a shimmering orange light on the walls cast by flames around the bend. "Wait. What . . . There was a tunnel under the building?"

"Noooo," she said, sounding a little impatient. Donny could see her better now. She was definitely pretty. Striking was more like it. There was something sly about her features. She had dark eyes, not quite black and maybe even purple, framed by lively eyebrows that angled wickedly down. Her hair was long, straight, and midnight black.

She offered her hand. "Angela Obscura."

What a name, Donny thought. He shook her hand. The flesh of her palm was feverishly warm. "Donny Taylor," he told her, adding another hacking cough at the end.

"Pleased to meet you, Donny Taylor."

Donny took another look around at the floor and roof and walls of solid rock, the fiery glow behind and the arch ahead. "I don't get it. Where are we? We must be under the brewery. But we were on the roof. How did we get down here so fast?"

Angela pursed her lips and tapped her cheek with

one finger. The other hand, Donny noticed, was clad in a tight red leather glove. Around that wrist she wore a thick timeworn gold band that looked like an artifact from a museum. "How do I break this to you gently?" she mused, almost to herself. "Let's start with this. Donny, you are nowhere near that old building, which I imagine is a steaming pile of rubble with a load of hunky firemen standing around it right now."

Donny frowned at her. "Nowhere near?"

Angela shook her head. "Far, far away."

Donny's frown turned into a glare. He had woken not long ago with his life in ruins, and then been scared half to death. Now on top of that, this weird girl was messing with his head.

"Don't give me that look," she said. She tugged at the bottom of her glove. It seemed like a habitual gesture. "Let me give you a hint."

Any other time, Donny would have been polite. But his nerves were shot, and that made it easy to be blunt. "I don't want a hint. Just tell me."

"Trust me, this news is best received in small digestible portions. You are nowhere near that old building. In fact, you are nowhere near Brooklyn. How far, I can't even tell you. We got here through a passage that was opened in the fire, because . . . well, because that's how I get around."

Donny let out a laugh, which turned into another cough that took a minute to rein in. "Oh yeah. Of course," he finally said. "We came through a magic passage."

"Was that sarcasm?" she asked, one elastic eyebrow arched high. "I *love* sarcasm. Good coping skill. Now, here's the next thing you should know: on the other side of that door is a place you have certainly heard of, but you weren't sure it was real. A place where sane people hope they never have to go."

Donny stood and brushed a fine layer of dark ashes off his shoulder. "This is getting creepy."

"You're getting warmer."

"What the heck are you talking about?"

"Exactly."

Donny opened his mouth to speak but suddenly couldn't find any words. Angela stared at him, nodding. "Take a good look at that door," she said, pointing over her shoulder.

He swallowed hard, ignoring the pain in his throat. He stepped closer to the door. The scarred, knobby, blackened wood looked almost petrified. *How old is this?* he wondered. Words were chiseled deep into the stone above the door, in a language he did not understand. HIC · INEST · INFERNUS. *Latin maybe?* There was no chance he could figure out the phrase, but that last word: INFERNUS. That was familiar somehow, and he knew words like it. Infernal. *Inferno.* He took a sudden sharp breath, and it stuck in his nose. It brought a smell with it. It wasn't just the burnt odor of his own hair—there was something new mingled in. A faint whiff of rotten egg. He leaned closer, and the smell was stronger, as if it had leaked through the cracks of the door.

Donny knew that smell.

Sulfur.

And suddenly he was aware of how warm everything felt, even the stone under his feet.

"You look a little pale," Angela said. She leaned closer. "Have you guessed?"

His voice fell to a whisper. "It can't be that place. It can't be."

"It is, though, Donny. This is the way into the Underworld. It's had lots of other names, though. Infernum. Hades. Hell. Gehenna. Baratrum. The Abyss. The Land of Everlasting Torment. The All-Inclusive Resort for the Terribly Naughty. These days, we like to call it *Sulfur*."

Her hand rested on his shoulder and steadied him, because he was wobbling. "I know what you're feeling," she said. "You're confused. You're sick with fear. But I bet you're curious, too. Are you ready to see what's on the other side of that door?"

Donny put a hand on his chest and felt it heaving under his palm. "I . . . I . . ."

"Oh, come on," she said, grabbing his wrist with her gloved hand. "You don't have a choice anyway. I can't leave you here. And I'm not taking you back. Let's face it: you didn't look like a boy who had someplace better to be, up on that roof. But you can tell me that story later. Now, before we go in—" She turned his wrist so his palm faced up, and pressed her other fist inside. She had a ring on that hand that he hadn't noticed, with a black insignia inlaid in gold. Donny felt the ring push into his flesh, and then a moment of tingly pain. He yanked his hand away and stared at his palm. The ring had left an impression of whitened flesh on his skin.

"What was *that*?" he asked, rubbing the spot with the thumb of his other hand. He thought he could massage the color back into it, but nothing changed: a symbol, an ornate fancy letter *O* with curling wings on either side, seemed to be there for good. "Did you just brand me?"

"Sorry, had to mark you as one of mine," she said. "You wouldn't last long without it. We have rules about unauthorized mortals wandering around. Actually, one rule: kill on sight. Now, enough with the preamble." She walked to the door. There was an enormous brass knocker mounted in the center, and she slammed it into the iron band below with three resounding clangs.

Donny held his breath for a moment and watched the dark door. Moments passed with only the sound of Angela's toe impatiently tapping the stone floor. A little rectangle of metal near the top of the door slid open and created a peephole. "It's me," Angela said. "Would you kindly let us in?"

Whoever was on the other side slammed the peephole shut. Then there came another noise as heavy things ground together. The door swung inward. Donny craned his neck to look through. A tall burly figure stood in the doorway, clad from head to toe in dented armor. If someone hadn't just opened the door, Donny would have thought it was simply an oversize, oddly shaped suit of armor standing on display.

Beyond the threshold was another, much shorter, tunnel. The opening at the far end was a rectangle with a rounded top. *Like a tombstone,* Donny thought with a shudder. The space beyond was orange-lit and, he was certain, immense. Angela stepped up beside him and slipped her arm inside his. "Come on, I'll prop you up. It can make you dizzy the first time you lay eyes on it. I promise you, it's not what you expect."

Donny gulped. What did he expect? Flames and creatures with pointy horns and pitchforks, he supposed. His joints felt weak, and tremors ran through his arms and legs. He might not have moved if Angela hadn't tugged him along.

Donny stared as they approached the armored figure. It was easily eight feet tall, and strangely proportioned with long arms and a grotesquely thick chest. It was so still and silent that Donny nearly shrieked when a cheery high-pitched voice rang out from within the helmet. "Lovely to see you, Angela."

"And you, darling," she replied. She stopped and smiled up at the hulking figure.

"Who's your little friend?"

"Oh, just someone I bumped into topside." She stared up, still grinning, and rocked on her heels. A long, strange, silent moment passed, and then finally she giggled and opened her red bag. "You thought I'd forgotten it, didn't you?" She pulled out an extra-large pack of beef jerky, ripped the plastic wrap off, and held it up. The armored thing squealed with delight and lifted its visor. A long pale tongue shot out, stuck to the jerky, yanked it from Angela's hand, and pulled it back in. Donny clapped a hand over his own mouth to stifle a shriek.

"Enjoy," Angela said, and she tugged Donny along.

"Mmm-hmmm," said the armored thing, waving a metal glove and then slamming the door shut.

"Grunyon loves the jerky," Angela said brightly.

Donny's brain felt like it was rattling loose inside his skull. *This must be what it's like to go crazy,* he thought. If Angela were to let go of his arm, he would simply fall over. The tombstone frame grew bigger with every step forward, and when he finally passed through the opening, Sulfur came into view.

CHAPTER 3

He rubbed his eyes with the heel of his hand and then opened them again. What difference that would make, he wasn't sure. Maybe the landscape would reorganize itself into something less surreal. But no. There it was again.

They had stepped through a wall of rock, onto the landing of a tall staircase. From there Donny had a view of an astonishing subterranean world. This was a cavern that dwarfed the grandest on earth and reached as far as he could see. Overhead arched a soaring ceiling that dripped with immense daggers of stone.

His mind fired questions and sought the answers. *How can the roof possibly stay up?* Then he saw the many natural columns of stone, each thicker than a dozen skyscrapers, that rose thousands of feet and melded with the rock above. *Where is the light coming from?* He looked up and saw billowing orange clouds floating under the roof, pierced by the giant points of rock. But they weren't the puffy vapors of the earthly sky. These were made of fire, burning from within like low-wattage stars. *Is that a river I see?* It certainly looked like a river, a glittering black ribbon that curled around the pillars and passed through what appeared to be ancient streets and towns. *And what are all those . . . things down there?* For that last question, there was no immediate answer—but roaming the land below were creatures of all shapes and sizes, some that looked human, some partly human, and some not at all human.

He couldn't absorb it all fast enough, so he closed his eyes again. Without realizing it, he had dropped to his knees and sat back. Angela must have made the fall a gentle one. She knelt beside him now. "Take your time," she said. "It's certainly an eyeful. You can sit here as long as you like."

Donny decided to voice some of his questions. It took a while to remember how to talk properly. "Why . . . how . . ." He shook his head. *Start again.* "Shouldn't it be hotter?"

"It used to be," Angela said. "Now it's a pretty steady eighty-eight degrees. Like I told you, things are different."

"But . . . ," Donny said. He kept his eyes shut but pointed up at the clouds of orange light.

"Oh, the clouds. They give light, not heat. One thing you'll learn about Sulfur: there are many kinds of fire. It's not just for burning."

16

Donny's eyes felt wet. He smeared the tears away with his sleeve. Another question had popped into his head. It felt more like a fact, one he barely wanted her to confirm. But he needed to know. "Angela. Am I dead?"

She chuckled. "I beg your pardon?"

"I'm dead. Right? The fire killed me, and now I'm here."

He felt a punch on his shoulder, soft and playful. "Silly boy," she said. "You're alive and mostly well. I saved you because you looked like you had nowhere else to go, and because I could occasionally use the help of a mortal. A live one, that is. If I need a dead employee, I can find one down here anytime. Come on now, on your feet. I think the first stop for you is the doctor."

"Doctor?"

"Yes, I assume you know what a doctor is. You're coughing a lot, haven't you noticed? I don't think all that smoke was good for you. We have a very fine doctor here. He died not too long ago, so his medical knowledge is reasonably up-to-date."

Died not too long ago? "I think I'm losing my mind."

"Then we'll find a dead psychiatrist next." Everything seemed to amuse Angela. She tugged on his arm. "Come along, and don't be so dramatic." She led him down the stairs, keeping him steady.

The year before, Donny's father had taken him on a trip to Europe, and they'd visited Athens and Rome.

17

Donny had been amazed to touch the ruins and walk down steps that had been built two thousand years ago. As he descended these stairs carved of rock, his hand sliding along the marble banister, he had the same awestruck feeling. It was like those antiquities, but better preserved. Everything he saw had been there for a long, long time.

He looked out again to see what other wonders lay ahead, but something caught his eye. A thing streaked toward them, bounding apelike across the ground on powerful arms and legs. It was squat and ugly, shaped and colored like a horned toad. Points jutted from the top of its head, and a bristly mane ran down its back. The mouth was wide and dangerous-looking with a forked tongue hanging out and plastered to the side of its face from the force of its acceleration.

Angela squealed, let go of Donny's arm, dropped to her knees, and opened her arms wide. The thing plowed into her and knocked her on her back. Its short tail whipped furiously from side to side. "Arglbrgl!" she said, laughing, as the creature licked her face. "How's my boy?"

The thing shouted, "ARGL! ARGLBRGL!" Angela kissed the horns atop his head and scratched the back of his neck.

The creature turned and looked at Donny, apparently noticing him for the first time. He leaped off Angela and crouched in front of Donny. The flaps of his loose skin sprung outward into pointy bristles. With the speed of an airbag exploding from a steering wheel, the creature doubled in girth. His lips quivered, and spittle flew from his bared teeth. Donny's eyes opened wide, because he was sure the thing was about to pounce and slash him to pieces.

"*Arglbrgl!*" Angela laughed. "Calm yourself. This is Donny. He's your friend now, you understand?"

The thing—which was apparently named Arglbrgl—looked back at Angela. "GRGLBRGL?" he asked. He looked at Donny again. The bristles retracted and then sprung halfway out again, then settled for good as the creature deflated with a loud *hisssss*. Arglbrgl hopped in front of Donny, and Donny held his breath as he was sniffed from his feet to his chest, which was as high as the thing could reach. "BLRGRL," Arglbrgl finally announced, and then hopped back to Angela's side.

Donny finally remembered to breathe. He faked a smile and talked slowly through his teeth. "What . . . is . . . that?"

"He's an imp, of course. You'll meet all sorts down here, Donny. We're just getting started."

CHAPTER 4

Donny's head swiveled and bobbed like a dashboard doll. There was insanity everywhere he looked: the friendly monster that had just joined them. The cliffs that towered on both sides. The immense, yawning canyon in the middle of it all that stretched for miles. Mountains that loomed, and maybe even smoldered, in the misty distance.

His legs wobbled, and Angela caught him by the arm. "Watch where you're going, Cricket. Last time I checked, you mortals were easy to break. And breathe normally. You're panting like a hyena."

"It's a little . . . overwhelming," Donny said.

Angela linked arms with him and pointed with her other hand. "That's where we're heading. The Pillar Obscura. Focus on that."

Donny stared. The pillar was one of the titanic columns

of rippling, twisting stone that reached from the ground to the roof, where the greatest stalactites above had merged with the greatest stalagmites below. A gently rising road had been inscribed in the exterior of the pillar. Along that spiraling ramp, niches, doors, windows, balconies, and statues had been carved into the stone, reaching several hundred feet high.

A small city wreathed the base of the Pillar Obscura. It looked like a greatest hits of the world's oldest structures: a Greek temple here, a stepped pyramid there, and domes, towers, arches, columns, and obelisks everywhere. Some oddly modern buildings made of brick, wood, or concrete were crammed between the antiquities, and telephone wires and power lines had been strung in disorderly fashion along the road and through the alleys. Road signs that looked like they had been pilfered from around the world were planted by the sides of the road, or hung on the building walls.

Strangely, a few sections of the city looked as if they'd been destroyed, reduced to heaps of broken stone.

"One of the pillar cities," Angela said. "This is my home. And now it's yours."

Donny followed her into the city, along a road of stone worn smooth over the ages. They passed others along the way. Donny didn't know what to call them. Creatures? Monsters? People? Some looked human enough. Others, less so. Reptilian beings were everywhere, from monkey-size things to hulking brutes. Some called a greeting to Angela, either in words or in a subhuman grunt or growl, and she smiled or nodded or waved in return. They looked at Donny, too, as if he were an object of curiosity. Every time they did, he averted his eyes and stared at his own feet. He had that awful feeling of sensory overload again, making him dizzy, and was thankful when Angela steered him to the right, onto a short narrow path that led directly to one of those strangely contemporary places. This one looked like a quaint white cottage from some New England seaside village. A sign hung over the door: MEDICAL DOCTOR, MORTAL CARE.

"Let's get you looked at," Angela said. She opened the door, and a bell jingled as they stepped inside.

"Who's that? What do you want?" a man said from down the hall. He stepped into view, a very human-looking fellow in a shirt and tie, with salt-and-pepper hair and a sour, put-upon expression. When he saw Angela, his attitude transformed instantly. "Miss Obscura. Well, this is an honor!" He clapped his hands. "What can I do for you?"

"Drop the act for one thing," Angela said. "And for the next, please do whatever medical stuff you ought to do with this mortal. I'll send someone to pick him up shortly."

"You're leaving?" Donny felt his chest clench like a fist.

"Don't worry, Cricket," Angela said. She pinched his cheek. "I'll see you soon. Oh, and Doc?"

The doctor straightened up and smiled too eagerly, at full attention. "Yes, Miss Obscura?"

"You're responsible for his wellness. And he is important to me. Understood?"

The doctor's head bobbed. "Certainly."

Angela left, moving briskly. The door closed behind her with another jingle.

The doctor let out a deep breath, and the smile evaporated. "Well, let's get it over with. Follow me, please." He led the way toward another room, and Donny heard him grumble to himself, "What have I done to deserve this?"

Soon Donny was sitting on a paper-covered bench in a strange imitation of a doctor's office. It had the trappings of modern medicine: a metal examining bench, a gleaming cabinet, and medicines and instruments on the shelves. But some of the light came from jars of blurry glass filled with balls of flame that swirled and pulsed like baseball-size stars.

"Anything I should know?" the doctor said.

Donny shrugged. "Like what, doctor . . . ?"

The doctor frowned. "Just call me Doc. I meant, what should I know about you? Your clothes reek of smoke. Am I supposed to guess what the problem is?"

"Oh. Yeah." Just the memory of the fire triggered another cough from Donny, which took a minute to contain. "There was a fire. Angela saved me. But I ate a lot of smoke."

"Right," Doc said. "Say *aaah*." He took out a little scope and peered down Donny's throat. "You'll live. But you probably shouldn't exert yourself for a couple of days." He leaned close and stared at Donny's forehead and cheeks. "You always this pale?"

"What? I don't know. I'm pale?"

"Clammy, too. And your hands are shaking. Eyes look dilated. How about your pulse?" Doc put his hand on Donny's wrist, and Donny gasped and pulled away.

"What?" said Doc, frowning down at him.

"Your hand . . . it's really cold." Donny wrapped his other hand around his wrist. The doctor's flesh had been like wax that had just came out of a refrigerator. He could still feel the oddly cold, almost plastic touch.

"Ah," said Doc. "Yeah. I'm the first one to put a hand on you, aren't I?"

Donny remembered something Angela had said. He'd thought it was a joke: *We have a very fine doctor here. He died not too long ago. . . .*

Donny leaned back, staring. "The first what?"

Doc rolled his eyes. "The first . . . I don't know. Resident. Inmate. Soul. Dead guy. You'd better get used to us. Now, do you mind if I finish up? Unfortunately, though I couldn't care less, I've been given responsibility for your health." He reached out again, pried Donny's hand off his own wrist, and put two fingers on the pulse point below the thumb. An old clock ticked on the wall, and

24

Doc counted silently while he stared at the second hand. Then came the blood pressure cuff, hugging Donny's arm. Finally Doc set the cuff aside, folded his arms, and looked at Donny again with a frown.

"You feel a little dizzy? Sick to your stomach? Weirded out? Not sure this is really happening?"

Donny felt his eyes watering up. He squeezed them shut and nodded.

"Look, it's not exactly an unusual reaction. Sounds like you almost died in a fire. Next thing you know, you turn up in this freak show. Monsters, demons, giant caverns, dead people. That's a lot to process. You have to stay calm."

Easy for you to say, Donny thought, but he just nodded again. None of what the doctor said was helping.

"I mean it. You can't really deal with another shock anytime soon. You might have a breakdown."

Donny finally opened his eyes and stared back. "It's not like I asked for this."

Doc raised his hands. "Don't bite my head off. I'm giving you the facts. Here's some advice: if you feel panicky, take a long, slow breath. Inhale through your nose, hold it, and exhale even slower through your mouth. That'll relax you. Got it?"

Donny tried it. "Yes. I got it."

"Isn't that nice? In the meantime, I got a bunch more questions for you."

"Okay."

"Are you on any medications, are you living with any diseases or disabilities, are there any health issues I need to monitor?"

Donny shook his head. "I'm good."

"We'll see." Doc reached for a clipboard. A flurry of inquiries followed about childhood diseases, symptoms, aches and pains, bodily functions, and more. By the end Donny had said no a hundred times and felt a little better about his physical health. His mental health was another question. *Twitchy* was the best way to describe it. His nerves jangled, and it was hard to focus on anything the doctor said.

Doc tossed the clipboard aside. "Now. Let's talk about your diet."

"My diet?"

"Great, you heard me correctly; we'll skip the hearing test. Obscura isn't your mother, and she's not exactly an expert on human needs, so it's up to you to eat well. I know how people your age eat when they're left to their own devices, and it's disgusting. That hole in your face is a mouth, not a garbage disposal. You need fruits and vegetables. And have . . ." Doc's voice trailed off, and he looked toward the doorway.

A noise came from outside the room, down the hall. A hinge creaked and a door banged. There was a moist, squishy sound, and the clatter of a chair tipping over. "Are you kidding me? Obscura left the door open, didn't she? And now they've gotten in again! I *hate* those things!"

26

Whatever was out there, it was coming closer. Doc stepped into the hall and shouted, shaking his fist. "Get out of here, you idiots!" The sound grew louder, and amid the grotesque squelching noises, Donny thought he heard the high-pitched chittering of some strange animal. "Back outside! You're making a mess!" screamed Doc, and he started kicking as a slithering flood of gray bodies engulfed his legs on either side.

They were worms, thousands of them, each as long as one of Donny's arms, with spiked heads and slimy segmented bodies. They swept the doctor off his feet, and he disappeared into the wriggling mass with only his legs kicking above the surface. The worms flowed into the room and surrounded the table.

Donny started to shout for help, but it turned into a violent cough instead. Then his mind did the strangest thing. It surrendered. His brain tilted like a pinball machine. The room faded into a shrinking circle of vision. He knew he was fainting, and he aimed his falling body onto the length of the table, so he wouldn't roll over and join Doc at the bottom of the mass of worms. But he was so dizzy that he didn't aim very well. His shoulder slipped over the edge of the table, and the rest of him followed. He landed on top of the squirming mass, and felt bodies engulf him, wriggling between his limbs as he sank.

CHAPTER 5

He woke slowly, rolling from side to side and back to belly for a while. The bed was plush and comfortable, and pillows surrounded him. The sheets smelled fresh and clean. He was afraid to open his eyes, but when he did, it was to a surprisingly pleasant sight. He was inside a four-poster bed with a canopy overhead and plush white curtains all around.

It wasn't his bed, or his bedroom. That was for sure. It wasn't any bed that he remembered, either. And this wasn't a hospital. Other than that, he didn't have a clue where he might be.

Donny sat up and rubbed his eyes. It felt like he'd slept for days. He had a vague recollection of running from home, getting caught in a fire, and finding himself in a bizarre underworld, delivered there by . . . what was her name? He could barely remember. His mind hadn't woken up fully. He craved tea, soda, or anything with caffeine.

With curtains all around it was hard to figure out which way to get out, but then he saw a gap to his left. He reached over and pushed the curtain aside. A scream caught in his throat when he saw the monstrous face that was inches away.

"ARGLBRGL!" the creature bellowed.

Donny rolled over, covered the back of his head with a pillow, and pulled it tight on both sides. "No. No way. Just no."

"BRGLGRGL?" asked the thing. *The imp,* Donny remembered. It had all really happened. And that woman, or girl, who found him in the fire, what was her name? Right. Angela. This thing, this imp from the underworld, was her pet or whatever. It was real, all of it, every crazy bit of it. Even the worms! Thousands of slimy worms the size of baseball bats, him sliding into the middle of the wriggling mass, certain he'd be gnawed to the bone.

If it wasn't real, he'd lost his mind for good. He didn't know which option he preferred.

"GRBRGLGRG!" cried the imp, hopping in place.

"Riiight." Donny crawled to the other side of the bed and opened the curtains there. He was greeted by a small, dark-haired, wide-eyed face and a piercing shriek. *"Eeeeee!"*

His legs kicked wildly and propelled him to the top of the bed, where he pressed his back against the wall on the other side of the curtain and clutched the pillow to his chest. He stared back and forth between the imp and the new face, a young Asian girl of maybe seven or eight, who had screeched from pure excitement upon seeing him.

"Who . . . What?" he said, gasping. His chest heaved and his heart thumped. A full spoken sentence seemed beyond him for the moment.

"I'm Tizzy!" shouted the new face.

"Tizzy," Donny echoed thickly.

"You're mortal, like me!" she said, with a wave of her hands.

"ARGLBRGL!" shouted the imp.

And then he heard Angela. "Is he awake? That took long enough." The voice got stronger and clearer as she entered the room. "Rise and shine, Cricket!"

The curtain was flung completely open beside the imp. Angela stood there, smiling down. She had changed into a bright yellow dress with a matching broad-brimmed hat and a single yellow glove on her left hand. In her other hand, she held a big plastic shopping bag that bulged with goods.

"Doctor Grumpypants said you had a panic attack, and that you might be suffering from mental shock," Angela said. She sat on the edge of his bed. "I told him it was a bunch of hooey. But anyhow, how do you feel?" She knuckled him on the shoulder.

Donny hugged the pillow tighter. "Like I had a panic attack and I'm suffering from mental shock."

"Oh, get a grip," Angela said. "So you had to hide in an abandoned building for some reason and nearly burned to death and then ended up in Hell. And then . . . what, do you have a fear of worms or something?"

Donny glared into space. "I do not have a fear of worms. I have a fear of thousands of giant monster worms and getting completely covered by them."

"Can I touch you again?" asked Tizzy. She reached out and put her hand on his arm.

Donny twisted away from her. "Did you say *again*? When was the first time?"

Tizzy clasped her hands behind her back and bit her bottom lip. "Um, a couple of times when you were asleep."

"And sedated," Angela added.

"I stared at you a lot too," Tizzy said. "But I only touched your arms. And your feet. And your face. No big deal." She reached out again. This time Donny didn't twist away, but he watched anxiously as she rested her hand on his arm, by the elbow. She closed her eyes and sighed. "See? You're a little warm. Just a little, like me."

"Ohhh-kay," Donny said.

"We're always excited to have a new mortal among us," Angela said. "Tizzy didn't believe you were one until she felt your skin. Denizens like me are hot. The dead are cold. And mortals——"

"Nice and warm," Tizzy said, hugging herself.

Angela shrugged. "Tepid, if you ask me. But, Donny!"

31

She clapped her hands and grinned widely. "It's time to face your new world. Unless your mind is permanently damaged, and then I don't know what we'll do with you."

"I'm fine," Donny said, but he found it hard to unclutch the pillow. "I think."

Angela tugged the sheet the rest of the way off of him. Donny noticed that his clothes had been changed—he was in black silk pajamas. His face flushed as the implications sunk in. "Uh. What happened to my clothes? How did I get into these?"

"Don't be so modest," Angela said. "Your clothes stank of smoke. And you were covered in worm slime. So we cleaned you up and got some jammies on you."

"We who?"

"ARGLBRGL!"

"Yes, Arglbrgl and I," Angela said.

Donny inhaled loudly. "You *stripped* me?" He shoved his face into the pillow.

Angela waved a hand. "You'd think that after everything you've been through, *that* would be the least of your issues. Now, come on. You've slept for nearly a day. I'm sure you have to eat. I'm sure you have to pee, too."

"Can I come along?" Tizzy said breathlessly. "For the eating part, I mean."

"Of course," Angela replied. Tizzy made a little squeaking sound.

"I got you some stuff I thought you might need," Angela

said. She tossed the bag onto the bed next to Donny. He put the pillow aside, sat up, and peered into the bag. Inside, at least on the top of the pile, he saw a bottle of baby shampoo, bubble-gum-flavored toothpaste, shaving cream and an electric razor, Band-Aids, deodorant, a twelve-pack of toothbrushes, mouthwash, cologne, talcum powder, bars of soap, baby wipes, contact lens solution, and gummy bear vitamins. It looked like she'd robbed a pharmacy.

"How'd I do?" she asked.

"Uh. Great." He didn't want to tell her that he didn't actually shave yet, or wear contact lenses, among other things.

"There was some guesswork involved," she added.

"It's perfect. Thanks a lot." He closed the bag, but not before spotting a king-size bottle of antiflatulence pills.

Angela slapped his knee. "Up and at 'em!"

"Right," he said. He swung his feet down and felt the warm stone floor. She had been right about one thing, at least. "Where's the bathroom?"

CHAPTER 6

I guess a normal bathroom is too much to ask for," Donny muttered to himself.

It was lit by what looked like an old streetlamp that stood in the corner, the globe filled with swirling, luminous gas. There was a modern toilet, but when he lifted the lid, he saw a shaft that ended hundreds of feet below in a distant inferno. The warm air gusting up while he used the toilet made for an interesting experience.

The brass fixture in the sink dispensed water that was too hot to touch. Fortunately, there was a regular water cooler next to the sink, and he mixed the two together to wash his hands and splash his face. He filled a paper cup from the cooler, and it felt good on his parched lips and tongue.

When he came out into the bedroom, the others were gone. He found a pile of new clothes on a bureau—jeans, shorts, underwear, shirts, jackets, socks, and sneakers. The house key and money he'd carried in his pockets were there too. He found the shirt and jeans that fit best and put them on, then stared into the mirror. "Too crazy," he said quietly. His face looked pale and twitchy. What had the doctor told him about relaxing? He inhaled through his nose, nice and slow, held it, and let it out through his mouth even slower. It did seem to help. He did it two more times and then stepped out into the corridor, where the others waited.

Angela apparently had a hundred ways to smile, most of them mischievous, and she gave him a toothy one. "Shall we?" she said, and led the way. The corridor ended in a large, high-ceilinged room with windows of stained glass, marble floors, a grand fireplace, and expensive antique furniture. One wall was practically covered with clocks, each with their hour hands set to a different time, and a sign underneath indicating a city: Washington DC, Buenos Aires, Reykjavik, London, Rome, Istanbul, Moscow, Islamabad, Mumbai, Bangkok, Kuala Lumpur, Shanghai, Seoul, Sydney, Kiritimati, Honolulu, San Francisco, Calgary, Mexico City, and more in between.

Extraordinary paintings lined the walls, with portraits of people, terrible beasts, gods and angels, landscapes of ruined cities, and depictions of great battles on land and sea. In niches and corners stood life-size marble statues straight out of Athens or Rome. Donny had spent enough time in fine art museums—his father loved to take him to museums of all kinds, and New York was full of them—to get a sense that these were the works of masters.

"Nice art," Donny said.

"Some beauties, right?" Angela said over her shoulder, without breaking her stride. "By some of the greatest artists in the world. I've even got a few that were done down here, postmortem."

"What? After they were dead?"

"Isn't that what *postmortem* means? We don't get loads of world-class artists down here, but when we do, we might as well let them be productive."

"GRGLBRGL," added the imp.

"Exactly," Angela said.

A winding staircase led to more rooms on an upper floor. Donny barely had time to examine the space any further before Angela heaved open the tall front door and they stepped outside.

"Oh," Donny said. When they emerged, he understood where he'd been: inside the gigantic pillar that Angela had called her home. The rooms had been carved from the rock, and the front door opened upon the road that spiraled around the titanic formation. He looked up and saw the stained-glass windows embedded in the stone. Angela's mansion was close to the bottom of Pillar Obscura, but still high enough to offer a breathtaking view from the railing on the other side of the path.

"Do you need a moment?" Angela asked. She eyed him warily.

"Why does he need a moment?" Tizzy asked.

"He has to adjust, dear. It's quite a shock, coming here for the first time. Yesterday he couldn't have imagined that all this existed. But he'll be fine."

Donny walked to the balcony, leaned out to look at the riotous blend of architecture below, and took a deep breath. *Will I be fine?* he asked himself. *Really?* The jury was out on that question. He did a little experiment. He raised his right hand and held it level, to see if it was shaking. And it was, but only a little.

A small hand reached out and clasped it. "You look okay to me," Tizzy said, smiling. "Come on, I'm hungry!"

They followed Angela again, nearly running to keep up with her energetic stride. They circled around the ramp until it reached the bottom and leveled onto a main thoroughfare.

Donny stared at the roof of jagged stone. It might have been a mile from there to the ground. The clouds of fire reminded him of the silky mantles of propane lanterns. Winged creatures flew among them. How large they were, it was impossible to say. They glided and swooped far above, and they had broad wings like bats, and narrow tails.

They passed a humanoid figure in a pair of farmer's

overalls. He was covered with skin like an alligator's, and a forest of horns grew from his skull. He smiled and nodded as he passed, and Donny made a valiant effort to smile back. The figure's demonic look prompted an unsettling question. "Uh, Angela? Can I ask you something?"

"Fire away."

"I hope I don't sound stupid asking."

"So what if you do? Go for it."

"Well . . . I never expected to come here. To the underworld, I mean. But if I did . . . there's something I thought would be here. Something terrible and scary. You know what I mean?"

"Nope."

"I mean . . . you know. The Big D."

She angled her head to one side. "Diarrhea?"

"No! You know what I'm talking about. *Who* I'm talking about. The guy in charge of all this." He almost didn't want to say it, and he found himself leaning close to her and whispering, "The prince of darkness, or whatever. The Devil."

"Oh, Lucifer!" she said quite loudly. It made Donny shrink back and hold his breath.

"Don't worry about him," Angela said. She waved her hand. "He's gone."

"He's . . . *dead*?" Donny asked. That possibility hadn't even occurred to him.

"Maybe. All we know for sure is, he's not here. Some

think he just got sick and tired of it all. It gets boring, you know, doing the same thing over and over for thousands of years. You can still see his perch above the Pit of Fire. He sat there since the dawn of human souls, overseeing the suffering. And then one day he simply wasn't there. He didn't say anything about leaving. In fact, he hadn't said anything for decades at that point. I personally never spoke to him."

"You actually *saw* him?" Shivers ran down Donny's arms. "How long ago was this?"

"Oh gosh. About a hundred years since he disappeared, actually."

Something about the roundness of that figure launched another wave of shivers. "Well . . . where do you think he went?"

"You want theories? Sure. Theory number one: he died. I mean, he was literally as old as heck. So he went off, crawled under a rock, and expired.

"Theory number two: there are passages in Sulfur that lead deep underground into lands unknown. We call them the Depths. They aren't safe to explore—anyone who goes down too far tends to not come back. A lot of denizens think Lucifer wandered down there. For some peace and quiet or to mull things over or who knows why.

"Theory number three: he went to your world. And he's been wandering on Earth ever since."

"Earth is scary," said Tizzy.

Donny felt a lump form in his throat. "What would he be doing up there?"

"Whatever he wants, kiddo. Checking you people out. Stirring up trouble. Taking a breather. There are other guesses about where he went, but the only thing that matters is, he left. When that happened, it wasn't clear who should be in charge, so the most powerful archdemons formed a council. And the rest is history."

They came to a ruined section of the city, which looked like it had been firebombed years before. What might have once been classical architecture was now just a heap of shattered marble and stone. Close to the street there was a row of fallen columns. Only one was partially upright, cracked in half with the base still standing. A feeble-looking creature squatted on the broken top. *Another imp,* Donny figured. From what he'd seen, most of them looked like gargoyles but without the wings. Their height and bulk varied wildly, along with the color of their reptilian or amphibious hides, and they might have any combination of spikes, horns, lumps, fins, boney plates, or fleshy whiskers. The one feature they shared was a short tail ending in an arrowhead.

This imp was old, pale, and blotchy, with milky, unfocused eyes. He seemed to hear them approach, because his ragged ear bent in their direction. He straightened a little, raised his head, and croaked out words like a talking bullfrog: "When eight sleeps, it is forever."

Angela called to it, "Hello, Sooth!"

Sooth turned their way as they passed, and said it again: "When eight sleeps, it is forever."

"What does that mean?" Donny asked quietly.

"Sooth is funny," Tizzy said. She had a musical way of speaking, her words going up and down the scale. "He'll only say that one thing, all day long, to everybody who goes by."

"Sometimes you can figure it out, sometimes you can't," Angela said. "Right, Sooth?"

"When eight sleeps, it is forever."

"You know what that means?" Donny asked.

"Duh," Angela replied. "Think about it."

Donny looked over his shoulder at the decrepit imp. Sooth had settled back down now that they had passed. They walked on and passed others along the way. There were imps of all sizes, and some creatures that seemed mostly human. Like before, they greeted Angela and stared at Donny, except for the oddballs that they encountered, like a plump little monster chewing on the corner of a building.

"I think I'll have pancakes," Tizzy said, squeezing Donny's hand. "Or waffles."

It sounded good, Donny had to admit. His stomach grumbled at the thought. But he had no idea where they'd find a place to get breakfast down here. And then he saw it, just ahead, tucked between something that looked like the Lincoln Memorial and something that looked like Stonehenge.

It was an actual old-fashioned diner, that kind that resembled a silver train car. Inside was a long white counter lined with red stools, and a row of booths along the windows. There was nobody inside except for the burly woman behind the counter. She wore a checked blue dress with a white apron and was reading a yellowed paperback detective novel. When the door opened, she put the book aside and wiped the countertop with a dishrag.

"Hungry guests, Cookie," Angela sang out.

"Good to see ya, Angela. What'll it be?"

"Pancakes!" shouted Tizzy.

Cookie smiled at Tizzy then jerked her head in Donny's direction. "That the new mortal?"

Angela tousled Donny's hair, which didn't annoy him as much as it should have. "Indeed."

Cookie slung the dishrag over her shoulder. "Got a note from Doc. He said I got to feed the boy healthy." She looked and talked like she'd stepped out of one of the black-and-white gangster movies that Donny's father liked to watch.

"After today, go right ahead," Angela told her. "For now he could use a treat."

"You're the boss," Cookie said. She winked at Donny. "Pancakes okay with you, sweetie?"

"Sure."

"Blueberry? Banana nut? Chocolate chip?"

"Chocolate chip!" shouted Tizzy.

"BLRGL, BLRGL!"

Donny would have said banana nut, but he didn't want to make things more complicated. "Chocolate chip sounds great," he said. He could hear his voice quaver as he spoke.

They took the middle booth. Angela sat on one side, and Arglbrgl hopped up beside her. Donny sat opposite, alone for a moment while Tizzy ran to a jukebox at the other end of the diner and punched its buttons. The jukebox was from another era, with an arm that plucked a shiny black record from a stack and played some tune from the fifties that Donny had heard but couldn't name.

"How are you feeling?" Angela asked.

Donny realized he had his arms folded tight across his chest, gripping the opposite elbows with each hand. He let his arms fall and shook them, trying to relax. "Better. I guess."

He turned to watch as Tizzy danced madly around to the music and jabbed her fingers in the air. If she could enjoy herself like that, he thought, maybe he could get over the shock too.

"Where did Tizzy come from?" he asked.

"As far as she knows, I found her in a field of flowers," Angela said.

"But where, really?"

The smile left Angela's face. "In an alley, next to a

Dumpster. In a bad country for abandoned babies."

There was no sound for a while except the music and Tizzy's laughter. Then Angela leaned forward on the table, resting her chin on the back of one hand. She wore a single glove again, Donny noticed. This one was yellow to match her dress. At her wrist, where the glove ended, and half hidden by the ancient golden bracelet, her skin looked different. There it darkened to a purple-red shade and broke into a fine diamond pattern, like the scales of a fish or a reptile. *A tattoo,* Donny figured. She must have noticed him looking, because she tugged the glove farther up her wrist, hiding the design.

"Speaking of origins," she said, "I'd like to know why you were in that burning building."

Donny stared out the window. "Not now, okay?"

"Right-oh," Angela said. Arglbrgl whimpered and patted Donny's hand.

Cookie brought orange juice and a pot of tea to the booth where they sat, and then went behind the counter to make breakfast.

"She seems nice," Donny said.

"She is," Angela said. "Unless you were married to her. Then . . ." She drew a finger across her throat.

"What? Wait, is she dead too?" asked Donny. It was hard to keep his voice down. He leaned over the table and whispered. "Are you telling me she's dead, and she killed her husband?"

"Husbands," Angela replied, stressing the plural. "But don't worry; you're perfectly safe. She knows this is a sweet gig compared to the punishment she could be getting."

"But . . . how did she kill them?"

"Poison, I think," Angela said, not keeping her voice down in the least. She called over to Cookie. "Cookie, did you poison your husbands?"

"Yes, dear," Cookie said as she poured something from a little bottle into the batter. "Arsenic. But have no fear, I have seen the error of my ways."

Donny slumped back and raised his hands in a helpless gesture.

Angela dismissed him with a wave. "Don't get your undies in a bunch. She's an amazing chef. Try her chicken Marsala, and tell me it's not worth the risk."

The pancakes came, still steaming, along with a pitcher of hot maple syrup and a bowl of whipped cream with chocolate shavings on top. Tizzy slid in beside Donny and dug in immediately. She didn't seem to suffer any ill effects, so Donny started on his. The cakes were so good that he shoveled three down in under a minute. Tizzy made *mmmmm* sounds the whole time, and Arglbrgl tossed his into the air and caught them whole in his mouth.

"So," Angela said, pancakes stuffed in one cheek. "You feeling a little better now?"

"I guess so," Donny said. "I think I'm still . . . What's the word? Processing."

Angela lifted the teapot. "You like?" Donny nodded. "I hope processing doesn't take too long," she said as she poured tea for both of them. "At some point I need you to help me with a chore."

"What chore? I don't know what you mean."

She sipped her tea and looked at him over the top of the cup. "I didn't rescue you just to be nice. I told you. I need some assistance now and then when I go topside."

Donny's brow furrowed. She had used that word before. "Topside?"

"Don't be dense. I mean the mortal world. Earth."

"Oh."

Tizzy shivered. "Scary!"

Donny stared at her. "You think Earth is scary? And this place isn't?"

"Eep!" Tizzy covered her eyes with her hands, smearing maple syrup on her forehead. "Superscary."

Donny shook his head. "I think you have it backward, Tizzy."

"Sulfur is all she knows," Angela said, smiling at Tizzy. "But we'll take another trip up there someday, right, darling? And you can be one of my special helpers?"

Tizzy still had her eyes covered. She shook her head vigorously. "Too bright. Too many colors."

Angela laughed and patted her arm. "Don't worry. Donny will help me. Won't you, Donny?"

He took a deep breath. Was he up for this? Whatever

Angela had in mind? "But why do you need me? What do I have to do?"

She sighed. "Do I really have to explain now? You'll see. But it won't be right away. I have some business down here first. In the meantime, I believe you need some orientation. I'll have Zig-Zag show you the ropes."

"Zig-Zag?"

"No better guide than Zig-Zag," she said. "You always get both sides of the story."

CHAPTER 7

Zig-Zag had two heads.

His body was stocky, but his necks were extra-long and elevated his faces to a normal height. Donny tried not to stare, or at least not to let his mouth hang open like a fool when he looked Zig-Zag in the eyes. But it was a challenge to decide which eye to look at. There was one eye on the right side of the right head, and another on the left side of the left head, and the same went for the ears. There was a nose on each side as well, but more like half a nose, with only one nostril. On one head, the silvery, almost blue hair was combed straight back and knotted tightly behind. On the other, it was the wild, unkempt hair of a mad composer.

But at least each head had a full mouth with which to speak. "Zig," said the shaggy head on Donny's right, with a nod and a smile. "Zag," said the other, also nodding, but with less of a smile.

"Donny." He stuck his hand out in greeting by habit—something his father had always insisted on. Zig-Zag had his own hands clasped in front of him, and he stared down at Donny's hand with wrinkled brows. Donny used the hand to wave awkwardly instead.

"Z, will you kindly show my new friend Donny around the place and give him the basics?" Angela said. "I'll need him back in a few hours, after council. Shall we say by two?" Among the buildings, one of the tallest was a soaring tower made of stone, with clocks as big as moons on all four sides. The hands pointed to almost nine—or at least, to where the nine would be on an ordinary clock but where some unreadable symbol was now.

"Very well," Zag said.

Angela pinched Donny's chin. "See you in a bit. Come on, you two," she said to Tizzy and Arglbrgl. They trotted off, trying to keep up with Angela's urgent stride. "Bye!" called Tizzy, and Arglbrgl shouted something incomprehensible.

Donny was left with his new two-headed guide, who didn't say anything for a while and just stared at Donny with both eyes.

"Um. So you're going to show me stuff?" Donny finally asked.

"Yes," Zig said. He tapped his lip with a finger. "I wonder where we should begin."

"The river, of course," Zag said. "What could be more important?"

"Hmmm," Zig said. "I hate to admit when you are right."

"You rarely do."

"You rarely are. The River of Souls, then? To the source?"

"Agreed. What do you say, young mortal?"

"Oh. Um. Sounds great," Donny said.

"Follow," said Zig, and the two-headed being set off. Just then a resounding deep-toned bell rang out. Zig-Zag stopped abruptly, and Donny nearly plowed into him from behind.

"Ah! The bells of nine! Look that way, pupil." Zag pointed to somewhere in the distance ahead of them, and Donny watched the spot as the bells tolled off the hours. *Gong . . . gong . . . gong . . .*

The bells finished, and as the echoes faded, Donny wondered if he were missing whatever it was he was supposed to see. There were holes in the ground ahead, like craters, of various sizes. He was about to ask what to look for when a bright glow filled the largest hole. His eyes widened as a column of fire slithered out and sprouted like an enormous tree. It twisted upward, growing limbs as it rose, and bloomed higher and higher toward the cavern ceiling.

"What . . . uh, what?" was all Donny could squeak out.

"The fire of illumination," Zig said.

"It lights our sky," Zag said. "On a regular schedule. At six in the morning, a touch of light for dawn. At nine

50

the full light of day, and by this evening the light will fade. What do you think?"

"Amazing," Donny replied. The fire looked like a gigantic oak by now, with a thick trunk and widely spread branches. Along the limbs clouds of fire blossomed, swelling in size until they broke from the stem and drifted away.

"Shall we?" Zig asked. Zig-Zag walked, and Donny followed.

"Do you have any questions?" Zig asked.

Donny thought for a moment. "Do you know what this means: 'When eight sleeps, it is forever'?"

Zig and Zag exchanged glances and a smile. "Sounds like something Sooth would say," said Zag.

"Yeah," Donny said with a chuckle.

"That imp is mad," said Zig.

"Not entirely," said Zag. "He has been known to foretell."

Zig snorted. "You will be mad too, young mortal, if you try to make sense of everything Sooth utters."

"Okay," Donny said. He looked back at the clock tower. "How about this: Are your hours and days the same as ours?"

"Why wouldn't they be?" asked Zag.

"Well, we have days because of the sun. But you don't have a sun down here. So why have days at all?"

"Clever boy," said Zig.

"We have days because you mortals have days," said Zag. "Our existence is tied to yours."

It was hard to figure out exactly how to talk to Zig-Zag, with two faces to consider. Donny decided he should look at the one who was currently speaking or had very recently spoken or was looking more in his direction. If none of those rules applied, he would glance from one to the other or find something else to look at altogether.

"I have another question. What's with all those worms?"

Zig chuckled. "Ah, the worm herd. I heard about your misadventure."

"Before the Reform, the worms were in the Pit of Fire, tormenting the dead," said Zag. "Now the pit is extinguished. The worms have nothing to do, so they wander around rather aimlessly. They are attracted to new smells, so they might have gotten a whiff of you. They're harmless enough, though. If you let them sniff you, they'll move on eventually."

Donny walked with Zig-Zag beyond the cluster of buildings at the base of Pillar Obscura. They were on a path that had been worn smooth and flat. At first he thought the surroundings were completely made of stone, but on closer inspection he realized it wasn't true. Things grew here that looked like moss, fungus, or lichen. Most were dark gray or black, with maybe a hint of green, but there was an occasional mushroom that added a dash of color.

The path out of town led to another, wider path that followed the river. Zig-Zag swept an arm across the vista. "The River of Souls," Zag pronounced rather dramatically.

"It's . . . cool," Donny said, staring at the water. Tendrils of mist hung over the flat surface. The river flowed in a channel carved into the stone, just a foot or two below the level of the cavern floor. A few bubbles rolled by and allowed him to see the leisurely current, not much faster than walking speed.

"The first thing you should know," Zig said, "is that it's not for swimming."

Donny almost laughed. Jumping in was the last thing on his mind. "Because it's cold?"

Zag sniffed. "Because it would be disrespectful. Also, you would be devoured."

Donny jolted. "Devoured? You mean *eaten*? By what?"

"Terrible, toothy things. You'll see soon enough," Zag said. Donny began having second thoughts about the tour, but he followed anyway as Zig-Zag led him beside the river, heading upstream. Donny kept to the far side of the road, away from the ominous waters.

They were headed toward the end of the underworld, where it terminated in a giant, sheer wall of rock. At the base of the wall, the river flowed from an arched opening.

A sound rang out from within the gap. It was a long,

low, mournful horn, deep and resonant. "Hurry," Zig said, and Zig-Zag walked quickly down the path to a bridge that arched high over the river. Donny followed them up onto the rounded span, where Zig-Zag stopped. They leaned on the stone balcony. "A barge is coming."

A thin mist wafted steadily out of the opening in the wall. Donny stared into it. The horn sounded again, much louder now, and the noise made the fine hairs on the back of his neck stand and salute. Out of the dark archway, through the mist, the front of the barge appeared. A huge horn was mounted at the front, curving down to sit just above the water. Instead of a bell at the end, there was an oversize skull with a yawning mouth that boomed out the note. The horn was being sounded by a tall cloaked figure at the front rail.

The rest of the barge drifted into view. There must have been a thousand people inside. They stood in rows twenty across, crammed in like cattle. Donny saw all sorts of faces, and all manner of clothing. The men outnumbered the women. They looked stunned or half asleep, blinking at their new surroundings or staring down at their hands and clothes or at one another.

"Who are they?" Donny asked.

"Arrivals," said Zig.

"Americans, I believe," said Zag.

"Could be Canadians," ventured Zig.

"The barge wouldn't be so crowded," countered Zag.

Donny stared at the masses. "You mean, these are people who just . . . *died*? And ended up here?"

"Thought that much was obvious," Zag muttered.

The boat drifted closer. From the bridge, Donny spotted a second cloaked figure who loomed above the crowd at the stern of the barge. He must have been nine feet tall, hidden utterly inside the loose-fitting cloak, the face invisible inside the shadows of the cowl.

"Those are the ferrymen at the fore and aft," Zig said, guessing Donny's next question.

The barge passed under the bridge. Most of the dead seemed to be in an almost hypnotic state, but a few were more alert. One woman looked up, gave the two-headed Zig-Zag a look of shock and surprise, and then focused on Donny. "You! Boy! Young man!" Donny gulped and pointed to himself. "Yes, you!" she cried. "What is this place? Where am I? What's happening?"

Donny's mouth went dry. "I . . . um . . ."

"You will learn all that soon enough," Zag called down to the woman. She looked desperate, like she wanted to run, but it seemed as if her feet were rooted to the deck, and the only movement she could make was to turn her head. As the barge passed under the bridge, she was hidden from sight. Donny sighed with relief.

"Who are they?" he asked.

"Just who you would expect," said Zig.

"Murderers, thieves, beaters, cheaters, slavers, predators, polluters, extorters, exploiters," said Zag.

"The selfish, cruel, sadistic, malicious, greedy, corrupt, and uncaring," said Zig.

"That list is by no means complete," said Zag.

Donny watched as the dumbstruck dead floated downriver, gawking at the weird grandeur of Sulfur. "Where are they going?" he asked.

"To their punishment," said Zig.

"To the wrong destination, if you ask me," said Zag. "But come along. More to see." Zig-Zag led Donny across the bridge, to the path on the other side of the river, and they walked to the arched opening that was the source of the river. Donny tilted his head and stared up, up, up to where the wall curved and merged with the ceiling full of stalactites.

"So this is as far as we go?" Donny asked.

"Hardly," Zag said.

"The really interesting part is still to come," said Zig.

Donny peered closer. "It looks dark in there."

"I have a vial of illuminating fire. But we probably won't need it," said Zag. There was a pocket in his garment, and he took out a baseball-size globe that was encased in a square golden cage and attached to a loop of chain. Inside the globe, a fireball swirled. "Would you like to wear it?"

"Isn't it hot?" asked Donny.

"You have a lot to learn about the fires of Sulfur," said Zag.

"There are many kinds. This one illuminates but does not burn," said Zig. Zig-Zag slipped the chain over Donny's neck. Donny held the globe up and stared into the ball of fire. It looked like an explosion in superslow motion. "That is awesome," he said.

"If you find that awesome, your mind will barely handle what's next," Zig said.

Zig-Zag led the way to the opening. Cool air whispered out, carrying an odd mingling of smells. Donny sniffed deeply and tried to puzzle it out. Something about the brew of odors made his stomach contract into a knot. It was dusty and musty, with a hint of formaldehyde and the antiseptic smell of hospitals. He detected flowers, freshly overturned earth, and whiffs of ash and decay.

Zig-Zag stepped into the opening, and Donny followed. The path narrowed to a table's width inside the crack. It was slender enough to make Donny nervous about tumbling into the black water. He stayed so close to the wall that his shoulder brushed the stone.

"Hold on," Zag said. He stopped and raised a hand. "Ah, as I expected. You don't really need that globe. More light is on the way."

Ahead, there was a light under the surface of the river. It moved toward them in serpentine fashion, outpacing the current. Beyond that, more followed, like submerged lanterns. When the first drew close and drifted toward the surface, Donny got a good look. He flattened himself against the wall as his heart whumped like an unbalanced washing machine.

It was an aquatic horror, like the fish that lived in the ocean's deepest places, creating their own light. A fleshy bulb of light grew from its head and dangled forward, poised in front of a yawning mouth with teeth as long and thin as pencils. It back-paddled with its fins and swam in place. The light pulsed and the jaw stretched even wider, inviting him in. It floated up, higher and higher, and touched the surface. Donny realized with a sick feeling that his entire head would fit in that frightful mouth.

Three more of the things appeared beside the first, and dozens more lights drifted toward them from every direction.

"See? The light-fish. Come to light our way," Zag said.

"They seem kind of dangerous," Donny said, panting.

"Oh, absolutely!" said Zig. "They'll eat anything, including us. But there is nothing they enjoy so much as mortal flesh."

"So you should try not to fall in," said Zag.

"I'll definitely try," Donny said.

"You see them now because we are closer to the water, and they can sense us," said Zag. "But they are everywhere, not just the tunnel."

Donny grimaced as he looked down at the monstrous fish, and ahead at the narrow path. "Um. Don't you guys believe in railings?"

"Are you nervous? Would you like to turn back?" said Zig.

"Don't coddle the boy," said Zag.

"I'm fine," Donny lied. That electric, panicky feeling was starting to surge through his veins again. He took a deep breath and then another. In the nose. Pause. Out the mouth. "Angela said I should see this, right?"

"So she did," said Zag. "Come along. We don't have far to go now."

They walked, and the dozens of light-fish swam below them, casting pale light in a rippling band on the walls of the tunnel, all the way up to where they met in a peak, high overhead.

The river ran straight between the walls, where the channel was narrower. It had to run straight, Donny figured, or else the barge would get stuck in the curves. The mist thickened and clung to the water as they advanced. It was deadly silent except for the scrape of their feet on the stone, and the water that dripped from above and struck the river with a plink or a plunk.

"There is no schedule for the barges, but they come frequently," said Zig.

"Can't the ferrymen tell you?"

Zig-Zag shook both heads. "The ferrymen rarely speak," said Zag.

"Look now," Zig said, pointing. "The end of our journey: the mouth of the River of Souls."

Donny saw it ahead, above the dense mist that carpeted the surface. The path they were on was a dead end, tapering to nothing. The mouth of the river was a literal mouth in an enormous primitive face carved from stone. It loomed over them with a heavy brow, blank eyes without pupils, and a crumbled nose. With the chin submerged, the river poured out of the yawning jaw, and the mist flowed out too, thick and milky-white. Inside, Donny saw nothing but dull illumination and occasional flashes of light. Thunder rolled deep within.

In an ominous and mysterious world, this place was the most ominous and mysterious of all. It felt as old as creation. Donny had the strangest compulsion to fall to his knees and lower his head. It seemed necessary to whisper. "What's that light?"

"A mystery," answered Zig.

"Where does the river come from . . . I mean, past here? What's on the other side?"

"Another mystery," answered Zag.

"Nobody ever tried to find out?"

"A few went in, paddling a boat against the current," said Zig. "They floated out dead, and the fish consumed them."

Zag shook his head. "Some things are not meant to be known."

"But you can understand the curiosity," said Zig.

Zag harrumphed.

There was a splash at the surface of the river. The glowing fish scattered suddenly, dove deep, and vanished. Inside the gaping mouth, the light went dark, as if something huge had snuffed it out.

"Ah. How well we have timed our visit," said Zag.

"Serendipity," said Zig.

Another barge appeared within the mouth and pierced the fog. The horn at its bow sounded, reverberating off the walls so loudly that Donny felt it in his chest. This time he did fall to his knees.

Zag lifted him by the elbow. "This, you have to see."

Donny stood again and looked into the barge as it slipped past. He expected a crowd of people, but there were none—only the ferrymen at the bow and the stern.

And yet, on the bare deck where the people would have stood, it wasn't empty. Many hundreds of things floated just above the planks: clouds of swirling gas and twinkling light, like celestial objects scaled down to the size of apples.

"Walk with the barge and watch," Zig said, prodding Donny along. Donny obeyed and stared, and something amazing began to happen.

The globs of light took shape. They stretched tall. Ovals formed at the tops, and tails oozed down below. When the tails touched the deck of the barge, they divided and formed legs. The ovals at the top became skulls and fleshed out into heads. Faces grew. Torsos formed and arms appeared, all made of mist and light, and hair bloomed on the heads. Finally clothing manifested on top of it all. Everything had just *appeared*, crafted from those clouds of mist and light.

Donny opened his mouth to speak but couldn't think of a thing to say.

The barge was now full of people standing shoulder to shoulder in rows, transfixed. They seemed to come from all walks of life. They were dressed like everyday folk, except for a few who looked more formal in suits or dresses. Here and there Donny saw people in uniforms. A nurse, a fireman, a chef, a soldier, a policeman, a baseball player. One or two wore hospital gowns.

Something about the crowd of people struck him. "Wait," he said.

"A question?" asked Zig.

Donny spoke quietly. "They're not old. Most of them, anyway. Shouldn't they be old?"

"What you see is not how old they were when they died. It is the way they always saw themselves," Zag explained. Donny scanned the faces on the barge. There were lined faces and gray hair among the crowd, but most were far younger. Some even looked like teenagers.

"And it is the same for the clothes they wear. Ask a mortal to close his eyes and picture himself. The clothes he sees in his mind are the clothes that will appear after death," Zig said.

Donny stopped walking. He didn't want to talk anymore while the dead were right beside him. It seemed disrespectful, no matter how awful those people were. He watched the current pull the ship away. "Where is the barge taking them?"

"To the place where the dead will disembark," answered Zag.

"Then where does the barge go?"

"To the end of Sulfur, far from here," answered Zig.

"What's at the end?"

"Another mouth, much like the one you see here," answered Zag. "The river vanishes inside. And then, in time, it reappears here."

"Are there lots of barges?"

"Oh yes. And lots of ferrymen, although you could never tell them apart," said Zig.

Zig-Zag gestured downriver, and Donny started to walk again, still thinking about what he'd seen. "Well . . . what do you do with all those people?"

"We show them the error of their ways," said Zag.

Donny tugged on his collar. "Um. How?"

"Not the way we used to, thankfully," said Zig.

"I beg to differ," countered Zag. "There was nothing wrong with the old ways. They worked perfectly well for a few millennium."

Zig sighed. "Zag doesn't believe in progress."

"I believe in tradition and fidelity. I don't believe in change where none is due."

"Let us bring the boy to the great pit, and show him how things used to be," said Zig. "Let him decide."

CHAPTER 8

They retraced their steps to the cavern and followed the river's course until they arrived at a place where the banks were carved into steps. "This is the first landing. The dead would disembark and march to the pit," said Zig.

"And so it was for thousands of years," said Zag.

They followed a path that led away from the landing, and within a few minutes they had arrived at the brink of the pit that Donny had seen from afar. Back on Earth, it would have been an attraction to rival the great canyons of the American West. The pit wasn't especially deep. It couldn't have been seventy feet to the bottom. But it was wide, and it went on for miles, with the other end out of sight in the distance. Narrow towers of rock rose from the canyon floor. Steps spiraled around them all the way to their tops, where thrones had been hewn from the stone. One throne towered high above the rest, and Donny shuddered to think whose seat that was.

The stone walls below were charred and blackened by fire. Steam hissed from cracks and fissures at the bottom. The rotten-egg smell of sulfur that rose up was almost overpowering. He held his sleeve across his nose.

"Come along," Zag said, and they followed the path out onto a long tapering fin of rock that projected a hundred yards into the pit. It stuck out like a diving board and thinned at last to a point that Donny could have covered with his foot. They stopped before it became dangerously narrow.

"Picture the dead, marching this way by the thousands, prodded from behind by an army of howling, giggling imps with pitchforks," said Zig.

"Loyal servants who willingly performed the task they were born for," said Zag.

"With the dreadful and heartless overseers watching from their perches atop the spires," said Zig.

Donny gazed into the pit. The drop was purely vertical at first, but then the walls curved out and flattened near the bottom. It looked to Donny like he could step over the side, slide roughly down . . . and then never be able to crawl out again.

"The fires are extinguished now. But in those days the pit was filled with Flames of Torment, a special fire that burned but did not consume," Zig said. "Can you picture it, Donny? The hopeless march to the edge?"

Donny could picture it, and the vision made his gut clench. He imagined the crowd forced onto this ramp. Those in front would see the path before them shrink to nothing. They might try to turn and push back, only to be bulldozed over the edge by the sheer mass of bodies, and they would slide and roll and tumble into the inferno below. He remembered his own brush with fire on top of the old building, and how the flames felt even before they'd reached him. The memory was so fresh that he had to remind himself to breathe. To suffer in flames for seconds, never mind centuries or an eternity or whatever the sentence might be, was a pain his mind could never comprehend.

"Let us not forget that these are the wicked we speak of," Zag said. "And this was the fate they earned."

"All of them?" asked Zig. "All of them earned it, forever and ever?"

"Can we go now?" asked Donny. His nerves had started to jangle again. Then he almost screamed when a new voice spoke behind them.

"And who do we have here?"

Donny spun around. A tall stout man stood there. He wore a white shirt and a striped apron, a red bow tie, dark pants, black shoes, and a paper hat atop his head that came to a point in the front and back. The man looked like a character from a black-and-white movie, the kind of fellow who might take orders behind the meat counter in a small-town grocery. It should have been a friendly face, with that broad, toothy smile under the thick shiny mustache. But there was a hungry look in the eyes that made it chilling instead. The man's chest heaved, his eyes watered, and his complexion was pink and red-cheeked, as if he'd been laughing too hard for too long.

Donny looked him over and saw more reasons for concern. There were frightening dark stains all over the apron, and the wooden handle of a blade stuck from the deep pocket at the bottom of the apron. And besides— whoever this was had crept up silently and cornered them on this point of rock.

"Mind your manners now, Butch," said Zag.

"Keep your distance," said Zig.

The man giggled. "It's a live one, isn't it?" He leaned over and gave Donny a wolfish grin. "Wherever did you *find* him?"

"That is none of your business, Butch," said Zag.

"Hmmm," said Butch. He tickled his chin and eyed Donny closely. "Aren't you going to introduce us?"

"Hardly," said Zag.

"My name was Marty," the man said to Donny, his hand cupped beside his mouth, whispering when there was no need to whisper. "But down here they call me Butch. Do you know why?"

There was something about this man and the appearance of his skin that reminded Donny of the other dead residents of Sulfur who he had met. Even before Butch had referred to himself in the past tense, Donny was sure this man had passed his expiration date. "Um. Because you used to be a butcher?"

"Right you are!" Butch shouted. It sounded all the more startling after his whisper. "But not just any butcher! No, not an ordinary butcher!"

"Enough of this," said Zag.

Zig gave a weary sigh. "Donny, it was long before you were born, but this wretched man was known in his lifetime as the Jolly Butcher."

"A murderer of some renown," said Zag.

Butch found this hilarious. He clapped his hands and danced in place. "A clever one! It took them twenty years to catch me!"

"He's also a madman. Obviously," said Zig.

"Putting a little more depression in the Depression," Butch added with a giggle.

"Run along now, Butch," said Zag. "This boy is under Angela's protection. If you cause any trouble, she'll make you pay for it."

"Under Angela Obscura's protection?" Butch tapped his fingertips together, an imitation of applause. "How wonderful! Does Havoc know?"

"What does that matter?" said Zig. "Run along, Butch. Don't you dare cause any trouble here."

"Wouldn't dream of it," Butch said. He grasped the

handle that stuck up from his apron pocket and pulled out a knife with a thick, nearly rectangular blade. Donny gulped and took another look at the sloping wall of rock below. He wondered if he might escape that way without fracturing half his bones.

Zig-Zag stepped in front of Donny. "Last warning," Zig said.

"I won't lay a hand on his head, shoulder, or flank," Butch said. "I just want to know if he's seen the trick!"

"Trick?" asked Zag.

"The trick of the dead!" Butch dropped to his knees and shuffled sideways until Donny could see him clearly. He put his free hand on the ground with his fingers fanned out, and he raised his knife with his other hand.

"Don't!" cried Zig, and he flung his arm in front of Donny's eyes as Butch brought the knife down.

"Ugh," said Zag.

Butch howled with pain and laughter. Zig dropped the arm in front of Donny's eyes, and Donny's stomach lurched as he saw three fingers on the ground.

But they weren't simply lying there. The fingers wriggled like worms and inched their way back toward the butcher. Where there should have been bloody wounds, instead there was vapor drifting out.

"That's not the trick," Butch said, barely getting the words out between his guffaws. "*This* is the trick!" He slipped the knife back into his apron, picked up one of the fingers, and brought it to the place on the hand where it had been severed. There, just below the knuckle, was another misty, bloodless wound. When he touched the finger to that spot, it healed instantly. The mist vanished, and the finger was whole once more. Butch laughed again and replaced the other two fingers, making his hand complete. "Ta-dah!" he cried. He held his hand toward Donny and flexed the digits. "Bet you can't do that!"

Donny was almost afraid to answer, because he was on the verge of throwing up. "You're right. I can't."

"No—we couldn't put *you* back together, could we?" Butch caressed the handle of his knife.

"Warning you again," said Zig.

"Didn't that hurt?" Donny asked.

"Oh *yes*," Butch said, getting to his feet. "The pain is just as exquisite as in life. But we dead can reassemble ourselves—and then do it all over again!" He rubbed his hands together and winked at Donny.

Zag was about to say something, but Butch just waved with his recently severed fingers and bounded away. He laughed over his shoulder. "I can hardly wait to tell Havoc about Angela's new friend!"

There was a long, stunned silence as they watched Butch depart. "Sorry about that," said Zag.

"Unfortunate, running into him," said Zig.

"Didn't know he was back," said Zag.

"That means Havoc is back too, I suppose," said Zig.

Donny realized that he had clamped his hand over his mouth, and had to remove it so he could speak. "So Butch is one of the dead, right? He came here after he died, a long time ago?"

"That's right," said Zag.

"But how come he's just running around free? Isn't he supposed to be somewhere? You know, getting punished?"

"Mmm," said Zig. "This is a special case. Unfortunately for the rest of us, somebody down here took a liking to Butch and now keeps him as a pet."

"Havoc," Zag said with a rueful smile.

"Yeah," Donny said. "Who is Havoc?"

"A rival of Angela's, and someone you ought to steer well clear of," said Zig.

"Havoc is angry and misguided," said Zag. "But he's not wrong about everything."

Butch was nearly out of sight, about to disappear behind formations of stone. He turned and waved again before vanishing for good.

"Well!" Zig said brightly, clearly trying to change the mood. "I'm certain Angela will have interesting news for us. Let us go to the Council Dome. The meeting should be nearly over."

CHAPTER 9

What is the council?" Donny asked as he followed Zig-Zag down the road.

"The powerful and wise archdemons who rule Sulfur," Zag said.

"Powerful, yes," said Zig. "Wise, occasionally."

Zag shot a sour look at his other head. "Have some respect, brother."

"So they're like senators or something?" Donny asked. "You elect them?"

"*Elect* them?" Zag guffawed. "Where do you think you are, your United States?"

"They represent the oldest families of Sulfur," said Zig. "The new council was created after the Great Reform."

"The ill-conceived reform," muttered Zag.

"What was the Great Reform?" asked Donny.

Zig raised his eyebrow. "You haven't been told? The Great Reform is why the pit is extinguished, and why the new method of punishment has been embraced."

"More coddling than punishing, if you ask me," grumbled Zag. "There was no reason for change. Even less reason for war."

"You had a war?" Donny asked. That explained some of the damaged buildings he had seen.

"A war like never before," said Zag, shaking his head.

"We only had a war because the Merciless would not budge an inch, and they turned violent against the reformers," said Zig.

"The war would never have started if the reformers hadn't turned their backs on the old ways," said Zag. "Old ways that had forever served us well."

"Come on, Zag, even you can't maintain that change wasn't needed. We imprisoned souls that were long since ready to move on."

"I can maintain, and I do maintain. Mercy and reform were never our calling. Imagine when Lucifer returns—what will he do when he sees what we have done?"

"Lucifer left. We chose our own path. If he wants the pit restored, he can come back and say so."

"Listen to you, so quick to part ways with millennia of proud tradition!"

Donny watched the conversation as if it were a tennis match, volleying from head to head.

"Proud tradition?" cried Zig. "Burning and poking

helpless souls for eternity, when a better way was right before our eyes? If only I could part from you so easily!"

"Bring me a saw and I'll oblige you, brother!"

"Do you guys agree on anything?" Donny asked.

Zig-Zag scratched both heads. "We like Angela," offered Zig.

"We despise Butch," added Zag.

They walked a little more, and the road snaked through rolling hills of smooth stone. Zig pointed. "The Council Dome. And those are the chariots of the council members."

Donny saw a stately dome of white marble, sitting atop the tallest of the hills. On the road at the foot of the hill were the chariots. They looked exactly as he might have expected—replicas of the chariots of ancient Rome, with one enormous wheel on either side. What he did not expect were the creatures that apparently drew the chariots. One or two of them rested on the ground beside each of the vehicles. These were imps too, Donny assumed—those creatures seemed to come in a lot of sizes and configurations. But these imps had the most startling proportions he'd seen yet. Their legs were so long that he could have walked between them without bumping his head. Their snouts were elongated and vaguely horselike, and their tall ears pointed straight up.

The Council Dome had a series of arches in its walls that allowed passage within. Under each stood an imposing figure—a monstrous, hulking imp, standing guard with weapon in hand. Donny caught glimpses of figures inside the dome, dressed in shimmering crimson robes. They sat on a ring of benches that encircled the interior, while one stood in the open space at the center and spoke to the rest.

"Angela is in there?" he asked.

"With the rest of the council," Zag answered.

"Watch out," Zig said. "Imp ball coming through."

Donny wondered what an imp ball was, but before he could ask, he heard a commotion on another of the hills nearby. Dozens of imps scrambled to the top. They giggled as they jumped atop one another. First they formed an unruly heap, but then they shaped themselves into a rough ball of arms, legs, and torsos. Their laughter grew as they tried to coordinate their motions and rock back and forth. They teetered on the edge of the slope. Finally one more imp clambered up the side of the ball closest to the edge, leaned out, and used his weight to tip them over. The knotted imps started to roll down the slope.

"Lunatics," said Zag.

"We ought to move," said Zig, and they stepped aside as the mass flew past them. The imps howled with crazed laughter. Their course took them directly into a thick spire of rock, and when they smashed into it, bodies flew every-where. The imps lay scattered on the ground and groaned for a while and held their skulls in their hands, until one of them started laughing again and the rest joined in. They wobbled to their feet and started jogging up the same slope, ready to do it again.

One of the imps skidded to a stop when he saw Donny. "GRBRBL!" he cried.

Donny laughed. "Arglbrgl, is that you?"

"ARGLBRGL!" The imp wrapped his arms around Donny and squeezed. Donny smiled, but at the same time having the air squished from his lungs brought on another fit of coughing.

Arglbrgl release him and frowned. "BGRGL?"

"I'm fine," Donny said into his fist as he coughed out the words.

"Let's get away from these hooligans," said Zag, "before they run us over."

Arglbrgl waved. "GLRG!" Then he raced up the hill with the others.

CHAPTER 10

The meeting ended. The imposing guard imps stepped aside from the arches, and the members of the council emerged from the building.

Donny watched the crimson-robed archdemons make their way down the wide steps carved into the slope, stopping to talk with one another. There were beings like Angela, who looked fully or partly human. Others were more terrifying to behold, humanoid creatures with reptilian faces, clawed hands, and skin covered in scales, lumps, and horns.

"Zig-Zag," called out a lanky, long-necked being nearby.

"Would you excuse us for a moment?" Zag asked Donny.

"Sure," Donny said. He watched Zig-Zag go to speak to whatever the thing was that had called him. When he looked up the stairs again to see if Angela was coming, he spotted a tall robed figure descending toward him, quietly and gracefully. This archdemon was entirely human in appearance, with sharp features, dark eyes, pale skin, and slick black hair. He was handsome in an old-fashioned way, like an actor from a silent movie. Following him down the stairs was a massive guard imp with a face that was covered with sharp, jutting thorns. The guard had an ugly weapon in his hands: a spiked ball at the end of a chain, attached to a club.

"Is this a living mortal I see?" the archdemon said.

Donny cleared his throat and improved his posture. "Yes, sir."

"Mortals are easy for us to spot, you know." The archdemon made a sweeping gesture around Donny's torso. "You have an aura about you. A signature. Now, I presume you didn't just wander in unauthorized?" He smiled, but Donny had the impression he was also poised to move quickly, like a mousetrap set to go off.

The question had seemed simple enough, but Donny felt it needed to be answered instantly and with certainty. "No, sir." He lifted his hand and showed his palm.

The archdemon cocked his head and stared at Angela's sign, embossed on Donny's flesh. His eyes narrowed. "Ah. Obscura has a new mortal. You will be assisting her?"

"I think so. I'm not a hundred percent sure what she wants me to do yet."

"I can guess," the archdemon said. He put a hand on

Donny's shoulder. "What she wants mostly is to fill your impressionable head with radical ideas. It's a sad thing, young friend. If you only spend time with her, you will never know the truth."

Donny started to feel twitchy. The hand on his shoulder was warm, and it gripped him a little too tightly. He looked toward Zig-Zag, hoping to be rescued from this encounter, but Zig-Zag was still engaged in his own conversation.

The archdemon followed Donny's gaze. "Ah. You have been with Zig-Zag? Zag will at least hint at the truth. But even he isn't as faithful as he ought to be."

Past the archdemon's shoulder, Donny saw someone else approach, and his eyes went wide. It was the Jolly Butcher, tiptoeing with a finger across his lips. "Sir—look out behind you," Donny whispered.

The archdemon turned just as Butch arrived. "Well, if it isn't the Jolly Butcher," he said. Butch responded with a ridiculous curtsy and another one of his high-pitched giggles.

"Master Havoc, I see you've met Angela's new pet," Butch said.

Every muscle in Donny's body went rigid. So this was Havoc.

"You two have already been introduced?" Havoc asked. "What is your name, young mortal?"

"Donny Taylor, sir," he answered without taking his eyes off the butcher.

"Donny. So you have met Butch. He is an interesting specimen, don't you think? I like to keep him around as a shining example of the depths of human depravity."

"I'm blushing," Butch said. He covered his cheeks with his hands.

"Butch serves as a reminder of the true mission of our world," Havoc said. "To punish the human souls who have gone astray. With fire. Forever. As it was meant to be." The grip on Donny's shoulder tightened, digging into his flesh. Havoc leaned closer, dropped his voice, and spoke into Donny's ear. "There will be a reckoning someday, when Lucifer returns. Those who choose the wrong side will pay the price. *And the mortals who serve them will suffer most of all.*"

"You have *got* to be kidding." It was Angela's voice, the sweetest sound Donny had ever heard. He saw her out of the corner of his eye as she trotted down the stairs. Another colossal guard imp followed her, an absurdly large battle-ax balanced in his hands. "Now you get your kicks scaring helpless mortals? So typical."

"Typical," echoed Angela's guard imp. He and Havoc's thorn-faced guard snorted and glared at each other.

"Hands off, Havoc," she said. "Or I will tear Butch apart and hide the pieces like Easter eggs." Butch circled around to put Havoc between himself and Angela, and watched with his mouth agape in a crazed smile, tapping his fingers together. Zig-Zag finally noticed what was happening, and ran over, looking aghast with both faces.

Havoc's hand did not move. It only grew hotter. "Young mortal, do you see what sort of character you've gotten mixed up with? She senses she fights a losing battle. It has made her prone to impulsive, erratic behavior."

"Seriously, Havoc?" Angela asked. She reached for the wrist of her gloved hand and grasped the battered golden bracelet as if she were about to take it off. "Take that hand off him in three seconds, or there's going to be an incident."

Havoc took his hand away and patted Donny's head. "There, there, little mortal, nothing to fear." He spun on his heels and faced Angela. "It really is lovely to see you again, Obscura. I missed you while I was on my expedition."

Angela had a remarkable catalog of facial expressions. On this occasion she rolled her eyes up, her eyelids fluttering. It was the most perfect look of irritation Donny had ever seen. "Feel free to take another one soon, and for longer," she told Havoc. "Maybe your next report will be more interesting, and even believable. You really found *nothing* in the Depths at all? No sign of Lucifer or the Merciless even after a month's exploration?"

Havoc did not reply. He chuckled and sauntered away, followed by the thorn-faced guard imp and the grinning Jolly Butcher.

Donny was about to thank Angela when he noticed something peculiar. Her hair, which had been pure black, was now auburn. He stared for a moment, and finally asked, "Are . . . are you wearing a wig?"

"Of course not," Angela said.

"Um. So. You colored your hair?"

"Not exactly," she said. She pinched some of her hair between her fingers and pulled it up to look at it. "Oh, I see what you mean. What, don't you like this shade?"

"Like it? Sure, it's great." He looked again, closer. It wasn't just a different color. It was shorter than before, barely touching her shoulders, and wavy instead of straight. "But how—"

She pretended to wipe her brow. "Whew. I'm *so* happy you like it." She swept her arm toward the huge imp by her side. "Now, I think you ought to meet my muscle. This is Echo. Echo, say howdy to Donny."

"Howdy," said the giant imp.

The imp was a head taller than the biggest man Donny had ever seen. His reptilian hide was gray with jagged stripes of blue. He was shaped like a titanic egg, with muscular arms and stumpy bowed legs. His eyes were wet black marbles set deep under his brow, so small they were hard to find. His nose was a pair of lopsided holes outlined by ridges of flesh. But the most extraordinary feature was his gigantic jaw, and a mouth so wide, it almost split the face in two. There was no neck at all. The mouth, when opened, would lead right into the vast belly.

"Hi, Echo," Donny said. He held out his hand.

"Echo," the hulking imp replied. His voice was a boom of thunder, and when the toothless mouth opened to speak, it looked big enough to crawl inside, over a tongue like a shovel. He stuck one of his powerful arms out, gently took Donny's hand, and gave it a shake that nearly tugged Donny's arm from its socket.

"Nice to meet you," Donny said, trying not to wince.

"Nice," said Echo. His king-size mouth curled into a crescent-moon grin.

"Obviously, Echo can speak, but he'll only give you one word at a time, and it'll be one of the words you just said," Angela said.

"Word," said Echo.

"But he's very wise," Angela said. "And strong, of course. Echo is my personal guard. He used to work in the Pit of Fire. He was a devour-and-regurgitation specialist. You know, wander around in the flames, grab a mortal soul, gobble up the whole body, and then spit it out again."

"That sounds kind of disgusting," Donny said. He wasn't surprised that Echo was capable of such a feat. He looked like he could swallow a refrigerator.

Echo nodded. "Disgusting."

"Echo, did you *like* your old job, or did you *hate* it?" Angela asked.

"Hate," Echo said. He lowered his head.

"You see, Donny, when the pit was extinguished, all those imps had to find new ways to make themselves useful. Many of them are fixing the damage from the war. Some still haven't figured out what to do, so you might observe some eccentric behaviors now and then. But Echo offered his services to me. Echo, do you *like* working for me or do you *love* working for me?"

Echo covered his grin with a massive four-fingered hand. If those gnarly, scaly cheeks could have blushed, Donny was sure they would have. "Love," Echo said from behind his hand.

"Thanks, buddy," Angela said. She patted Echo's mountainous gut. "Would you mind sending a chariot this way? A big one, please, with two runners. We have an errand. Then I'll see you later, okay?"

"Later," Echo said. He lumbered away.

"Something urgent has come up," Angela said. "Donny, are you ready for a little travel? You don't have to walk this time."

Donny took a quick deep breath to test his lungs. He managed to do it without coughing. "I'm all right."

"What is the trouble?" asked Zag. "Aside from Havoc returning."

"He's as intolerable as ever, by the way," Angela replied. "Wait until you hear about his phony expedition. But this is something else. Trouble at the refinery."

CHAPTER 11

Donny heard the clatter of wheels on stone, and turned to see a chariot roll up. It was drawn by an identical pair of the long-legged imps that Angela had called runners. There was a bench inside where a few people could sit.

"In we go," Angela said. Donny and Zig-Zag sat on the bench, but Angela stood at the front of the chariot and called to the imps. "To the refinery!" There were no reins to hold. The runners nodded, and the chariot lurched into motion. Its unexpected burst of speed rocked Donny backward. They flew down the path, away from the dome, and turned onto a road that led toward the cavern wall beyond the pillar city.

Donny saw dark shapes ahead on either side of the road. They were like trees at the bottom, with broad leathery umbrella shapes on top, nearly a dozen feet high. Imps were cutting some down with two-handled saws and piling them into carts.

"Are those mushrooms?" Donny asked.

"Delicious," Zag replied.

Well, they have to eat something, Donny thought.

The chariot rolled on. They passed through meadows of black ferns and then a tortured terrain with pools of boiling mud and steam whistling from cracks in the ground.

"What's the refinery?" Donny asked, this time raising his voice so Angela might hear him better. But she didn't answer. She appeared to be deep in thought as she gripped the front of the chariot and stared at the road ahead.

Zig spoke for her. "Fire is everything in Sulfur, young mortal. You have seen how we use it to illuminate the skies, and you have seen the pit where the Flames of Torment once burned. But those are only two of the types of fire we employ."

"In Sulfur, all fire comes from below," Zag continued. "We call that the Crude Fire. At the refinery, the Crude is separated into the many useful types."

It didn't make sense to Donny. "Where I come from, fire is just fire. You can't just break it down into other things."

Zig nodded, encouraging, and Zag shook his head, bemused. "So I have heard," said Zig. "The natural laws of the infernal realm are not the same as the mortal realm.

We are almost there—now you will see how it is done."

They drew close to the outer wall of Sulfur. Donny had started to orient himself to this strange world, using the river that ran through the center. He thought of the river's origin as north, with the water flowing south past the great pit and beyond. And so the side that they now approached—which was within a mile of the river at this point, where Sulfur was still quite narrow—to him, that was west.

A wagon rolled toward them along the road, and the chariot slowed and veered toward the side to let it pass. It was pulled by a lumbering beast that looked like a lizard-skinned rhinoceros walking on two legs. The wagon was loaded with barrel-size ceramic vessels, a few of which glowed red-hot.

A small imp was perched on the seat at the front of the wagon, picking his nose with unusual vigor. He wiped his findings on his leg when he saw Angela, and tipped his floppy hat. "You here because of the theft?"

Angela nodded.

"Well," the imp said as he plunged his finger into the other nostril. "Better get to the bottom of that." The wagon rolled on.

Zig and Zag glanced at each other with brows raised. "A theft, Angela?" Zig asked. "Has there ever been one before?"

"Not that I remember," Angela said. "That's why we're here."

"See?" Zag said to Donny. "You break with tradition, and bad things follow."

Zig sighed heavily, and rolled his eyes.

The refinery was inside a long curving wall that had been constructed near the side of the cavern. Bursts of fire billowed up from the other side, along with clouds of smoke and steam. Things rumbled, rattled, boomed, and hissed. Donny felt adrenaline course through his veins. Inside that wall, it sounded like two things he had always enjoyed: construction sites and the Fourth of July.

The chariot halted outside, next to a basin filled with water. "Thank you, gentlemen," Angela told the long-legged imps as they unharnessed themselves and headed to the basin for a drink. "Wait here if you don't mind."

They stepped down from the chariot, and Angela walked up to a pair of huge black wooden doors. They were tall and wide, reinforced with iron bars, and shut tight. "We close the doors now?" she said quite loudly.

A voice answered from above. "After the first theft in a thousand years, we do. Hold on, Obscura." Donny looked up. He was getting the hang of not crying out when he saw something strange or awful. That skill came in handy just then, because the person, or thing, who had spoken was a terrifying sight: a gnarly, piggish face with charred, ragged ears, and a pair of goggles pushed high on the forehead.

One of the doors screeched open a minute later. They

stepped through, and Donny's eyes opened wide when he saw the refinery inside.

Dozens of smoldering cones of rock, like miniature volcanoes, jutted from the ground. Some looked extinct, while others had fire, smoke, or steam gushing from their tops. In other places, the imps had dug wide holes in the ground, with ramps that dove into the openings. Flames belched from the depths, and imps hustled wheelbarrows up and down the ramps, oblivious to the heat and fire.

"The Crude," Zig said. He pointed at one of the smaller cones nearby. It looked like a witch's hat made of stone, as tall as a telephone pole. The fire that flowed from its top was like no fire Donny had ever seen. It glowed with neon intensity, bursting with yellows, oranges, and reds that bathed every surface with rippling multicolored light. The flames rolled and curled at an unnaturally slow pace, like a form of matter somewhere between liquid and gas. He could have stared at it for hours, but there was too much else to see.

The larger cones within the walls were surrounded by scaffolding, ladders, and old machinery, with tubes, stoppers, and spigots embedded at various heights. Imps of all sizes crawled up the wobbly scaffolding. They turned valves with fat wrenches, checked dials, and hoisted vessels with chains and pulleys. The vessels, which looked like they were made of black glass, were everywhere, in stacks against the wall and loaded onto carts.

"Holy smokes," was all Donny could say.

The being who had spoken to them before came down along a staircase that hugged the inside of the wall.

"Hello, Flint," Angela said.

Flint jabbed a thumb at Donny. "That a mortal?"

"You can talk to him as if he's standing right there," Angela replied. "Which he is."

"Hmmph," Flint said. "Didn't mean to be rude."

"That's okay, sir," Donny said. Flint was amazing, if a little disturbing, to look at up close. He seemed to have spent his entire existence in the flames, because his whole scaly body was scorched, blasted, and scarred, except for where goggles protected his eyes. He wore a heavy leather apron, also blackened by soot and fire.

"Show me what happened," Angela said. "Donny, you seem enchanted by the refinery. Z, do you mind?"

Zag sighed. "Yes. We will instruct him."

Angela and Flint walked away toward a smaller building within the walls. Donny heard the beginning of their conversation.

"What type was it, Flint? Not annihilation, I hope."

"No, Obscura. Destruction, but a very specific type, heavily refined."

"How strange. What do you mean, specific type . . . ?" They wandered out of earshot.

"Well, mortal, would you like to know about the refinery?" Zig asked.

"Oh," said Donny. "Sure. Please!"

He soaked up what Zig-Zag told him. Apparently, the process was similar to what he'd learned once in school about oil refineries. When the cones were capped, the fire separated into layers. Then, by tapping into the cone at various levels, the engineer imps isolated the different types of fire.

"Depending on where the holes are drilled," Zag explained, "you can extract the Flames of Torment. As you know, those once filled the Pit of Fire. Or you can extract the Flames of Destruction, which can eat through flesh or stone. Or the Flames of Illumination, which bring light but not pain or heat. Or the Flames of Annihilation—the most deadly and powerful of all."

"How is that more deadly than destruction?" Donny asked.

"Annihilation," answered Zag, "is the end of all things. If I burn you away with the Flames of Destruction, your mortal form is gone, but your soul remains. But if I destroy you with the Flames of Annihilation, you are gone forever. No body. No soul."

"Yes, that would be worse," Donny agreed quietly. "Um, does anyone ever actually get annihilated?"

Zig and Zag looked at each other. "It has happened," Zig said.

"When the punishment deserves it," said Zag.

Zig frowned. "Annihilation is never deserved."

"Typical weak-spined drivel from you, brother," Zag said. "When the crime is sufficient, the guilty should be removed from society so they can cause no further harm."

"And typical cruelty from you, brother," said Zig. "Who are we to decide when annihilation is the solution?"

"Criminy," Angela said. "Are you two at it again?" Donny hadn't noticed her return. She smirked at Zig-Zag and folded her arms. "Put your debate on hold, boys. I need to think on the way back."

CHAPTER 12

Angela asked the runners for speed, and they obliged. The chariot rumbled along so fast that Donny clutched the edge of the bench, afraid of bouncing out.

Back at the pillar, Angela hopped out and walked a few paces ahead, muttering quietly to herself. Donny walked with Zig-Zag as the two heads traded angry looks, still inflamed from their debate. They didn't look open to conversation, so with questions piled up in his brain, Donny trotted ahead to walk beside Angela. He hesitated to say anything, because she looked so deep in thought, but eventually she peered at him from the corner of her eye. "Strange doings, Cricket."

"What exactly was stolen? Do you mind if I ask?"

She exhaled through her nose. "The Flames of Destruction. We use it to build things, because it cuts through stone. But it was also used in the war."

"Did they steal a lot?"

"It doesn't take a lot. The stuff is potent. It goes through rock like scissors through paper. But yeah. A lot was stolen. A bunch of barrels."

"Didn't anybody guard it?"

"Three guards. All vanished. Either they were in on it, or . . ."

"Or what?"

Angela shrugged. "They could have been burned away by the same fire that was stolen. There was plenty of scorching, that's for sure. I think they're goners."

Zig spoke up from behind. "It's the Merciless. They're coming back."

"You don't know that," groused Zag.

"Who else?" replied Zig. "And can it be a coincidence that Havoc returned from his 'expedition' just in time for this?"

"So quick to accuse," said Zag.

"Boys . . . ," Angela began, but she didn't say anything else. Instead she looked up, because the sky suddenly had brightened, as if stadium lights had been flipped on. She shielded her eyes with her hand. "What the Sulfur?"

Great billowing clouds of illumination spread in every direction. All of Sulfur turned red and gold as the shadows sharpened.

"What's wrong with that?" asked Donny.

"It's the end of the day, not the beginning," said Zig.

"Remember when you saw the clouds released this morning? They should never be released at night," said Zag.

Angela frowned and puckered her lips. "I can't deal with one more issue right now. Z, can you go find out what happened?"

"Of course," said Zig and Zag together. They headed down the path toward the source of the cloud, bickering along the way.

Donny stared up. The clouds pulsed with orange light as they engulfed the enormous stalactites and left only the points sticking out below. "Kind of pretty," he said.

"Hmmph," Angela replied. Her brow was deeply furrowed. "I like the night."

They stood quietly for a while. Donny sneaked a sideways glance at Angela, who wasn't even looking at the clouds anymore. She stood with her arms folded, tapping one toe, eyes focused on nothing. Finally she came out of it with a toss of her head. "I want you to know something. Come with me." She walked off briskly and headed up the road that spiraled around Pillar Obscura. Once again Donny raced to catch up.

CHAPTER 13

They circled the pillar, far above Angela's rooms, and gained altitude quickly. On Donny's right, there was a low balcony carved out of the rock at the ramp's edge. On his left, in the pillar itself, they passed the occasional doorway and window. Some openings had wooden or metal doors, or leather curtains. Some were completely open and revealed simple dwellings inside, mere niches in the stone.

"Who lives in those?" Donny asked.

"Imps," she replied.

Donny stopped for a moment to catch his breath, and looked again at the swollen clouds. They began to drip fire. Giant blobs formed at the bottoms, tethered by strands that thinned and snapped, and then the luminous bubble that broke away fell slowly, twinkling and withering to nothing before it touched the ground.

"Are you all right to keep going?" Angela said. "Need a piggyback ride or something?" She tapped her back.

That sounded kind of wonderful, but Donny would never admit it. He fought back the grin that wanted to creep over his face. "I'm fine. Let's go."

The flying creatures that Donny had seen before were at eye level now. Dozens glided about, in and out of the fiery clouds, while more clung to the sides of the lower-hanging stalactites. One swooped by, close to where they stood, and Donny got his first good look. It was batlike, as big as an eagle, with a slender body and humanoid head with a pointed crest. The membranous wings were pointed and thin, with tiny hands at the tips. "What do you call those?" Donny asked, pointing.

"Gargs," Angela said. "They're harmless."

His legs and lungs burned as they climbed beyond the last of the doors and windows, until the spiraling path ended at last on a simple flat lookout. Donny had not seen Sulfur from such a height before, and more of it was visible than ever, bathed by the harsh light.

Angela seemed to appreciate the vantage point as well, because a minute passed before she spoke. "Zig-Zag told you about the war?" she said.

"A little."

"Did he tell you why it happened?"

Donny tried to remember what he'd heard. "There was a disagreement about the Pit of Fire. Reformers wanted to do something different with the dead people. But the other guys—you call them the Merciless?"

"They came up with that themselves. No mercy for the dead."

"Okay. They didn't want anything to change. So there was a war, and the reformers won."

"There's more to it than that, obviously. Do you know who started the reform?"

"No."

Angela raised her hand over her head. "That's who."

Donny stared. A strange feeling swept over him and left him weak in the arms and legs. He had gotten the sense that Angela was an important figure in Sulfur, but he never imagined just how important. It made him wonder why she wasted her time with a nobody like him.

"Really?" he said. "Why . . . I mean, how? What did you do?"

There was a low stone railing at the edge of the lookout. Angela sat and slid her legs through the space below the rail and let them dangle. Donny sat the same way beside her.

"You know how the Pit of Fire used to be," she said.

"Uh-huh. Zig-Zag told me."

"This was about sixty years ago. Lucifer had already been gone for decades, leaving the council in charge. That pit—what a horror show. So many bodies. We would constantly have to expand it because the souls piled up and spilled over. Crazy stuff went on down there. Every once in a while, a soul would get tossed right out of the pit. You know, off the end of a swinging pitchfork or something.

"Normally, I didn't like to go near the pit—it made me sick, honestly. But that one day, there I was, and a soul landed right at my feet. I looked down at that poor sucker, who I would guess was a peasant from maybe the seventeenth century. All of a sudden the guy got a weird smile on his face. A fire imp ran up, ready to spear him and toss him back into the flames, but when he got there—there was nothing to spear. Nothing but a glob of twinkling lights."

"Like I saw on the river," Donny said.

"You saw the souls before they take shape? Good. Yes. It was exactly like that. The soul of that peasant returned to its immaterial form. It floated for a moment, and then it drifted like it was a feather caught in a breeze. I followed it because I had to see where it would end up. It floated to the river and then downstream. All the way to the end, where the river disappears into another hole filled with mist." She turned and looked Donny in the eye. "And that was when I realized: we might be doing something wrong. That soul was ready to move on to whatever came next. But we had kept it here for who knows how long. You understand what I mean? The flames weren't just tormenting souls. They were *trapping* souls."

"What did you do?"

"First? I ordered the imps to throw more of the dead out

of the pit. Before long it happened again—poof! Another soul went on its merry way! Not all of them, of course, but enough of them to convince me that I was right.

"Of course, what I wanted was completely radical. I was proposing that we extinguish the pit and use another means to punish the souls that allowed them to move on when their time had come. I wanted to put a stop to the endless, mindless torment, and I had a pretty good idea how. I knew there would be resistance. Was it even worth it to try? So, I went topside for a while, just to clear my head and think about it. And when I traveled the world and took a good look around, I realized that something amazing was happening."

She paused, and the moment of silence begged the question from Donny. "What was happening?"

She pushed her hand through her hair and smiled. "Humanity was getting better."

"We were?"

"Absolutely. Are you a history buff?"

"Sort of," Donny said. He wondered if watching *Gladiator* counted.

"Well, then you should know. For as long as you knuckleheads have been around, you've been murdering, mutilating, terrorizing, persecuting, and enslaving one another."

"Speaking of enslaving," Donny said. He raised his hand to display Angela's mark on his palm.

"Oh please," she replied. She waved him off. "That's for your protection. See how long you last in Sulfur without it. What was I saying? Oh yes. You people. Somewhere along the sad trajectory of your rotten history, you started *improving*. Don't get me wrong—loads of horrible things still happen around the globe on a daily basis. But as bad as you are today, you're a bunch of pussycats compared to your ancestors. Genghis Khan murdered tens of millions. Alexander was mostly great at slaughter. Caesar was a homicidal thug. Show me an empire, and I'll show you a bloodbath. And do you know what they all did it for? The loot, mostly. And personal glory, as if butchering and plundering is something to be glorified.

"You'd never know it from your news shows, Donny, but humanity has gotten nearly respectable lately. More educated. More rational. More tolerant. Less prone to war and atrocities and mayhem.

"There was nearly a major exception: back in the sixties you came darn close to blowing yourselves off the planet. It seemed so inevitable that we were trying to figure out how to expand the pit to accommodate all the new bodies we were expecting! But you pulled back from the brink—and, by and large, you've gotten more peaceable. Then, finally, you people did something so amazing that I knew the time had come."

Again Angela let the silence linger. Donny didn't wait so long to ask this time. "What? What did we do?"

She threw her hands up. "You went to the *moon*, for crying out loud. You sent people in a rocket to the moon, and they walked around for a while, stuck a flag in it, picked up some rocks, and flew back home. Do you even appreciate how outrageous, how audacious, how supremely wonderful that was? I bought a bunch of newspapers. 'Man Walks on Moon!' 'One Giant Leap for Mankind!' And I brought them to the council. 'Look at this!' I shouted. 'Look what these numbskulls have accomplished! And what about us? Down here, nothing has changed at all! If Earth can make progress, why can't Hell?' And that was when the debate truly started. All I got back at first was ridicule, scoffing, and two scoops of outrage. But slowly I won some converts. And something else worked in our favor. The imps in the pit? Turns out a lot of them weren't too happy with the work and would be delighted to put out the fires.

"One by one, we picked up more votes in the council. It was funny how it went. Some of them simply agreed with me. Some of them thought that if we extinguished the pit, it would get Lucifer's attention and he'd come back. It took years and plenty of arm-twisting, but we gained momentum."

Donny could see the pit from there. It yawned across the landscape, ominous even without the flames and writhing figures. "So you guys just voted on it?"

"It never came to that," Angela said. "Once the Merciless saw that change was inevitable, they went a little crazy."

"Crazy how?"

"Oh, they called us traitors, started riots, assassinated a bunch of us. Finally they decided that they wanted to split away, form their own realm, and take all the souls with them. Apparently, the bigger a change you try to make, the more violently the other side reacts. Anyway, things escalated, and pretty soon we had a war on our hands. You can still see the damage. Look there, and there." She pointed to other pillars like the one they were on, where the base was surrounded by rubble, and straight below to the ruined section near her own home.

"Now, look that way—all the way across. See the far wall with the jagged peaks?"

Donny looked. Far away, beyond the pit, the river, mushroom forests, and miles of strange stone formations, lay what he thought of as the eastern side of this cavernous world. Out there stood mountains with narrow tops—really a series of colossal stalagmites that had merged together in a range that ran for miles.

"We call those the Dragonbacks," Angela said. "Now look there, between the two tallest peaks, at the bottom. See the dark space?" Donny looked at what seemed to be the mouth of a cave. In front of that opening was a wall of stone.

"Inside those mountains there are enormous passages and caves," Angela said. "Those are the Depths. We don't even know how far they go, or how deep, or what's down there. When the Merciless lost the war, that's where they retreated. We built that wall you can just make out from here, and we keep an army there to guard the cave. But we haven't seen them since."

Donny looked again at that opening, so dark in contrast with the harshly lit peaks around it. "What do you think they've been doing all this time?"

Angel tapped her chin with one finger. "According to Havoc and his fraudulent expedition, they're searching for Lucifer, and they've gone so deep, they can't be found. I don't buy it. I think he's gone there to scheme with them. The Merciless care too much about their precious pit to give up. They're either plotting a comeback, or they're biding their time, hoping that things change in Sulfur. That last thing is what worries me the most."

"Why?"

She brooded for a while. "Now that years have gone by, some on the council wonder if we did the right thing. There are thirteen members, you know. Right now if it came to a vote, it would be eight to five in favor of keeping the pit extinguished. But a couple of council members could be swayed."

"Why would they change their minds?"

"Different reasons. It might be nostalgia. They miss the fire, the heat, and the howls. Or Havoc is winning them over. Havoc thinks what we're doing is an abomination. He preaches that we've abandoned our traditions and our duty.

As far as he's concerned, roasting mortals in the fire is the only reason we exist."

"But eight to five is still pretty good," Donny said.

She frowned at that. "Do the math, Donny. If two members change their votes, we lose everything we've fought for."

Donny looked up at the billowing, incandescent clouds dripping fire. They were so bright, he had to squint to see them. Angela had just stuffed his brain with an overwhelming feast that would take a while to digest. There was a long silence, both of them lost in their own thoughts.

One of the gargs swept past them. It dove steeply from above and chirped as it passed. Two more dove by, and then another. "Odd," Angela said. She stood and shaded her eyes as she gazed into the cloud.

A terrible screech, as harsh as nails on a blackboard, rang down from above. The noise alone was enough to make Donny cringe. "What was that?"

"Hope it's not what I think it is," she said. A dozen other gargs left their perches on the stone and rushed away from the cloud in a panic. Donny glimpsed a larger shape inside the cloud as it swooped by.

Another garg dropped from the cloud, but this one was injured, one of its wings in bloody tatters. It flapped awkwardly and lost altitude fast. Unable to glide like the others, it aimed for the pillar and a place to land.

"What do you *think* it is?" asked Donny. He got up and backed away from the edge of the landing.

The thing revealed itself, dropping out of the clouds. It was a larger, nastier version of the gargs, gray and black except for the red of its mouth when it screamed. A serrated horn jutted from its snout, and the talons on its feet looked like knives.

"That is a shreek," Angela said.

The shreek closed in on the fleeing, wounded garg. The smaller creature just made it to the pillar. It grabbed the rock with its hands and feet and tried to squeeze into a crevice. But the shreek soared by and raked it with those awful talons.

The garg toppled off the pillar and fell limply past them. The shreek arced past the ledge where Donny and Angela stood, so close that Donny ducked low. With nothing else to throw, Angela took off one of her shoes and flung it at the creature. "Hey! Knock it off! Go back to the Depths!"

The shreek seemed surprised to see her there. It screeched at her as it went by, such an awful sound that Donny jammed his fingers in his ears. The cry was answered by others hidden in the clouds.

"Wish I had my sword with me," Angela grumbled. "I'd have shut him up in a hurry." She looked out at the bottoms of the fiery clouds. In the distance, above the Council Dome, smaller gargs were driven out of the clouds by the larger, fiercer shreeks. "I can't even tell how many there are."

"Is this unusual? Aren't they always here?"

She scrunched her mouth. "No. Not since the war. They were allies with the Merciless. They would carry barrels of fire and drop them on us. When the Merciless were forced into the Depths, the shreeks followed. We'd see one or two every once in a while, but nothing like this. I guess they're back."

Donny saw another poor garg drop lifelessly from the cloud. "They're horrible."

"Ugh," Angela said. She shook her head. "Let's get out of here."

Going down the spiral path was easier with gravity on their side. The commotion above had died down now that the gargs had been driven away. The shreeks were quiet and stayed hidden in the clouds.

Without the noise, Donny was able to think again, and he realized there was an important question he'd never asked. "Angela?"

"Mmm?"

"How did you know what you would do with the souls once they weren't going to be in the pit?"

"Cricket, that's enough history for one day. I want to get my mind off this stuff that's been happening. It feels like everything's going here in a hand basket." She put her arm around Donny's shoulder and jostled him. "Are you ready for some fun?"

Donny gulped. He wondered what Angela's definition of *fun* might be. "Um. I guess so?"

"Swell! We'll pack some things and leave tomorrow."

"Where are we going?"

"Topside, of course."

"What are we going to do?"

Her smile widened. "We're gonna catch a monster."

CHAPTER 14

Donny's eyes fluttered open. He lifted his head and saw the canopy all around. At least this time he knew where he was when he woke up. He parted the material on both sides, half expecting to find Tizzy peering at him, but the room was empty. There was a clock on the table beside his bed. It was four a.m. Sulfur time.

All night he'd dreamed about the astounding things he'd seen since arriving. It was almost too much to absorb, and the sheer volume and intensity of the memories had woken him in a dizzy state. Amid those confused thoughts, a word floated up: *infinite*. Why, he wondered, had that popped into his head? It was connected to something. Then he realized what it was. That strange old imp named Sooth had said that puzzling phrase over and over: *When eight sleeps, it is forever.*

"Eight sleeps," Donny muttered. He closed his eyes and pictured the word *eight* sleeping, and then the number 8 sleeping. And then he started to laugh. "Oh," he said, grinning. "I get it." He turned over again, laughed into his pillow, and dozed off once more.

CHAPTER 15

Wake up," said a musical voice. Little hands bounced
Donny's shoulders into the mattress.

"Hi, Tizzy," he said through a yawn.

She fired words like machine-gun bullets. "Angela says
you're lazy and you sleep too much and you have to go have
breakfast with me right now because you're going somewhere with her later."

"Oh. Yeah, I guess we are."

She bit her bottom lip. "Are you going home?"

Donny laughed. "No. Not home. She has something else
she wants me to do."

"Are you from New York?"

"Yes."

"Is that Gotham?"

"Well, some people call it that."

"Do you know Batman?"

Donny looked at her and tried to figure out if she was clowning around. She stared back with wide eyes. "Batman isn't a real person, Tizzy," he said.

"I know that." She looked over her shoulder, then leaned closer and whispered, "It's his secret identity."

"That's not what I mean," he said. "I mean . . ." He took another look at those wide, dark, unblinking eyes. She was holding her breath. "I mean, no. I've never met Batman. Maybe someday, though."

She nodded and then rubbed her stomach. "I want scrambled eggs and bacon! Cookie makes them into a smiley face."

"Sounds good," Donny said. "I'll meet you downstairs in a little while."

After he washed and dressed, he found Tizzy in the main room below, slapping her knees and clapping her hands to amuse herself. "I'm hungry," she said when she saw him.

Echo waited by the door. "Hello, Echo," Donny said.

"Hello," the giant imp replied.

"Where's Angela?" Donny asked Tizzy.

"She said go and eat, and she'll meet you here later," Tizzy told him. "And she said Echo has to go with us, but it's not because weird stuff is happening and she's worried."

"Okay," Donny said. He watched Echo pick up the

lethal club that leaned against the door. "Echo, are you coming along so you can protect me?"

"Protect," Echo said. He rested the weapon on his shoulder.

"Thanks," Donny told him. He didn't want to wander around alone, or just with Tizzy, with Butch in the vicinity.

They went through the tall doors, down the steps and the ramp, and took the same road toward the strangely out-of-place diner. When they approached the shattered building and the broken column where Sooth had been perched, Donny looked for the old gray imp. He planned to call out the answer to yesterday's riddle, and wanted to hear if Sooth had a new one. But the little imp wasn't in his usual place.

Tizzy noticed too. "I wonder where Sooth is."

Donny was about to answer, but instead he gasped as a hand clamped on his elbow. He looked down and saw Sooth staring wildly up. "After the light comes the fall," he said in that froggy voice.

"Right," Donny said. "Hey, I figured out the last one. The number eight looks like the symbol for infinity when it's sideways."

"After the light comes the fall," Sooth repeated, louder this time. He squeezed Donny's arm until it was nearly painful and his breath wheezed through his nose.

"Why aren't you up there?" Tizzy asked. She pointed at the broken column.

Sooth let go of Donny's arm and repeated the riddle again, reaching for Tizzy. She backed away. "After the light comes the fall," he croaked at her. The ancient imp turned to Echo next. "After the light comes the fall!"

"Are you feeling all right?" Donny asked. But Sooth wasn't paying attention to them anymore. Someone else was walking down the street. Donny was pretty sure it was another one of the council members who he had seen outside the dome. Sooth stumbled toward the newcomer and repeated the riddle again, louder still.

"He's acting funny," Tizzy said.

"Funny," Echo said.

They went on to the diner, and Donny turned the phrase over in his mind. He wondered if it could be solved as easily as the last one.

After the light comes the fall.

CHAPTER 16

Y ou're back," Angela called down when they'd returned from the diner. It sounded like she was in one of the rooms upstairs.

"Sooth was acting weird!" shouted Tizzy.

"Isn't he always? Donny, come up here, will you?" When Donny went upstairs, he saw the door to her room open, and rapped his knuckles on it.

"Come in, Cricket," she sang out from within. Donny stepped inside, and almost whistled in admiration when he looked around the room. The ceiling was twenty feet tall, and the frame of her bed reached almost as high. Murals of cherubic angels covered the walls. But the most curious feature of the room was that the bed, the shelves, the bureaus, and the tables were littered with stuffed animals of all sizes: teddy bears, dogs, cats, lions, giraffes, pandas, and more, as if she'd cleaned out an aisle at the toy store.

"Almost time to go," she said. She stepped out of a smaller connected room that must have been a huge walk-in closet. Donny saw clothes inside, hanging in long rows, with hundreds of shoes in racks and dozens of hats on shelves above. Angela was dressed in a black shirt with silver embroidery, a jacket with tails, and dark jeans with leather boots that came to her knees. The matching glove on just one hand was an eccentric touch, but even with that she'd blend in easily on the streets of New York.

"You should grab some money," she said. As she put on a glittering necklace, she gestured with one elbow to a table in the corner.

"Are you kidding me?" Donny asked. The table was littered with piles of money. He stepped up to it, his mouth hanging open. There were stacks of bills, euros, and other currencies he could not identify. "You just leave this sitting here?"

"Who's going to steal it? It's not like anyone can use it down here," she said. "Go on, grab some good old American buckaroos."

"This is crazy," Donny said. He picked up a bundle that was an inch thick. On top was a hundred-dollar bill. He riffled through the stack. They were all hundred-dollar bills. "This isn't real, is it?"

"Of course it's real."

"But . . . how much is there?"

"I haven't the slightest. Loads."

"But . . ." Donny's head wobbled. "How did you get this?"

She stepped up beside him and shoved some of the bundles into a purse. "You know all those people who arrive here by barge every day? The wicked dead? There are plenty of rich ones among them, with a lot of ill-gotten gains. If we ever run low on money, we ask the new arrivals to tell us where the loot is hidden. They're so eager to help! The embezzlers, the bank robbers, the tax cheats, the drug lords, the grafters, the white-collar weasels . . . They all figure that, if they give it up, maybe we'll go easy on them."

"Do you?"

"You're so funny." She thrust another stack into his hands. "Come on, fill those pockets. New York is expensive, you know."

Donny stared at the pile of bills again. He shook his head and stuffed one of the bundles into his pocket. "Hey, did you find out what happened with the clouds?" he asked.

"The strangest thing. There's a natural vent for the Fire of Illumination over yonder—no need for refining at all; it just comes out that way. The imps who run that operation keep the vent capped. While it was unattended, the machinery collapsed into the vent, and a huge amount leaked out. Now the skies will be bright for days. No nighttime at all."

Donny looked at the intense shaft of light that came through the window. "Was it really an accident?"

"That's a good question," Angela said.

"Is it weird that first the fire got stolen, and now this?"

"That's an even better question. Go on downstairs, I'll be right behind you."

Donny was halfway down the steps when a metallic clang rang out three times from the front door.

"Can you get that, Cricket?" Angela called from above.

Donny went to the front door, turned the lock, and pulled it open. An odd sight was on the doorstep. It was an imp about his size, in a housedress with a flower print. She—if it was a she—had a pair of old-fashioned round spectacles, a huge paisley carpet bag slung over one elbow, and an umbrella that seemed entirely unnecessary in Sulfur. Topping it all off was an obviously fake granny wig.

"Is that Nanny?" Angela shouted.

Donny stared. This ridiculous creature *looked* like a nanny, more or less. Or at least like a bipedal toad dressed up like somebody's idea of a British storybook nanny.

"I Nanny," the imp finally said, settling the question. She handed Donny the umbrella and brushed past him and into the room.

"I guess it's Nanny," Donny called back to Angela.

Tizzy bolted into the room with her arms flung over her head. "Nanny!"

"Tizzy breakfast?" asked Nanny.

Tizzy screeched to a stop. "Yes, I had breakfast."

"Tizzy nap?" asked Nanny.

"I'm too old for naps," Tizzy said with her fists on her hips.

"Tizzy Candy Land?"

"Yay, let's play!" The two of them headed for the cabinet in a corner of the room that was stuffed with books and board games.

Angela came down the stairs. "Isn't she just the perfect nanny?"

"Uh. Sure," Donny said.

"Well, maybe not perfect. She can barely talk, and she can be surly at times. But back in the day you should have seen her changing diapers."

"Stinky diapers," said Nanny.

"Gross," said Tizzy.

"She keeps an eye on Tizzy when I'm gone," said Angela. "Speaking of which, away we go."

CHAPTER 17

They left Sulfur the way Donny had first entered, up the tall stone steps and through the passageway guarded by the enormous armor-clad figure. "Any requests, Grunyon?" Angela asked as the thing opened the door.

Grunyon tipped his head to one side and thought about it. His voice rang from inside his helmet. "Crystal Pepsi?"

Angela rolled her eyes. "They haven't made that since the nineties, sweetheart."

"Oh, right. Vanilla extract, then?"

Angela's head rocked back a little, but then she grinned and double-pointed. "Vanilla extract. You got it."

They stepped through the door. The last time Donny was here, he had been sick from smoke, disoriented, and on the brink of hysteria. Now, as the door slammed shut behind them, he looked with clear eyes at the passage curving out of sight. Around the bend, a dim orange light flickered. "So, this is the way up?"

She raised her eyebrows at him. "It's not literally *up*, you know. I mean, people on Earth used to think the underworld was down. Obviously, or you wouldn't have named it the *under-world*. Coincidentally, all of us down here used to think that the mortal realm was up. But then you guys invented a little thing called science, and the evidence seemed to rule that out."

"But you don't know for sure?"

"Nobody's ever gone to the roof of Sulfur and started drilling up, if that's what you're asking. Look, I don't think you appreciate just how inquisitive you mortals are. You people need explanations for *everything*. How did the universe begin? What's on the other side of the moon? Where did the dinosaurs go? Why was *Two and a Half Men* on TV for so long? Here in Sulfur, most of us aren't that nosy. The only thing we're curious about is human nature."

"Well, if you're not up and we're not down, where is Sulfur?"

"Darned if I know. One time we had this evil dead astrophysicist down here. I asked him that very question, and he could only guess. He prattled on about parallel universes, quantum physics, alternate dimensions, wormholes, a planet with the same mass as Earth but with an unusual layer of open space between its surface and its core, blah blah blah."

Donny's brain was aching, and he clutched his forehead. "Okay. So we don't take an elevator or anything like
that. How do we get to Earth then?"

"Follow me."

When they rounded the bend, Donny saw the source
of the light. Where the passage ended, there was a wall
of ruby-red flame. It rippled upward like an inverted
waterfall.

A small figure, hooded and cloaked, no bigger than a
toddler, sat on a tiny chair beside the fire, maybe sleeping.
Leaning against the chair was something that looked like
a medieval weapon, a short club with nasty spikes at its
round head. "That's Porta, the keeper," Angela whispered.
"Don't do anything to annoy her. She gets her dander up
in a hurry."

When they were still several paces away, the keeper
moved. The cloaked head rose up, and a snout poked out
and sniffed the air. It was long and narrow and reminded
Donny of a baboon snout, but with scales instead of fur.
The keeper reached down with arms that were far too
long for her tiny body, and wrapped her hand around the
shaft of the weapon.

"Yes, Porta, it's a mortal," Angela told her. "The same
one I brought down not long ago." She spoke to Donny
over her shoulder. "Show her my mark."

Donny frowned a little—he still wasn't happy about
this apparently permanent mark on his palm—but he

raised his hand and displayed the winged *O*. That seemed to placate the keeper, who settled back on her seat.

Porta raised one of her sinewy arms and made a sweeping gesture across the wall of flame. The fire transformed quickly, with a large round section that bulged from the center. It looked as if an oversize beach ball were pushing in from the other side. Shapes appeared on the bulge, and Donny recognized the continents of Earth surrounded by the dimmer orange of the oceans. The wall of flame had become a giant globe, gently spinning. There were tiny pinholes, whiter and brighter than the rest of the flame, scattered across the nations.

"See the dots?" Angela said. "That's everywhere we can go."

It looked as if they could travel practically anywhere. Europe rolled by, with those intense points everywhere. Then came the ocean. "But there are dots in the middle of the Atlantic," he said. "There aren't any islands there."

"Boats," she told him, and then she spoke to Porta. "Manhattan, please," Angela said.

The keeper nodded then flicked a hand as if to spin the globe. It turned faster. With her spidery fingers she made a beckoning motion, and it pulled the features of the globe closer. Soon Donny could see the east coast of the United States. She drew the globe nearer again, and there was the familiar shape of the island of Manhattan.

Porta turned to look at Angela. Inside the hood, Donny

caught a glimpse of glazed white eyes, and he tried not to shudder. The keeper simply stared at Angela, her head bent to one side.

"Right, more specific," Angela said. "Greenwich Village, please."

The keeper looked at the flames for a moment, and then turned back to Angela and shook her head.

"Not available? Let me see—I think that's Midtown West? Well, we have some shopping to do anyway. I haven't gone that way in a while."

The keeper nodded. She nudged the globe until the pinpoint she wanted was centered. Then she held both hands up, forming a diamond of space between her thumbs and fingers. In the middle of the globe, the flames darkened in a diamond shape like the one she had formed. As she drew her hands apart, the shape stretched wider and taller, and it darkened until it was almost black. The flames within the shape burned out and left behind a flimsy, wavering parchment.

"Thank you, Porta!" Angela said. She took Donny's hand and led him into the dark shape. It was merely the thinnest layer of ash, and it disintegrated as she passed through it. Donny felt a blast of heat on both sides for a moment as they stepped into what looked like a basement utility room.

Donny turned to look behind him and saw Porta in the space they had left, waving the flames back together to seal the opening. Then all he saw was ordinary fire. *I guess we're in Manhattan,* he thought. In a basement in the city, someone had kept a fire burning. It looked like a large version of a gas fireplace, with brick all around and flames shooting from metal tubes connected to a propane tank nearby. A vent was above the fire, and a fan whirred noisily.

There was a man in the room, dressed in a sleeveless T-shirt and plaid flannel shorts, oblivious to their presence. He sat at a folding card table covered mostly by a jigsaw puzzle that had his full attention. On a second chair there was a pizza box. He had a pepperoni slice in his hand and chewed noisily while he stared down at the puzzle. A large messy pile of brown glass bottles was in the corner.

"Incoming!" Angela bellowed through cupped hands.

The man shrieked and shot up from his chair, upending the table. Jigsaw pieces rained onto the floor. The pizza landed with a splat, sauce side down.

He clutched his chest with one hand. "I nearly wet my pants."

"There are products for that," Angela said.

"You scared me, that's all. I never know when you're coming."

"Well, here I am. Thanks for the fire."

"Anytime," the man muttered. It sounded like "no time" was his actual preference.

"Toodles," Angela said. She tugged Donny behind her.

"Er, thanks a lot," Donny added. "And sorry about the puzzle."

The man watched them go with his fingers on his wrist, checking his pulse. They left through a door that latched behind them. Cement stairs took them up into the lobby of a rundown apartment building. They stepped outside onto the bustling streets of midtown Manhattan in the middle of a bright summer day. Donny took a deep breath. There was that familiar scent of New York, an urban odor that assaulted the nose like no other. It wasn't altogether pleasant, with its whiffs of garbage, motor oil, hot-dog carts, automobile exhaust, pizza grease, dog pee, and stale air wafting from the subways. But it smelled like home.

"I can't believe we're back," he said.

"Remember, I can take you just about anywhere. We could go to Paris just to get French fries."

"People just keep all those fires going for you? Why?"

"Gee whiz, let me think. Because we pay them?"

"Aren't you afraid somebody will, you know, tell the world about you?"

"Ha! Would you take that chance and double-cross me, knowing what you know?"

Donny thought about that. "I would not."

"Of course you wouldn't. It's unwise to get on our bad side." Angela took a phone from her pocketbook and turned it on. She pulled out another, hit the power button, and handed it to him. "Here," she said.

"You're giving me a phone?"

"Yup. You shouldn't use your own phone, I assume. Being a missing person."

"Oh, right." He had lost his phone the night of the fire anyway, dropping his bag while his father had chased him. His heart sank a little. *A missing person.* That was exactly what he was. Suddenly the idea of popping up in New York didn't seem so smart, and he instinctively looked up and down the street. Was anyone looking for him? He jolted a little as the phone rang out in his hand.

"Hey, it's ringing."

"Maybe you should answer it."

He raised it to his ear. "Hello?"

He heard Angela's voice beside him and through the phone. "It's me, you nitwit. I'm making sure it works."

"Oh. Yeah. It works." Donny laughed and ended the call.

"Come on," she said, and she was three steps away before he took one.

CHAPTER 18

Angela took a lot of strides in a hurry, and Donny had to speed-walk to keep up. He couldn't go faster without breaking into a jog.

She stopped abruptly and stared ahead with her mouth agape in a delighted smile. "Doggies!" she said. An elderly man came toward them down the sidewalk with a pair of bristly white terriers on leashes. She put a hand on Donny's chest and pushed him against the wall, then joined him there. "Act normal," she said.

"You're telling *me* to act normal?" Donny said. He rubbed the back of his head where it had struck the brick.

"Shush now." Angela peered sideways at the dogs and put on an unconvincing display of casual behavior. She even puckered her lips to whistle.

"What's the big deal?" Donny asked.

She whispered from the corner of her mouth. "I want to see how close they'll get. They're so *cute!*"

The dogs approached, tails wagging furiously. Their mouths were open in canine grins, tongues lolling. Donny wondered why getting close would be a problem. The sidewalk wasn't wide, and the man was about to walk right past them.

When they were still twenty paces away, the tails fell still, and the ears that had pointed high flattened against their heads. The dogs slunk low and finally spun and turned the other way. Their leashes tangled around the man's legs. The man laughed. "What's the matter with you guys?" He stared up the sidewalk, probably looking for another dog, but only saw Donny and Angela. "Something spooked my babies!" he said.

Angela scowled and grumbled. "Mmm-hmm."

"That's because of you?" Donny asked quietly. "No way."

"They *hate* me," she pouted back. "Watch." She grabbed Donny by the wrist and hauled him down the sidewalk toward the dog walker. As they passed, the dogs backed away, over the curb and into the gutter. One snarled at Angela and the other whined.

"Jeez," the man said. "They never do this."

"Maybe they have rabies," Angela shot back over her shoulder. She dropped Donny's wrist. As she stalked away, Donny trailing, she stuck her lower lip out. "All I want to do is pet a stupid dog. Just once."

Danny trotted up beside her. "Dogs don't like you? Like, all dogs?"

"Not just dogs. Animals. All of them."

"I can't believe it. Have you tried cats?"

She glared at him. "Of *course* I've tried cats. They absolutely *freak* when I try to touch them. Once, I cornered one and grabbed it. It tried to scratch my face off." She closed her eyes and stroked the air. "But it was so soft. One cuddle, I'd be happy. One stupid cuddle."

"Grown-up cat or a kitten?"

"Doesn't matter."

"How about a guinea pig?"

"They squeal bloody murder in the cage. Or they have a heart attack and go belly up."

Donny stared. "Rabbits?"

"Likewise."

"Birds?"

"Tell me if you ever see a bird anywhere near us, ever. Pigeons fly away, and they're *disgusting*. Even turkeys run away, and nothing's dumber than a turkey. Forget it, okay?"

"Did you ever go to a zoo?"

"Worst day of my life. It caused a riot. Every last animal went berserk. Monkeys, elephants, camels, zebras, all of them. The tigers tried to jump the fences. The pandas fainted."

Donny thought for a while. "How about spiders?"

Her nose wrinkled. "Who wants to pet a spider? I

want to touch a sweet, fluffy thing, all right? Spiders! Cripes. For the record, bugs get out of my way too. Like I'm made of citronella. Stay near me and you'll never get a mosquito bite."

There was an intersection ahead, where birds sat on wires that held up the traffic lights. Sure enough, as Donny and Angela reached the corner, the birds took flight in the opposite direction.

"But . . . why?" Donny asked. "What makes the animals afraid?"

"They know what I am," Angela said quietly. She stared at the sidewalk. "And you know what else? There are some people who sense it too. And a few people, one in a thousand maybe, they get seriously unnerved. I call them canaries. I have to avoid those." Donny looked at the crosswalk sign, waiting for it to tell them to walk, but out of the corner of his eye he sensed Angela looking at him.

"What about you, Cricket?"

"What?"

"You sense anything when I'm around?"

"Uh." Donny thought about how to answer this one. It wasn't fear he felt, that was for sure. "No. Nothing like that. I'm fine when you're around. I feel good." He felt a twitch in his gut. Was that the unnerved sensation she'd talked about? He didn't think so.

She narrowed her eyes and smiled a little. "Right back at you, Cricket. You know what I like about you?"

He shook his head. His legs felt a little shaky.

"Hanging with you, I feel like a kid." She hopscotched for a couple of steps, then stomped the pavement with two feet at the end. "Now I think we need to do some shopping."

CHAPTER 19

Angela dragged Donny into three separate stores. She picked out clothes for both of them then thrust piles of bills at the bemused cashiers. In a grocery store, they cleared out the entire stock of vanilla extract. Then they walked to Madison Square Park, bought cheeseburgers and shakes for lunch, and found a bench.

Donny looked over his shoulder now and then, still nervous he might see someone he knew. But he reminded himself what a huge, crowded city this was, and how few of his friends tended to venture into Midtown from Brooklyn.

Angela finished her burger and leaned back on the bench with arms spread wide. "So, Cricket. What about your parents?"

Donny dropped his gaze. "What do you mean?"

"You haven't said a word about your mother or father

since we met. As in, 'I want my mommy' or 'I want my daddy.' Shouldn't a kid your age be freaking out, torn away from the parental bosom? Any particular reason you're not talking about them?"

Donny dropped his gaze. "No reason."

"Maybe it has something to do with you hiding in a filthy brick heap in the middle of the night?"

Donny sagged in his seat. The cheeseburger was delicious, but suddenly he didn't want the last few bites. He rolled it up in the wrapper and dropped it into the empty paper bag. "No. I mean, yeah. Sure. Of course it does."

"You wanna tell me about that?"

"Do I have to?"

"Not at all." She leaned toward him with glittering eyes and a tiny smile. "I'm just so darned curious."

Donny rocked his head back and let out a deep breath, straight up. It occurred to him that it might be a relief to talk about it. "It was just me and my father."

"No mother?"

"Well, there was. My dad said she just left one day. Without saying anything. She just . . ." The words trailed off as dark thoughts clouded his mind. He was young when his mother left, so young that he only had the dimmest memories of what she looked like. He and his father had talked about her over the years. His father always said she hadn't been happy being a wife or a mother, and that was why she'd left. But now, after what Donny had learned about his father, he wondered if that was the real story. What if she'd made the same discovery he had?

"Something on your mind?" Angela said.

He lifted his head and shook it as if coming out of a dream. "No."

"So your dad raised you by himself?"

"Yeah."

"How nice of him."

"Wait until you hear the rest before you decide how nice he is," Donny said. He stared at nothing for a while, and then went on. "When I was growing up, though, I never really missed having a mom. I had the coolest dad in the world. All my friends were jealous."

"Really. What was so cool about him?"

"He looked like an action movie star. Dressed like one too. He had a mysterious job that he said he couldn't talk about much. The most he ever said about it was 'security consultant.' My friends used to joke he was a spy or something. It paid really well, because he had a lot of money, and we lived in a great place in Brooklyn. It wasn't far from where you found me, in one of those brownstones with the big flight of steps in front."

"Love those," Angela said.

"Uh-huh. So he had to travel for his job a few times a year, and he was gone for weeks. He hired a nanny to watch me while he was gone. We changed nannies a lot— he said he didn't want me to love any nanny more than him, but now I think he just didn't want any nanny getting to know *him* too well."

Angela arched an eyebrow. "Good story. I'm hooked."

"When he was back, all he wanted to do was have fun. We played cards, we went to the movies, we went to basketball and football and baseball games, and we always had amazing seats. But it wasn't just fun stuff. He always told me, he wanted me to be smart."

"You *are* smart," Angela said. "I can tell by the way you talk. And you're confident, too. A lot of kids your age are insecure dopes."

Donny smirked. It made him glow a little inside, to get a compliment from her. He could thank his father for those qualities at least. He made a mental note to use big words in conversation. "Yeah, my dad said I should speak up for myself but not be obnoxious about it. But mostly he wanted me to know stuff. He made sure I did my homework and got me tutors if I ever needed them. And we went to all kinds of museums. We traveled a lot too. He wanted me to see the world."

"Really. Have you ever been to Europe?"

"Oh yeah. My dad took me one summer. The whole summer. He said he had the kind of job where he could take as much time off as he needed. Now I think he had to get out of the country for a while. But it was great. We went everywhere. Edinburgh, London, Paris, Vienna, Prague, Rome . . . I'm forgetting some."

"All that travel? But you're so young. You're like a fetus."

"It was cool. And my dad was with me the whole time."

"Well," Angela said. "That does sound delightful. Your friends were right about your father. Even I'm a little jealous. So how do you go from that to the top of a burning building?"

Donny cleared his throat and rubbed the back of his neck. "I found out what my dad's real job is."

Angela leaned in, staring avidly. "Hmmmm?"

"He kills people for money."

She pushed his shoulder and nearly toppled him off the bench. "Shut up!"

"It's true."

She shook her head with a little smile. "A *hit man*? This is just like the movies! How'd you find out?"

"I was supposed to sleep over at my friend Kevin's house, but he got sick and started throwing up, so Kevin's mom drove me home. My dad didn't hear me come in—I actually snuck in because I thought it would be funny to surprise him. He was talking to some guy. . . . First I thought it was a joke. But it wasn't. They were talking about somebody my dad was supposed to kill, and my dad was arguing about the price and talking about all the other people he'd killed, and that this one would be hard and it would cost more."

"Golly."

"Yeah,'" Donny said. "I just stood there and listened. And then I tried to leave, and my father must have heard me, because he came running with a gun in his hand."

Angela listened with her mouth open.

Donny closed his eyes and rubbed them with his fingers. "He looked so mad until he saw it was me. I never saw him look like that before. I just ran, with him after me, telling me to stop. I didn't know what he would do. I don't think he'd ever hurt me. But what about that other guy? Maybe he'd do something, even if my father didn't."

He felt Angela's hand on his arm. She pulled Donny's hand away from his face and clasped it in hers.

"I didn't know where else to go. If I went to a friend's house, I might've put him and his family in danger. I thought about going to the police, but I wanted to think first. So I ran to that brewery. I knew where it was because Kevin and I had been there before, just exploring. And that's how you found me."

"Aw, Cricket. That's terrible. No wonder you haven't talked about it." Angela squeezed his hand. "But look at the bright side."

"What bright side?"

She grinned and leaned in. "Stick around Sulfur long enough, and you'll probably see your daddy again."

CHAPTER 20

Angela led Donny to a handsome old building a few blocks away on Fifth Avenue. She used a key to get into a lobby, and used the key again once she'd summoned the elevator to unlock the button to the highest floor.

"This is your place?" Donny asked as the elevator hummed ten stories upward.

"Mine to use," she said. "I don't technically own it. We have to hide our tracks pretty well with fake companies and aliases."

"You can do that?"

"We have clever people like my friend Howard to do it for us. If you have enough money, they can do anything." The elevator chimed and opened into a foyer with a single door. Angela unlocked it, and Donny stepped inside a jaw-dropping apartment. It looked like it belonged in an architectural magazine. The ceiling was absurdly high. The kitchen was vast and gleamed with polished wood and stainless steel. Against one wall was the biggest television Donny had ever seen.

"Drop the bags anywhere," she said. "And make yourself at home. I have some errands to take care of, but I'll see you in a bit."

"Errands?" Donny tried but failed to keep the sound of disappointment out of his voice.

"Check the place out! The guest room—the one with the blue walls—is over there. And don't miss the round room, up those stairs and through the door. Watch TV, play some music, pig out, whatever you want. I'll be back by dark."

"By dark?" That was hours away.

"Have you gotten hard of hearing? Yes, by dark. You might want to get a nap in. We'll be out late tonight, and you'll need your energy."

She was gone a moment later, shutting the door behind her. Donny stared at the door for a while. He heard the ding of the elevator and the subtle hum of its machinery as it took Angela down.

There was a terrace outside the main room. He went onto it, leaned over the railing, and tried to spot Angela on the street. If she was there, she was lost in the crowd.

He killed the afternoon wandering around the place. The apartment was beautiful but hardly lived-in. He opened cabinet doors and bureau drawers, but almost all of them were empty. The kitchen at least was well stocked, but only with items that wouldn't go bad. He found a bag of Oreos, checked the expiration date—still good for a few months—and opened it up. As he munched on the cookies, trying not to spill black crumbs everywhere, he looked at the views from the terrace and every window, and appreciated the familiar skyline. The dazzling Chrysler Building was visible to the north, the soaring new Freedom Tower to the south.

He wandered up the stairs, went through a door, and found himself in a remarkable room—round, with tall windows around its perimeter. A little gas fireplace was in one wall, unlit. The ceiling overhead was domed, and painted white and gold. He whistled to himself. He didn't know much about New York real estate, but a place like this on Fifth Avenue had to be worth millions.

There were weird, modern pieces of furniture all around. One sofa looked odd, with its wavy contours, but when he lay down, it was surprisingly comfortable. The sun fell across that spot, but despite the warmth, a chill swept over him. He thought about the city outside and his house not far away, just over the bridge to the south. Was it really possible that Brooklyn wasn't his home anymore? That he didn't belong to this world at all, but to Sulfur instead?

He always had a general idea of how his life was

supposed to go. Middle school, high school, college. Get a job. Start a family. Something like that, anyway. But suddenly he could not imagine what the next day would bring, never mind the next year.

As he worried about what he'd gotten himself into, he felt his pulse quicken. His thoughts swirled like a tornado. He closed his eyes and tried to calm himself with Doc's breathing trick. In the nose, slowly. Pause. Out the mouth, even slower. He did it over and over until the sun warmed him again, and he finally fell asleep.

Even after a long nap, he had time to watch a few movies before Angela returned. It was after dark, as she'd predicted. She came in holding a big brown paper bag. "You like Thai food?"

Donny nodded. "Definitely."

"Great." She unpacked an absurd number of white boxes and sauces. "Let's eat—and then it's game time!"

When they were done, she told Donny to change into the black jeans and black hooded sweatshirt she'd bought for him. When he came back, she was at the kitchen counter, holding a tiny glass jar with an eyedropper for a lid. The stuff inside swirled and glowed like a miniature lava lamp. "You need some demon drops for tonight," she said.

Donny shook his head. "I'm not swallowing that."

"Of course not. It goes in your eyes."

He took a step back. "Nuh-uh. You're not putting something called 'demon drops' in my eyes."

"Oh, did I say demon drops? I meant fuzzy bunny juice."

"No way."

Angela puckered her mouth to one side. "For crying out loud. It won't do any permanent damage."

"Oh, just temporary damage?"

"No damage at all. In most cases."

"Most cases!"

"I'm *kidding*. It's harmless. And it's the only way for you to see."

"I have twenty-twenty vision."

She scrunched her face. "I have no idea what that means. But *this* is the only way for you to see the creature we've come to catch. Your mortal eyesight isn't enough. You need a little help." She waggled the tiny bottle.

Donny eyed it doubtfully. "You're sure it's safe."

"Absolutely," she replied, wearing one of her wicked grins. She unscrewed the top, squeezed the bulb on the dropper, and lifted it. The thin glass tube glowed with the liquid inside. "Now tilt your head back and don't blink."

Donny took a deep breath and did as she'd asked. Her hand came into view, and the shining eyedropper was poised above his eyeball. "Wait," he said as second thoughts occurred, followed by third, fourth, and fifth thoughts. He closed his eyes. "What's that stuff really made of?"

"Oh, this and that," she said. "Come on, open up and hold still."

As soon as he did, a glowing drop hit his left eye. Then another hit his right. His eyes grew warm, almost until it was uncomfortable, but the heat soon faded. He blinked, and looked at Angela and the room around him. Everything had taken on an amber hue.

"Thank goodness," Angela said. "You're still alive."

Donny's mouth fell open. "What!"

She laughed. "Just joshin'. I told you, it's perfectly safe. How does everything look?"

"A little not right."

"Perfect. Wait till we get outside."

"The drops will wear off by dawn," Angela told him as they stepped onto Fifth Avenue. It might have been after midnight, but this was New York, and the streets were still lively. Cabs sped past, a distant siren wailed, and a light crowd roamed the sidewalks. "Look at the people," she said.

Donny watched a group go by, young men and women dressed mostly in black and gray, talking about music. Each was surrounded by a glow, mostly orange, that pulsed like a heartbeat. One of the women smiled warmly at Donny as they went by—her glow was the brightest and most orange of all. The last of the group was a man who peered at them sideways as he passed. His glow was different: a dim, grayish purple, like a bruise.

"What'd you see?" Angela asked once they'd passed.

"There's light coming out of them," Donny said.

"Auras," Angela said. "That was a pretty decent bunch, if you ask me, judging by their light."

"But one of them——"

"Yes. That last fellow better watch himself. He's either done some things he shouldn't have, or he's thinking about it. With an aura as ugly and purple as that, he may end up on a slow boat to Sulfur."

Donny watched the group move down the street. They stopped to wait for a crossing signal. "Why don't we tell him?"

Angela sniffed and shook her head. "We're not here to fix people."

The pedestrian sign glowed white, and the group crossed the street. "But what if he does something bad? Maybe those people are in danger."

"Donny, I'm not running around fighting evil like some comic book character. We don't intervene. We let life happen then check the scorecard after the buckets are kicked."

"But——"

"But nothing. Butt out. Right now you and I are here to collect a troublemaker from downstairs who's gotten loose in the mortal realm. When *that* happens, I step in. You people get into enough mischief on your own. You don't need a nasty little demon stirring things up. Let's go." She strode off quickly, as usual.

Donny took one more look at the group, almost out of sight now, and then ran to catch up to Angela. "Did you say nasty little demon?"

"Yes. A specific kind of demon," she answered. "A murmuros, we call it. It's a weak, pathetic creature. It chooses a human victim and pours poisonous thoughts into his or her ear. The person doesn't even know it's there. You'll see." She turned into a subway entrance and hurried down the steps. "You ever ride the subway?"

"I grew up around here—of course I rode the subway. But usually not this late."

"Why not?"

"It just . . . It feels kind of dangerous."

"Kiddo, you're singing my tune!"

Angela hummed and checked her phone as they waited on the platform. Headlights glared in the tunnel, and then the train roared into sight. It slowed with a whine and hiss of brakes as it neared the platform. They stepped through the doors and took a pair of seats. There were only three other people on the car with them—a trio of unkempt, unshaven men who stopped talking and stared at Angela as she took the opposite seat. Their auras were like that of the man in the group they'd just seen. They were an ugly, grayish sort of purple, but even darker. Donny sat beside Angela. He wished she'd moved to the other end of the car.

Angela hummed to herself and glanced at the trio. "I

wonder if I have enough cash on me," she said, more to herself than to Donny, and louder than Donny would have liked. She reached into her bag and extracted one of the thick stacks of hundred-dollar bills held together with a blue rubber band. Donny's eyes widened. Angela thumbed through the bills and counted to herself. "Eight hundred, nine, a thousand, eleven hundred . . ."

The men stared at the cash. Donny lowered his eyes but knew they were watching. He saw the one on the right move his foot over and tap the boot of the man in the middle.

"Thirteen, fourteen, fifteen hundred . . ."

Donny felt sweat bloom on his forehead. He nudged Angela with his elbow and whispered out the corner of his mouth. "Put that away."

Angela looked at Donny with her eyebrows raised. The postures of the men across the car shifted. One uncrossed his legs. Another put his hands on his knees and leaned subtly forward. The one on the left glanced over his shoulder to see if anyone else was in the car, and to the upper corners, maybe looking for security cameras. Donny sensed their hungry energy.

Angela smiled at the men. "What are you guys staring at? The money?" She riffled the stack of bills with one finger. "Sure is a lot of cash, isn't it?"

The man in the middle stood up. He seemed to be the leader. There was a faded tattoo on his neck. "Sure is."

"You think *that's* valuable?" Angela asked. She dropped the money into her bag and lifted her gloved hand, exposing the thick golden band around her wrist. "Did you notice this bracelet, Mr. Neck Tattoo? Solid gold. Thousands of years old. It really ought to be in a museum. I can't imagine what it's worth."

The other men stood up. The one on the right was alarmingly muscled. The man in the middle reached inside the front of his jacket to some inner pocket. The jacket bulged as his fist closed around something. "We're gonna have to take that," Neck Tattoo said. The hand came out with a gun.

Donny groaned, and Angela laughed. "I don't think you really want this bracelet. Because I'd have to take it off, and you don't want that, I promise you."

"Next stop's coming up. Let's do this," the muscled man said to Neck Tattoo.

"Give it up," Neck Tattoo said as he curled the fingers of his free hand.

Angela stood, radiant and excited, as if she'd been asked to dance. Donny started to stand too, but she pushed him down with two strong fingers and stepped in front of him. There was a strange sound in the air—a low tone almost beyond the range of human hearing. It was like distant thunder, or the crackle of power lines overhead. Donny felt a wave of gooseflesh sprout on his arms. He held his breath.

The men sensed it too. The hand that held the gun began to shake. The muscled man's face twitched madly. The third man uttered a strangled, high-pitched noise, the kind a puppy might make. He backed away from Angela and Donny, toward the door between the subway cars.

"Frankie, I don't like this," the muscled man said to Neck Tattoo.

"*Frankieee!*" Angela repeated, like it was the name of an old friend. "You pull that trigger, Frankie, and things will get a lot scarier in a hurry."

Donny peered around Angela. She was projecting something at the men, a beam of pure terror. He sensed it emanating from her. It was focused on them, but it still leaked out in all directions, and brushed against him, too. It felt like spiders crawling up his spine.

Tears trickled from Frankie's eyes, but he gritted his teeth and tried to hold his ground. The muscled man stared with his eyes practically exploding from their sockets. The third guy pulled open the door between the cars and darted through, and the squeal and slam of the door finally broke the spell for the other two. They turned and bolted. Frankie looked over his shoulder with animal panic in his eyes, and the side of his head clipped the door as he ran through.

"Ouchy," Angela called after him. The subway reached the next station, and Donny saw the three men bolt from the next car and dash for the stairs, Frankie holding a hand to his head.

Angela chuckled to herself and sat down next to Donny again. She returned the money to her bag, sat back, and crossed her legs.

"What is that thing you do?" he asked.

"To freak them out?" She put the back of her hand to her forehead and made a flicking motion with her fingers. "I just unleashed a little terror in their direction. If I give 'em a little, they get nervous. If I go full throttle, I can sometimes make 'em pass out."

Donny took a moment to absorb the information. "That's amazing, but you wouldn't have had to do it just now if you hadn't started the whole thing."

"What's that supposed to mean?"

"You created that situation. Nothing would have happened if you hadn't shown off all that money."

"So? I was just entertaining myself."

"But I thought you didn't do that."

"Do what?"

"Intervene. You scared those guys. Maybe they'll think twice about robbing someone from now on."

She laughed. "I doubt that!"

"Okay, comic book hero."

"Give me a break."

"Fighter of evil doers. Sulfur Girl."

"Shut your pizza hole. I was having fun."

The subway rumbled on. Another stop came and went, but they were still alone. Donny turned a thought over in his mind, and wondered if he should voice it.

"Angela."

"Hmmm?"

"Would you do me a big favor?"

She looked at him sideways. "Depends."

"Would you scare my dad like that?"

She sat up and arched an eyebrow. "You say the nuttiest things."

Donny's nerves were on fire with the possibilities. "You could scare my dad like you scared those guys. But worse—a lot worse! Tell him he has to go straight, or something awful will happen to him. That could work. It could really work!"

She rested her chin on her knuckles and stared back. "Sorry, kiddo. No dice."

"But you could save him. You could save his soul!"

"Donny, you're a sweet kid. I see where you're coming from. But that is not the way I operate."

"But—"

"*No,*" she said, and for an instant Donny felt a tiny hint of that beam of terror she could project. His breath caught in his throat. He turned away and looked straight ahead, his hand clutching the front of his shirt.

CHAPTER 21

"There," Angela said. She pointed up at the apartment building that loomed overhead. It was four stories tall with five windows across. The brick had been painted years before, but only flakes remained, like peeling skin. Black fire escapes formed a stack of Zs in front of the windows. "Third floor, on the right."

Donny stared at the dimly lit rectangle. "And this thing—people can't see it?"

"It's not exactly invisible. You might have caught a glimpse of one yourself."

That stopped the breath in Donny's throat. "What? Really?"

"Have you ever thought you saw something move out of the corner of your eye, but when you looked that way, you didn't see anything?"

P. W. Catanese

"Um. Sure. Hasn't everybody?"

"Did you ever hear something whisper, but you couldn't figure out where it came from?"

"You're creeping me out right now."

"You ever just get the chills for no reason at all? You'd swear that something was in the room, even though you couldn't see it? Everything's normal, and suddenly, you just got . . . *scared*?"

"Please stop. I'm really sorry I asked."

"I'm just saying. That's what it's like when one of these things is around. Scoping you out to see if you're vulnerable. You ought to know what we're dealing with. It's a troublemaker of the worst kind."

Donny looked at the window again. It dimmed for a moment as something moved in front of the light source. "So this whispering thing . . ."

"Murmuros."

"Murmuros. It lives in an apartment in Brooklyn?"

She shook her head. "Temporary residence. A murmuros roams the world and looks for someone to latch on to. This one's name is Gustus. I chased him in Pakistan and Denmark and then Missouri, and I almost had him in Greece. Wherever he goes, he wants to stir up hate, and when he finds a good vessel for making that happen . . . that's what makes him happy. And that's what he's up to right now. He found a patsy, and that patsy lives three stories up, on the right."

154

"Patsy?"

"Sorry, old-fashioned term. Gustus found a sucker. A victim. This guy—he's an easy mark for the murmuros. Weak of mind. Inclined to hate. Simple to manipulate."

Donny heard footsteps and turned to see a man approaching down the alley. A streetlight behind him cast an elongated shadow. "Don't worry, Cricket," Angela said. "That's Carlos. He's here to help."

Carlos wasn't very tall, but he was wide and strong. He had a friendly face, framed by a narrow beard that ran along his jawline. Like Donny, he was dressed mostly in black: wool cap, jeans, boots, and leather jacket, and he had a long black bag slung over his shoulder. "Good evening," he said quietly. He smiled at Angela and then at Donny. "Angela, who's your friend?"

"Carlos, this is Donny. Donny, Carlos." They shook hands.

"Thanks for your help tracking this one down," Angela said.

"De nada," Carlos said with a shrug.

"Is Victor coming?" Angela asked.

Carlos shook his head. "Still afraid, after the last time."

Still afraid. Those words echoed inside Donny's head.

Angela tapped her bottom lip with a finger. "Hmmm. Well, I think we should go for it anyway. We need to catch Gustus before he moves on. Donny can help you."

Donny wasn't sure how he felt about the "helping"

part. His eyes bulged, but he didn't say anything.

"So, here's what we do," Angela said. "There are only two ways out of that dump. The door that leads to the hallway, and those windows that lead to the fire escape."

"Correct," Carlos said.

"I'll go to the apartment door. If I can get the patsy to open the door, and Gustus doesn't sense me coming, then I can handle this myself. If he heads for the window, you boys will use the net. You have the net, Carlos?"

Carlos patted his black bag. "Right here."

"What's this fellow's name, anyway, the patsy?"

"Massey."

Angela rubbed her hands together. "Won't this be fun!"

"Or terrifying," Donny suggested.

"You're both right," Carlos said.

Donny looked up at the glowing window. "This thing can sense you're coming?"

"Right," Angela said. "Kind of like animals. Moments like this are why I need mortal helpers. Gustus won't know you're there."

Donny felt a twinge in his chest. "That's why you saved me? To do this?"

She reached out and bopped the end of his nose with a finger. "Aww. Also because you sounded so pitiful, calling for help!"

Donny knew from the warmth in his cheeks that his face had gone red. He looked away from her, up at the fire escape. It began like most of them, one story above ground level, with a ladder that was raised out of reach. He was relieved to find a flaw in the plan. "Angela, there's no way for us to—"

His question was interrupted, and the air forced out of his lungs, as Angela seized him from behind with her hands under his arms. She tugged him down a little and then tossed him in the air. Suddenly the ladder was directly in front of him, and it was simple enough to grab the railing with both hands and plant his feet between the rungs.

If they hadn't been about to sneak up on a monster, he would have shouted from surprise at being launched. Instead he just gaped down, stunned at how absurdly strong Angela was. "Move," she told him. He climbed onto the landing of the fire escape and watched in amazement as she repeated the feat with Carlos, who must have outweighed Donny by sixty pounds.

"Give me a few minutes to find a way inside," she called up quietly. "Donny, I'll text you when I'm ready. See you boys later." She sauntered down the alley and headed for the front of the building.

"Quite a woman," Carlos said.

"Yeah." Donny looked around them. It seemed safe enough to talk. Their target was still two stories above, and the closest windows were boarded up with plywood.

"She saved you, huh? Where you from, Donny?"

"Just a few miles from here, actually, Prospect Heights.

At least, I used to be. Now . . ." Donny wondered exactly how to phrase it. "I live in, you know, Angela's place."

Carlos gave him a much closer look. "You've been . . . *there?*"

Donny nodded. It was still hard for him to believe.

"Wow." Carlos looked at Donny some more. His head wobbled in a compromise between nodding and shaking. Then he looked down the alley, where Angela had gone. "She haunts my dreams."

Donny had no idea what to say in response. The best his brain came up with was, "That's too bad, sir," which sounded even dumber when his mouth said it.

Carlos shrugged and jutted his chin upward, toward the stairs. "Never mind. Let's go. Nice and quiet now, like ninjas."

Donny pulled the hood over his head. It made him feel stealthier. They snuck up the fire escape, Carlos leading. Donny planted every step carefully to stay silent. His nerves jangled, and it wasn't just because of the demon he was about to see, or the fact that they were creeping like burglars past windows where other people might be asleep. It was also unnerving to find himself on a fire escape again, so soon after he'd done the same thing to avoid a fiery death in the old brewery. If he breathed in deep enough, he still felt the damage that smoke had inflicted on his lungs.

As they approached the third floor, Carlos lowered

himself until he was crawling on his hands and knees. When he was outside Massey's apartment, he raised himself up slowly and tilted his head back so that only his eyes rose above the windowsill, and risked a quick peek inside. He ducked his head and waved for Donny to join him.

Donny felt sweat forming on the top of his scalp. A squeak of metal made him freeze for a moment. His arms and legs quivered. Carlos waved again, more emphatically, and Donny crawled up the last few steps.

"Go on, take a quick look," Carlos whispered so quietly, Donny barely heard. "That's one ugly mother in there. Did Angela give you the drops?"

Donny nodded. He took a deep breath and let it out, and then slowly raised his head and peeked into the apartment.

CHAPTER 22

The apartment was a mess. Dirty clothes were everywhere. Piles of mail cluttered the kitchen table. Filthy dishes were stacked high in the sink. Newspaper stories, ripped by hand from the pages, were taped on the walls and scrawled with red ink.

Massey was hunched in front of an outdated computer at a rickety desk. He leaned in to stare at the screen, and pecked furiously at the keyboard with two fingers. He had a shaved head and wore a stained white T-shirt and sweatpants.

A nightmare squatted beside Massey, one long sinewy arm around his shoulder. The murmuros had a monkey's shape with the lumpy, scaly hide of a lizard. His back was turned to the window, so Donny felt safe taking a longer look. He shuddered as he absorbed the features: feet that were clawed, birdlike but with five digits. A short tail that ended in a leather diamond, flicking from side to side. Bony spikes that ran down his back. Quivering ears that stuck out like batwings.

The murmuros whispered into a cupped hand by Massey's ear. Massey never looked at the thing. He only paused in his typing while the creature spoke, and stared at the wall as if deep in thought. When the whispers stopped, he hunched over the keyboard and typed some more.

Carlos put a hand on Donny's shoulder and tugged him down. "You see it?"

"Yeah. It's gross," Donny whispered back.

Carlos nodded. "That guy, Massey. He's been spreading nothing but hate on the Internet since this bad boy moved in. Whipping up anger, spouting bad ideas. Suggesting violence as the solution. It wouldn't be so bad, but some people actually read that stuff. A man can do a lot of damage from his computer." He took the bag off his shoulder and unzipped it slowly. "Let's get ready. Shouldn't be long now."

Donny jumped a little as his phone vibrated in his pocket. He took it out and saw a text message from Angela: *I have entered the Taj Mahal. At the door in five.*

Donny shared the message. Carlos hit a button on his digital watch, and it counted up the seconds and minutes. Then he reached into his bag and pulled out yard after yard of black netting. "Commercial fishing net," he whispered, his mouth close to Donny's ear. "Heavy-duty nylon. A shark couldn't get through this." He gave one end to Donny. "Take your end to the other side of the window. Hold it like this, and pick it up high when I tell you, all the way to the top. But first . . ." He took a pair of clear plastic goggles out of the bag. "So you don't get your eyes clawed out."

Donny gulped. *Gee thanks,* he wanted to say. Nobody had warned him about the potential for loss of eyeballs due to murmuros claws. He exhaled deeply, put the goggles on, and grabbed the net the way Carlos had showed him. Then he backed across the fire-escape landing until he was in position.

Carlos kept an eye on his watch and held up two fingers. *Two minutes,* Donny thought. He felt his heartbeat in his ears, and suddenly needed a drink of water badly. Time slowed to a crawl. His mind went into overdrive. *How did I get into this? Shouldn't I be wearing a helmet? And Kevlar? What if Angela's early? What if she's late? What if the monster already left?*

The last thought gave him pause. He raised his head again, tilting it so only his eye would rise above the windowsill. Inside, he saw a water-stained ceiling with a bare lightbulb illuminating the apartment, and then the tops of the walls. He saw Massey bent over his keyboard. And then the murmuros sprang up like bread from a toaster, inches away with only a windowpane between them.

Donny screamed. If he thought the murmuros was hideous from behind, that was nothing compared to the front. A catfish was the closest thing he'd seen to that terrible face—tiny gray wriggling eyes and a wide ugly mouth, fleshy barbs jutting from the jowls.

The murmuros leaped across the room and headed for the door. Massey woke from his trance and reached for something on the desk that Donny hadn't noticed before. A handgun. Massey stood up, groggy, and stumbled toward the windows.

Carlos peered over the sill. *"Dios mio!"*

The murmuros flung the door open and slammed it closed again. While it was open, Donny caught a glimpse of Angela on the other side, her knuckles raised, ready to knock. She looked startled and amused at the same time.

"Get down!" shouted Carlos, because Massey was at the window. He raised the gun with a wobbly hand and squeezed the trigger. A shot exploded, and a splintered hole appeared in the window over Carlos's head.

Donny heard a crunch and splinter of wood from inside the apartment. It had to be the door getting smashed open. There was a second roar of gunfire with a different sound—fired in the other direction, Donny thought. He heard Angela's voice. "Idiot! You want to get someone killed?"

Then came another, louder crash. Glass rained on Donny's shoulders and bounced off his goggles. The murmuros had burst through the window. He jumped over the net they'd failed to raise and landed in a crouch, facing Carlos. The creature swiped at Carlos, driving him back, and then turned to head for the stairs, where only Donny stood in the way of escape.

"Oh, crap," Donny said as the murmuros ran toward him with one arm poised to rake him with claws. An explosion of nerves made Donny do the only thing he thought might protect him: he threw the net up in front of him.

The murmuros charged into the net. Donny ducked low to avoid the swiping arm. The monster was partly entangled, his toes and one hand caught in the mesh. The murmuros hissed, an awful sound made up of a thousand hateful whispers. With his free hand, the creature reached down for Donny, grabbed him by the front of the sweatshirt, and threw him aside. Donny's back struck the railing, his legs flipped up, and his momentum carried him over. Then he was falling, three stories toward the ground.

CHAPTER 23

Donny saw the hard paved surface of the alley a fatal distance below. He tried to grab the top of the railing, but he was too late. Instead his arm went between the bars and closed on a handful of net. It slithered out between the bars as he fell, and he thought for a moment the whole net might come with him. But he jerked to a stop and winced as the net cut into his fingers. There was another awful snarl, and he saw the murmuros tumble down the stairs, tripped up by the net that had tangled around one of his feet.

Momentum swung Donny in, and when he looked down, he saw the second floor of the fire escape just below. He let go of the net and sprawled onto the grating. When he looked up, he found himself in the exact same predicament, but one floor lower. The murmuros had rolled down the entire flight of iron steps and smashed into the railing. He got to his feet, wobbly at first, but then his eyes focused on Donny.

The murmuros rushed at him, claws first. Donny saw Carlos race down the steps to help, but there was no time. He threw himself sideways to get out of the thing's way, and hoped he would be more interested in escape than in tearing a boy to pieces.

Apparently he was, because the thing headed straight for the next flight of stairs and didn't bother to slash him. As the creature went by, Donny did something that surprised even himself. He stuck his foot out and caught the creature's ankle.

The murmuros hissed again, and Donny thought he heard a rude word mixed in there somewhere. This tumble down the stairs was even more spectacular than the first. It ended as the murmuros's head slammed straight into the railing on the next floor below. It rang like a gong, and Donny felt the vibration run through the iron grate where he sat.

He figured the thing would be dead after that crushing blow, but the murmuros staggered to his feet again. The chase ended there, because something dropped from above—a sleek, acrobatic human form who used the fire escape like a gymnast. It was Angela. She landed next to the murmuros and grabbed him by the neck in one smooth motion.

"That thing almost killed me," Donny squeaked.

"Sure, but now you have a fabulous anecdote," Angela replied.

The murmuros stared up at her. "Is that you, Angela?" he asked in a perfectly civil voice.

"Hello, Gus," Angela told the thing. "Been a long time. I'll snap your neck if you make one move I don't like."

"I understand completely," Gustus said.

Angela reached into a pocket with her free hand and pulled out a vial with a cork stopper. She bit on the cork to extract it.

"Is that absolutely necessary?" the murmuros inquired.

"Afraid so," said Angela, and she tossed the liquid contents of the vial into the creature's face. Gustus went limp immediately and his eyes rolled up, his tongue drooping from the side of his mouth.

Carlos trotted down the stairs and stood next to Donny. "Uh, Angela. Witnesses." He pointed to the windows along the side of the apartment. Lights had come on, and curtains parted. Angela stared up at the building, and a fierce expression came across her face. Donny stepped back, careful to avoid the beam of fear she was projecting. Still, the skin on his arms erupted in gooseflesh again. One by one, wherever Angela turned, the curtains closed again, and the people backed away from the windows.

Donny was sure police lights would start to flash during the next part. Angela lowered Donny and Carlos by the arms until they could drop safely to the ground, and then hopped down herself with the insensible demon draped over her shoulder. She landed easily, despite a drop that would have shattered Donny's ankles.

Carlos led them to a battered sedan around the corner. Angela tossed Gustus into the trunk and covered him with a blanket. "Can I drive?" she asked Carlos hopefully.

Carlos shook his head and replied to Donny. "I let her drive once. She has no idea what she's doing."

"I did fine," she snapped.

"She has never taken a lesson, and she does *not* respect the rules of the road," Carlos said as he took the driver's seat.

"Nobody died," Angela pouted. She stomped around to the passenger's side. Donny had the backseat to himself. They drove to a narrow two-story house a few miles away, sandwiched between other slender homes with strips of lawn in front. Carlos squeezed his car down the skinny driveway and into a cramped garage, and killed the engine. "Donny, can you do me a favor?" he asked.

"Sure." *Please don't be something horrible,* he begged.

"I have to bring my dog out so Angela can come inside. Would you watch him for a few minutes?"

Angela bristled and huffed. "Sorry," Carlos told her. She gave him a dismissive wave.

Carlos went inside and came out with a black-and-white mutt on a leash. "This is Rocco," he said.

"Hi, Rocco," Donny replied, but Rocco wasn't interested in saying hello. He strained at his leash, trying to get away from the car where Angela sat. Rocco didn't relax until Angela got out of the car, took the murmuros out of the trunk, and carried the unconscious creature through the back door. Even then, the dog looked nervously back at the house and whined every few minutes.

Donny walked Rocco to the back of the yard to give him some distance from the source of his fear. Carlos, or somebody before him, had built a stone grotto in the corner of the yard. A fountain sent water trickling over stones. Behind that stood a statue, nearly life-size, of a stern-faced, long-haired angel. A wing was broken on one side. She wore an armored breastplate and held a flaming sword.

A cement bench with ivy clinging to its legs faced the grotto. Donny took a seat and scratched Rocco's ears while he waited.

Twenty minutes later Angela and Carlos were back again. Carlos walked Rocco into the house after Angela returned to the passenger seat of the car. "Easy-peasy," she told Donny. "I dropped the little rat off in Sulfur, and he'll be locked up good and tight. Carlos said he'll drive us back to Midtown."

CHAPTER 24

Back in the apartment on Fifth Avenue, Angela stood in front of the broad window, her hands on her hips. The lights of New York sparkled like stars. "Egad, what a beautiful city." She heard Donny chuckle and gave him a withering, narrow-lidded glare. "Did I say something funny?"

He shook his head and smiled. "No. You just use some words that we don't hear a lot these days. Like egad. Or jeepers or golly or hooey."

She crossed her arms. "Listen, buster. I've been around a lot longer than you. Sometimes I forget what the current lingo is, and the old stuff slips out."

Donny peered at her closely. Anyone on Earth would have sworn she was a teenager. "How long *have* you been around?"

"Shucks, I don't know exactly. We're not good with dates in Sulfur. Have I mentioned that? Let me think. When I was born, must have been around"—she wiggled her fingers, counting silently—"1860, something like that."

Donny gaped. "1860?"

"You got wax in your ears?"

He shook his head and tried to process this information. "So you were alive at the same time as Abraham Lincoln."

"The tall one with the beard and the speech? Yep. Never met him though." She drummed her chin with her fingers. "I didn't go upstairs until . . . let me think, who was the president? I'm not good with presidents. The Odyssey guy. The one with the tomb."

It took Donny a second. "Ulysses S. Grant?"

"That's the one."

Donny rubbed his hands up his face and into his hair. "Angela, will you live forever?"

She rocked her head back. "Of course not. Archdemons like me get about ten years for every human year."

Donny did the math in his head. "So in people years you're . . . about fifteen?"

"Going on sixteen," she sang.

"Oh." Donny smiled. The idea made him dizzy but strangely happy. "We're closer than I thought."

"Don't get any ideas, hot stuff." She laughed and twirled

with her arms outstretched. "You know what I feel like doing now, Cricket?"

"No. What?"

"Dancing."

Donny's eyes widened. Was she serious? Dancing? In this apartment?

She whirled to a stop. "You wouldn't mind, would you?"

He cleared his throat and put his hands on the arms of his chair, ready to stand. "Um, no. Of course not."

"Wonderful. Don't wait up for me. You'll find plenty of snacks in the kitchen and a zillion channels on the TV. I'll just change real quick, and then I'll be on my way." She jogged, humming, into her bedroom, and shut the door behind her.

Angela had been gone for hours. Donny found a carton of ice cream in the fridge and gorged on it. While he ate, he used his phone to see what the Internet had to say about a killer from the Depression called the Jolly Butcher. The answer turned out to be "plenty." He found black-and-white pictures of Butch, grinning at the camera from behind a meat counter in 1933. His real name was Martin Franklin Whitehead and, apparently, he was a popular figure in his picturesque Missouri town, famous for his big laugh and ready smile. That popularity waned when someone got a closer look at his meat locker. After too many grisly details about cleavers, hooks, and meat grinders, Donny stopped reading.

He turned on the TV and watched the end of a Jackie Chan movie. When it was over, he turned the TV off and tossed the remote aside. Then he walked around the place again.

Angela had left the door to her room open. He poked his head in and saw an enormous bed with an amazing brass frame. Everything here was modern, unlike the antique look of the rooms in Angela's pillar home.

More stuffed animals with long plush fur were all over the bed and the bureaus. He remembered their encounters with animals, and it clicked for him: these were the only kind she could touch.

It felt like a violation, peeking into her room with her not there, and his heart thumped wildly when his phone buzzed in his pocket. He took it out and saw a text message: *Cricket, still awake? Having fun?*

"Not really," he said aloud. But he typed: *Yes. You coming back soon?*

The answer came quickly. *Not yet. Get some sleep. More fun tomorrow. Emoticon.*

Donny thought about replying but didn't know what to say after that. Although he wondered if he should explain that normal people typed a smiley face instead of writing *emoticon.*

He stared at the phone. Suddenly, out of nowhere, he ached to know what was going on with his father. And were people looking for him? Donny Taylor had disappeared, after all. He was a missing person. And a few days had gone by. Would his father have even reported it, considering why Donny had run away from home?

For a moment he thought about calling his dad. But he couldn't bring himself to do that. Then he thought about Kevin. His best friend. There was someone you could trust. Would Kevin be awake? No. But he kept his phone by his bed, and he usually forgot to turn it off, which drove Kevin's mother crazy. With his hands trembling, causing mistakes he had to fix, Donny entered Kevin's number and composed a text: *It's Donny. Can I call u? Don't let anyone know.* His thumb hovered over the send button, and then he pressed it. He put the phone on the coffee table and waited.

It buzzed a moment later. He scooped up the phone and read the reply: *Yes, call now!!!*

Donny smiled and hit call. The phone rang once, and Kevin's familiar voice came through, whispering close to the phone. "Donny! Donny?"

"Yeah, it's me."

"I can't believe it! Dude, everyone's looking for you! Even the police!"

That answers that question. "Yeah, I thought that might be the case."

"Where are you? Are you home?"

"I'm not home. I . . . I can't tell you where I am."

"What? Donny, where you been? You gotta come back.

174

This is crazy. What happened? We thought you got murdered or kidnapped or something."

"I'm fine, Kev. I really am. But I can't go home, not yet. It's . . . it's hard to explain."

"Explain it anyway! Wait, are you with your mother? Did you find your mother?"

Donny sighed. "No. I told you, my mom was never in the picture. Listen. I just wanted you to know that I'm okay. And I was wondering . . . what's going on with my dad."

"He's going crazy looking for you, that's what's going on! He thought you might be hiding out with me. And he begged me to tell him if I knew where you were. He was crying, man. I can't believe I saw your dad cry."

Donny felt a twinge in his chest, and his breath hitched. "Kevin, you *cannot* tell him I called. It's really important."

"Are you nuts? You can't just stay missing. Your dad is gonna lose his mind. He has the police looking for you, he's hired people to look for you, there are posters with your picture all over the place."

"Kevin—"

"Wait, I gotta tell you this, too. Your dad was here a couple times, and the last time he took me aside and said the weirdest thing."

Donny clutched his throat. "What'd he say?"

"Okay, okay, I can't remember exactly, but it was

something like 'Kevin, I know Donny and you are best friends. He might call you before anyone else. You have to tell him, I need him back. He's everything to me. You tell him that. And you tell him, no matter the reason he left, I'll fix it. Everything will be all right.' Something like that, anyway."

Donny squeezed his eyes shut and shook his head. "Right. I get it. Look, I'll think about it. But you still have to promise, Kevin. Don't tell anyone I called. Not our friends, not your sister, not your mom or dad or anyone. I mean it."

Kevin's voice got lower. "Are you in trouble? Is someone there, listening?"

Donny had to smile over that one. "Not in trouble. Nobody's listening. I'm telling you, I'm fine. I'll come back eventually." As he said it, he wondered if that was even true. "I think I should go. But, seriously, don't talk about this. Promise me."

"Donny—"

"Promise!"

"Okay. I won't tell."

"Good. Thanks, Kevin."

"This is so messed up."

"I know. But remember, you promised. Bye, Kevin." As the last words came out of his mouth, he knew they sounded permanent. He hung up before Kevin could say anything else.

He dropped the phone onto the table, leaned back, and covered his face with his hands. His cheeks were wet a moment later, and he made a wailing sound that he'd never heard from himself before. He flopped sideways, curled up on the couch, and pulled a pillow over his head.

CHAPTER 25

Donny woke when he heard the door to the apartment close, and sat up on the couch and rubbed his eyes.

"There's a bed in your room, you know," Angela said.

"Uh. Yeah. I fell asleep."

She kicked her shoes off and flopped down next to him. "It was a very exciting night all around. You didn't miss me too much, did you?" She patted his knee.

He looked away and shook his head. Angela yawned. "Well, I think I'll crash for a while. See you in the morning?"

Donny nodded. She started to get up, but he said, "Angela?"

"Mmm?"

"I did something that might have been a bad idea."

She stiffened and swiveled toward him. "Would you care to be more specific?"

"I used the phone you gave me to call my best friend. I wanted him to know I wasn't dead."

She shot to her feet. "Where's the phone?"

"Right here," Donny said. He held it up.

She snatched it from his hand and crushed it in her grip, pulled the battery out of the wreckage, and let the pieces drop to the floor. "That was dumb, all right. You know phones can be tracked, right? If your friend told the police that you called, you know they could find us? Right here in this apartment?"

"I . . . I . . . don't think Kevin would do that."

Angela's phone rang. She pulled it from her purse. "Hello?" She listened and scowled and rolled her eyes. "How long ago?" She paused, listening. "Got it," she said. "Thanks for your help." She hung up, closed her eyes for a moment, took a deep breath, and glared at Donny. "You messed up, big-time."

Before Donny could open his mouth to respond, the door to the apartment burst open. Policemen in protective gear with helmets and faceguards, all carrying rifles, poured into the room. "Get on the floor!" the first one shouted.

Angela grabbed Donny, tossed him over her shoulder, and bolted for the stairs. She slammed the door behind her and sprinted up, toting him like he weighed less than a cat. When she entered the round room, she shut that door too. She dropped him on the floor and heaved furniture into a pile in front of the door. Donny heard the policemen stomping up in pursuit.

"Close the shades!" Angela snapped. She started at one end, and Donny went to the other. As he started to pull one shade down over the tall window, a powerful beam of light shot from the next rooftop. Donny yelled and shielded his eyes. He had caught a glimpse of a figure on the roof, holding a spotlight.

"Police on the roof, too! For crying out loud," Angela said. "Like you're that important."

"Open up!" shouted the cop on the other side of the door. "You have no way out. Let's not make this harder than we have to."

"No, let's not," Angela muttered as she tugged down the last of the shades.

"I'm so sorry," Donny said.

"Save it," Angela told him. She ran to the fireplace and turned a dial on the wall beside it. A propane fire whooshed to life and formed a knee-high curtain of flame.

"We can use that?" Donny asked.

She sneered at him. "Get ready. I set the timer, and the fire will go out in sixty seconds." There was a loud crash by the door, and the pile of furniture shifted. Angela went to the fireplace, cupped her hands, and spoke into the fire. It was a strange, hoarsely whispered series of sounds, like no language Donny had ever heard. The only thing that sounded like a word, somewhere in the middle, was *Porta*.

There was another loud crash, and the furniture shifted again. The fire went ruby-red, and a diamond shape appeared. It was no bigger than a playing card at first, but in seconds it grew big enough to crawl into. "Get in before I bowl you through," Angela snapped.

"Yes, ma'am," Donny said, and he scrambled into the dark space. He felt only the slightest resistance from the parchmentlike film that had appeared within the diamond, but the heat of the fire nearly scorched his shoulders and legs. On the other side, he tumbled into the stony corridor where the keeper, Porta, stood.

Through the opening, he saw the apartment. The pile of furniture lurched forward as the door was forced open, wide enough to enter. There was a shout: "Police! Don't move!" Angela rolled through the low space and sprang gracefully to her feet. "Close it up, please," she said. Porta waved an arm, and the opening vanished just as a policeman rushed into the room with his rifle raised. Donny thought he looked a little stunned to find the room empty. Then the flames filled in the open space and erased the apartment from sight.

Donny got to his knees and stared at the fire. His heart thumped and his chest heaved. He turned to Angela, meaning to apologize again, but the words froze in his throat when he saw her expression. When she spoke, it was like a snarl. "Do you realize what you just did?"

"I'm sorry. I didn't know—"

"You didn't know *what?*" She paced back and forth as she ranted. "You didn't know that you were going to ruin everything? I can never use that apartment again! Who knows if I can even go back to New York! The police will ask questions. And if they got a look at me, I'll be a wanted woman." He'd never seen this from her before—a vivid, white-hot anger. She stuck a finger to his chest to punctuate her words, and he stumbled back with every jab. "I *like* New York, you stupid mortal. It's my *favorite* city. And you messed it all *up!*"

Donny's stomach was knotted tight. "I just . . . ," he said, but the words crumbled on his tongue. "I wanted—"

"You know what? I don't want to hear it!" she raged. "I don't even want to *look* at you. I should just drop you off where I found you. Let the police find you on the streets. What do you think they'll do when you tell them where you've been? They'll think you've lost your mind, that's what they'll do!"

Donny put his head down and clasped his hands behind his neck. "Don't do that. Please don't. I can't go home. I don't have anywhere to go."

Angela growled through her teeth and stomped away. Donny lifted his head. Porta stared up at him without expression, her baboon snout twitching. Angela rounded the corner and headed for the barred entrance to Sulfur. Donny's eyes bugged wide—he was about to be trapped in this corridor with only Porta for company, and she didn't seem the friendly type.

"Wait, please," he moaned, and he got to his feet and ran after Angela. She knocked on the door to Sulfur and swept through as it swung open. Donny arrived a second later, barely in time to grab the edge of the door and keep it from shutting. Grunyon's hand went to his sword but relaxed when he saw Donny.

"Vanilla extract?" Grunyon asked. Angela had already stormed away, moving even faster than usual.

"I'll bring you gallons next time, I promise," Donny said as he went by. The vanilla extract, at least twenty bottles of the stuff, was back at the apartment, soon to become a puzzling piece of evidence.

He stayed far behind Angela, who never turned around to see if he was there. She just went on slapping the path in her bare feet, swinging arms that ended in fists.

CHAPTER 26

Angela stomped all the way to her pillar home and up the circling road. Donny hung back, just close enough that she did not vanish around the curve. She reached the door, unlocked it, stepped inside, and slammed the door behind her without a backward glance. Donny heard the bolt slide from within.

For a while he just stood and stared at the door, bathed in the harsh light of the fiery clouds. Then he sat with his back to the wall and his arms folded across his knees, and put his head down.

He looked up again a few minutes later when he heard feet scuffing the stone.

"ARGLBRGL," said Arglbrgl.

"Hey," Donny said. With an effort, he mustered the faintest of smiles.

Arglbrgl looked at Donny and cocked his head to one side. He made a fist with one hand, put it next to his eye, and twisted it back and forth. "GRBLRGL?"

Donny shrugged. "Yeah. I'm sad. I messed up."

Arglbrgl sighed. He plopped down next to Donny and leaned against him. Donny put his arm around the imp's shoulders. Arglbrgl started to snore a minute later.

"Donny?" said a familiar voice. Zig-Zag was approaching and had just come into view around the bend.

Donny waved. "Hi," he said quietly.

Both heads stared down at Donny, then at the door, and then at the higher windows of Angela's home. "Why are you out here?" asked Zig.

"I made a huge mistake," Donny replied. "I don't think Angela likes me anymore."

Zag rubbed his chin. "Is that so?"

Zig and Zag looked at each other, then whispered into the other's ears and nodded.

"Why don't we continue with your orientation?" asked Zig.

"There's much more to see," said Zag.

Donny looked up at the two-headed being and saw two kind smiles. "Really? I mean, I don't even know if I'm supposed to be here."

"The last we heard, we were supposed to go on educating you," said Zig.

"Those are the standing orders. We'll sort your dilemma

out later," said Zag, and he nudged the snoring Arglbrgl with his toe. Arglbrgl woke with a start and snarled. His skin began to bristle, until the sharp points stuck through Donny's shirt and he winced. Arglbrgl whimpered and jumped aside, and his points melted away. "RGBR?" he asked Donny, putting a paw on Donny's shoulder.

"I'm fine," Donny said as he rubbed the wounds.

Zig held out a hand. "Come on. It is time to see what replaced the Pit of Fire."

Donny took the hand and was pulled to his feet. "Thank you, Zig-Zag."

"Our pleasure," Zag said with a nod. "Arglbrgl, please join us. If we run into Butch, we could use your protection."

"ARGLBRGL!"

Donny's mouth trembled when he smiled. "I'm really glad to see you guys."

"We came by to deliver some interesting news for Angela," said Zig, "but that can wait until we return."

Donny hesitated to ask, but his curiosity got the better of him. "What was the news? I mean, is it okay to tell me?"

"Of course. The riddling imp is missing. Nobody can find Sooth. This has never happened before," said Zag.

CHAPTER 27

How many types of infernal beings have you encountered so far, Donny?" asked Zag.

Donny searched his mind. "Well—there are the ones like Angela."

"The archdemons," said Zig.

"And there are imps," Donny said. "Lots of imps."

Arglbrgl raised his clawed hand. "ARGLBRGL."

Zig and Zag nodded.

"And the flying things. The gargs and the shreeks."

"Those are imps as well," said Zag.

"And that murmuros. Angela said it was a demon."

"A lesser demon," said Zig.

"And the worms," Donny said with a shudder. "And those nasty fish in the river. And . . ." He paused to try to figure out the best way to phrase the next thing. He looked at Zig, then Zag. "There's you?"

Zig-Zag was not offended. "We are demon too," said Zag.

"But there are more creatures down here, especially in the Depths," said Zig.

"And another being, which you are about to see," said Zag.

"The strangest and most wondrous of all," said Zig.

"Not all of us find it wondrous," said Zag.

Donny tried to imagine what that could be. "Great," he said.

Zig-Zag took Donny down the street that led to the diner. Along the way they again passed the broken column where Sooth should have been perched. Donny looked at the mounds of shattered marble behind the column, and scanned the niches and alleys, but he saw no sign of the old imp.

They turned another corner, and that byway led to a circular path where chariots seemed to gather. Zig-Zag led Donny to one of the smaller chariots, drawn by a single long-legged imp. "To the Caverns of Woe," Zig told the runner. Soon they rumbled down the road, out of the city that wreathed the Pillar Obscura, and into the lands Donny thought of as south, or downriver.

The road followed the path of the river, more or less, but without hugging every curve. They passed more jagged formations, fields of dark moss and lichens tended by imps, a pond of boiling water, and a craggy land with geysers blasting high into the air.

Ahead stood another of the enormous pillars that supported the roof of Sulfur. Like the Pillar Obscura, this one had a city around its base—but in this case the city lay completely in ruins. Even the pillar itself had been blasted and gouged.

"Look over there," Zig said. "See that smoking cone of rock on the other side of the river?"

Donny looked beyond Zig's pointing finger, and saw the formation. It looked like a stumpy volcano, not much bigger than the brownstone where he grew up. Smoke trickled out of the jagged opening at its peak. "Yes, I see it."

"Stay clear of that. It's where Havoc lives."

"He lives in *that*?" Donny stared at the lump of rock. Sure enough, even from this distance, he could make out the door that had been carved into the base, the porthole windows on its slopes, and a terrace near the flat top.

"He does now. Before the war, he lived with his family in the Pillar Arcanus—the one you see over there. That city was ruined in the war, and only Havoc survived. His parents, his brother and sister, all were lost. In his grief, he moved to that former refinery. Staring every day at his ruined ancestral home has only stoked his fury over the reforms. He doesn't like anyone getting close to his home, never mind stepping inside. And he has some nasty imps for guards. Butch loiters there too, of course."

Just the mention of the Jolly Butcher was enough to set Donny's nerves on edge. "Yeah, no problem. I'll keep away from there."

The chariot rumbled on. An hour later, much farther down the road, the river curved so close that the road nearly touched its bank. Donny saw another barge, the ominous ferrymen fore and aft of the anxious dead. The craft had come to a stop at a landing, where steps in the riverbank led to the deck of the barge. There the dead filed onto the shore in an eerily organized manner.

"Where are they going?" Donny asked.

"The same place as us," said Zag.

Zig pointed down the road, where the western wall of Sulfur vaulted to the roof. "There."

Donny looked at the dark space at the foot of the wall. It looked like the entrance to a train tunnel, although an exceptionally wide one. The shadowy space looked blacker still against the harsh light of the fiery clouds.

The chariot was there a minute later. It slowed to a halt, and he and Zig-Zag stepped down. Arglbrgl hopped out and growled and bristled in every direction before taking his place by Donny's side. "Thanks, buddy," Donny told him. "I think I'm safe."

Something was in the tunnel, coming toward them. It glowed softly within the dark and bobbed through the air.

Donny recognized it, because he'd seen it before at the source of the river: the bundled, pulsing lights of a human soul. When the soul emerged into the bright light, it was harder to see, but Donny watched it float past them and head toward the river.

"Another soul on its way," Zig said.

Arglbrgl watched it pass right over his head and sniffed as it went by. "GRLG?"

"Shall I do most of the talking this time, brother?" Zig said to Zag. "I know this is not your favorite subject."

"Go on," Zag said, rolling his eyes. "In fact, would you mind if I napped?"

"Certainly not," said Zig.

Zag closed his eye, and his head listed to one side.

Zig smiled and cleared his throat. "Donny. You have been wondering, I am sure: Once the Pit of Fire was abandoned, how did we punish the wicked dead? The answer, it turns out, was in front of us all the while. It lies down that passage, in the Caverns of Woe." Donny looked into the tunnel, but all he saw were the thick tendrils of mist that slithered out from the depths. There was an unseen source of inner light, dim and silvery like moonlight. Even as he watched, another cluster of lights floated out into the open, and another soon after that.

"These caverns were always here, but very few of the denizens of Sulfur were willing to enter them. Mysterious entities live inside, and they are unlike anything else in the underworld. We call them sorrowmongers. They have the ability to cause fearful hallucinations. If you went too far inside the caverns, a sorrowmonger might come upon you and envelop you within a spell that forced you into a dreamlike state. Your memories would bubble up from inside your brain—and those would not be your happy memories. It was a deeply unsettling feeling. So most of us preferred to stay out of the caverns."

Zig put a hand on Donny's shoulder. "Are you ready to go in?"

Donny stiffened. "Based on what you just said, no, I am not at all ready."

Zig laughed. "Don't worry. We have an understanding with the sorrowmongers now. They will not bother you, with so many souls to tend to. Come, this is too important to miss." He gave Donny a gentle push, and against his better instincts, Donny walked into the long passageway.

Donny heard a high-pitched whine and looked back to see Arglbrgl pacing back and forth at the entrance. "Aren't you coming?" Donny asked.

Arglbrgl shook his head.

"He doesn't like it in there," said Zig. "We'll be back soon," he told the imp.

It was cool inside the passage. For the first time in Sulfur, Donny wished he had a jacket with him. As they walked along, the mist grew thicker, the tunnel brighter. The mist itself, Donny realized, was the source of the light.

"In the old days," said Zig, "a soul would occasionally escape from the pit and go on the run. There were imps whose job it was to track it down and bring it back. Sometimes a runaway soul would be discovered here. That is how we learned about the power the sorrowmongers have over the dead."

Where the passage ended, a vast cavern began. It sloped downward ahead of them, and Donny could look at least a mile into the distance.

Countless people were on the cavern floor, frozen in place, a sea of statues. The thick, nearly liquid fog pooled around their feet, as high as their knees. From that ocean of fog a thinner vapor swirled up and enveloped every figure in sight. It was like looking at them through silken veils.

Donny tried to guess how many people there were. Thousands upon thousands, and that was just in the space that was visible to him, before the distant mists hid the rest from sight.

"How big is this place?" he asked. He rubbed his arms. It was even cooler in the cavern than in the tunnel.

"We don't know," Zig said. "Bigger than the Pit of Fire for certain. Bigger than all of Sulfur, perhaps."

A sound came from everywhere at once. It was a low, ominous, unsettling noise, like the hum of a million bees. Donny felt it in his ribs and spine. It made him want to stick his fingers in his ears.

Some of the people below stood, some knelt, and sometimes all Donny saw was an arm that rose up with fingers bent and grasping. None of them moved, even when striking awkward poses that should have made them topple over.

"There," Zig said, pointing. Not far from where they stood, something tunneled through the fog, causing the vapor to bulge where it passed. It was like watching a snake crawl under bedsheets. As it slithered its way toward where they stood, Zig put his arm around Donny's shoulders.

Donny held his breath and bit his lip as the thing drew near. It finally rose out of the sea of fog just below where they stood. It seemed to be made of fog itself, until it solidified before Donny's eyes and formed a tall, wormlike figure, ghostly white.

The thing had no legs, just a tail of insubstantial fog that turned solid near the waist. There were three delicate arms on each of its sides, its hands clasped in front. The face was something like a goat's, with white whiskers sprouting from the chin and horns curving from its skull. Where the eyes should have been, there were only vacant holes.

"This is a sorrowmonger," Zig-Zag said quietly.

Donny tried desperately to keep his fear from showing, but his shivering legs betrayed him. He clutched his stomach, afraid he might get sick.

"A living mortal," the sorrowmonger said. His voice

was a whisper but somehow easy to hear. Vapor drifted from his mouth when he spoke.

"A friend," Zig-Zag replied. "Here to understand."

The sorrowmonger nodded. Without another word, he turned and drifted back down the slope toward the frozen figures. With one of his six hands, he beckoned for them to follow.

There were spaces between the people, but not much. As they passed among the petrified crowd, Donny got a better look at their expressions. Everywhere, he saw anguish, sadness, terror, or pain.

The sorrowmonger paused beside a man who was on his knees, his hands raised to ward off something terrible. Donny looked at the wreath of mist around the man's head and saw that it moved and swirled like a thunderstorm blooming. There were fingers of vapor that plunged into the poor fellow's eyes.

"What do you see?" the sorrowmonger said.

It took Donny a moment to realize that the sorrowmonger had spoken to him. He bent closer and peered into the mist. The face of the frozen man was contorted. His mouth twisted, and his eyes were squeezed halfway shut. "He looks . . . afraid. And guilty, I guess." Donny said. When the sorrowmonger said nothing in return, Donny added, "Why is he afraid?"

"Because he understands what he has done. From the outside looking in, you see the mist that surrounds him. But from the inside looking out, he experiences the pain he has caused. Imagine the worst moment of your life, mortal—the time you were most afraid, most anguished."

That was easy for Donny. It was when he was in the brewery, heartbroken, his life ruined. Even before the fire had nearly killed him, that was the darkest point. His heart had felt like it was rotting inside his chest.

"Now," the sorrowmonger said, "imagine that lasting a hundred years. And when that is over, another terrible fraction of time replaces it. That is what this man will feel. But it will not be *his* anguish. He will know the terror his victim knew—bottled up inside that instant as if he were the victim himself. Never will he become accustomed to the feeling or grow numb to the fear. The last second will be as horrible as the first."

Donny stared at the man. He couldn't imagine it. *Is this really so much better than the fire?* he wondered.

"But that is only part of what the dead will know," the sorrowmonger said. "They will also understand the things in life that formed them—the things that made them the way they were."

Donny stared at the man's face and wondered what terrible vision he perceived in the mist. As he watched, he noticed that the man's eyelids were closing, but moving as slowly as the minute hand of a clock. He was *blinking*. Donny turned his head and put his ear by the man's face.

This close, he heard one specific sound that he could pick out from the eerie hum that was everywhere at once.

The man was *screaming*.

The hairs on Donny's neck stood up as he realized that this was just one of the countless voices, one buzz in the hive. That awful pervasive noise was the grand total of every one of them screaming, wailing, or weeping in the slowest of motions.

Donny looked around at the countless figures. He tried to imagine how many more must be deeper inside, trapped in their own terrible moments. Were there hundreds of thousands? Millions? Sure, each had done wrong in their lifetime, but how much pain would they endure before they moved on? He thought suddenly of his father, Benny Taylor, the killer for hire who was destined to become one of these frozen figures. Would his father see the pain he'd caused? Would he become one of his own victims and stare down the barrel of a gun?

Donny covered his eyes with his palms. "Zig, can we go, please? I've seen enough."

Zag was awake now, frowning at his surroundings. He and Zig nodded together and led Donny back toward the tunnel. The sorrowmonger melted into the fog. Of all the beings and creatures he had seen, that ghostlike figure had filled Donny the most with dread. "How many of those sorrowmongers are there?" he asked.

"As many as there need to be," answered Zig.

"Or perhaps only one," said Zag. "The fog and the sorrowmongers may be one and the same."

That idea sent Donny's brain into a tailspin. He couldn't get out of those caverns fast enough, and so his heart sank when he looked down the tunnel. The dead from the barge were marching toward them, and they filled the tunnel from side to side. He and Zig-Zag had to stand with backs pressed to the wall to let them pass. There was a ferryman at the head of the group and another behind, looming over the crowd.

Donny didn't want to look at the faces of the dead, but he would have felt like a coward if he didn't. It surprised him again that so few of the people seemed old. Once again, they were dressed in everyday clothes, except for the occasional work uniform, although the uniforms did not look entirely familiar. *What would Dad be wearing?* he wondered. Somehow he knew it would be one of those sharp Italian suits his father loved.

The dead plodded along, their arms limp by their sides. They walked almost in lockstep, without bumping into one another or trying to turn and run. Donny was sure they were under some sort of spell cast by the ferrymen. Only their heads seemed free to move at will. The dead looked around and strained to see what lay ahead. They talked to one another with panic in their voices, but in a language Donny did not understand. That was why the uniforms looked unfamiliar, he realized. They were not American.

Some tried to talk to him, asking questions he couldn't answer. "I'm sorry," he told them, and he held up his hands in a helpless gesture. "I don't speak your language."

A few heard him and called to him in accented English.

"What is happening to me?"

"What will they do with us?"

"Where are we?"

Zig-Zag stepped in front of Donny. "Don't trouble the boy," said Zag. "You will see soon enough what's to become of you."

CHAPTER 28

They were back in the chariot again. Donny stared at the barge in the river nearby. It was empty of the dead, thick ropes mooring it to the landing. When the ferrymen returned, it would move on and vanish into mystery at the far end of the river.

More clusters of lights floated out from the tunnel, like swarms of fireflies. They drifted to the river and joined its course, hovering a few feet above the water. It made Donny feel a little better to see those souls moving on. But after how long?

"What do you think of the Caverns of Woe?" Zig asked.

"They were terrible," Donny said.

"I agree," said Zag. "They should all be back in the Pit of Fire, as it was meant to be."

That wasn't exactly what Donny had meant. As bad as

the caverns were, the pit must have been worse. In the caverns, a soul might eventually move on. In the pit, there was nothing but hopeless torment, forever and ever.

"Well," said Zig, "what shall we show you now, young mortal?"

"The fungus farms? The quarries? The Infernal Sea? Another pillar city?" asked Zag.

Donny shook his head. "Can we go back to Angela's place? I really need to talk to her."

"If you must," said Zig.

They had just set out again when Donny felt a great weariness come over him. It was hard to keep track of time, with the nonstop daylight of the clouds, and the leaps between hours as they had ventured from Sulfur to New York. But it had been a long while since he'd slept. He rested his head on the back of the bench and let the motion of the chariot lull him to sleep.

Shouts and mutters woke Donny from a deep slumber. He lifted his head, blinked at the harsh light, and wondered where he was. The Pillar Obscura loomed overhead, but they'd stopped in the city, a short distance away. The diner was nearby. A crowd of imps and other denizens had gathered around an alley that was choked with debris from the long-ago war. He saw Zig-Zag among them, staring at something.

"GRGL?" asked Arglbrgl, still beside him.

"I don't know what's going on," Donny said.

Cookie, the cook from the diner, stepped out of the crowd and dabbed the corners of her eyes with the bottom of her apron.

Donny cupped his hands around his mouth and called to her. "Cookie!" She saw him and came over to the chariot.

"What happened?" Donny asked.

"An awful thing, a terrible thing," she said.

Donny heard a mournful cry, and then the crowd parted. A tall imp walked forward, a familiar form cradled in his arms.

"Poor Sooth," Cookie said.

There was a terrible deep wound across Sooth's skull. The imp who carried him raised his head and howled to the sky. Other imps in the crowd did the same. Beside Donny, Arglbrgl joined in. The chorus sent shivers down Donny's spine.

"Was it . . . Was it an accident?" he asked, raising his voice over the din.

Cookie wagged her head while she blew her nose into the apron. "I don't think so. You see that cut on his head? Somebody killed Sooth. Hid the body in the rubble. Who would do a thing like that to such a harmless imp?"

A murderer, Donny thought. In his mind, he saw the loathsome, smirking face of the Jolly Butcher. *A murderer would do a thing like that. But why?*

CHAPTER 29

Tizzy told me Sooth was acting strangely," Donny said as the chariot rolled on.

"Sooth was always a strange one," Zag said.

Donny looked back toward the street where the imp had been murdered. "Yeah, that's what Angela said. But maybe Tizzy was right. He was down from his column. He seemed nervous." The imp's riddle had almost slipped his mind, but it came back to him and he said it aloud. "After the light comes the fall."

The question was still on his mind when the chariot stopped at Pillar Obscura. Was it just a coincidence that Sooth had been killed after behaving strangely? He looked at the luminous clouds. They still burned, but not as brightly, and they showed signs of breaking up. Here and there he caught glimpses of the stony ceiling as gaps appeared between the clouds. Sooth's final riddle, the one that seemed so urgent to the imp, echoed in his head. *After the light comes the fall.*

"I'm going to find Angela," he told Zig-Zag.

Zig-Zag nodded. Arglbrgl was still on the bench. The imp gripped his head in his hands and moaned softly, mourning the loss of Sooth.

Donny ran up the path that curved around the pillar. First he wanted to beg Angela for forgiveness. But it was more than that. A feeling had grown in his mind, gathering strength. Something was wrong. He just wasn't sure exactly what.

After circling entirely around the pillar, he arrived at her door, out of breath. There was a huge brass knocker on the door, big enough to fit a dinner plate inside. He raised it and slammed it against the metal plate three times. Then he stepped back and listened for footsteps.

None came. He looked at the windows above the door in time to see Tizzy pop her head out. Her mouth opened in a wide smile, and she waved. "Hi, Donny!"

"Hi, Tizzy. I need to talk to Angela."

Tizzy shook her head. "She's not here. Plus I think she's really mad at you. Did you do something bad?"

"Something *dumb*," Donny clarified. "Where did she go?"

"There was a council meeting and she didn't want to go but she had to go 'cause it was important but it was the last thing she felt like doing and she went."

Donny looked at the white dome perched on those low hills across the river. "Okay, thanks!"

Nanny's ridiculous wig emerged from the window, followed by Nanny's scowling face. She looked at Donny, bared her teeth, and growled.

"Gotta go," Donny said.

"See you later!" Tizzy cried.

"Hope so," Donny called back. He wasn't so sure he would ever be welcomed back.

When he got back to the street, the chariot was gone, and Zig-Zag with it. Arglbrgl moped on the curb, staring at the street, his head in his hands. Donny thought about asking the imp to come but decided to leave him to mourn in peace. He jogged down the road, heading for the bridge that would take him over the river and to the Council Dome.

Along the way, he slowed to give his lungs a break. He stopped, his chest heaving, his hands on his hips. Ahead of him, the clouds parted for a moment, and he caught a fleeting glimpse of the ceiling.

"What was that?" he muttered to himself. The image was fixed in his head. He closed his eyes and studied the memory, trying to make sense of it.

Up there, thousands of feet above, he thought he'd seen a fine white-hot line running across the width of one of the great stalactites. It wasn't part of the cloud—it was on the rock itself. He rubbed his eyes, opened them again, and stared at the spot, hoping for another, better look. But the clouds had rolled back in. He wouldn't see it again soon.

Something else emerged from the cloud for a moment. It was little more than a speck from that distance, but Donny was sure he'd seen that shape before. It looked like a shreek, one of the nasty flying imps that Angela hated. The thing quickly wheeled and hid itself in the cloud again, heading back toward the same stalactite.

Donny looked at the tip of that enormous dagger of rock pointing down from the cloud like the tip of a spear. Then he looked down to see what was directly underneath.

It was the Council Dome.

Things connected inside Donny's brain. A handful of clues, oddities, and incidents. Taken separately, none of them made sense. But when he considered them all together, it added up to something terrible, and he couldn't imagine it meaning anything else.

He might still be wrong—epically, idiotically wrong. And he was in enough trouble with Angela already. Their relationship was in ruins, and the thought of angering her further was enough to make him waver and doubt. He stared up again, but everything was hidden by the clouds of fire.

"What if I'm right," he said aloud, and when he said it, he pictured it happening. The image sent electricity through his veins. He ignored the pain in his lungs and started to run again.

The bridge was ahead. The dome was maybe a half-mile beyond it. He raced onto the bridge, which arched over the river high enough to allow barges to pass below. With his eyes raised up to the clouds that covered the stalactite, he barely saw the man who stood in the middle of the bridge, gazing the other way. But the fellow heard Donny's footsteps and turned to see who was coming. With a look of surprise, and then dark delight, he spread his arms wide.

Donny almost stumbled into the embrace. Then he staggered backward and held up his hands to ward the man away.

The Jolly Butcher giggled. "Angela's pet! Where are you rushing off to without your master?"

CHAPTER 30

Donny looked to the right and left of Butch, but the madman had positioned himself in the middle of the bridge. It was just wide enough for a chariot to cross, with precious little room on either side.

"Let me go by, please," Donny asked. "It's important."

"Go right ahead," Butch said. He raised his arms a little wider.

Donny shook with fear and anger. "Seriously. Step aside."

Butch didn't move. "Can't you stay and chat instead? Come, enjoy the view with me. I'm sure we'd have lots to talk about." The mouth was grinning, but his brow was lowered cruelly, shading the butcher's eyes.

Donny was ready to scream. It would cost him a half an hour to run to the next bridge up or downstream, and he felt sure time was running out. He eyed the spaces beside Butch one last time. Maybe if he feinted in one direction and darted in the other. But he was already tired. And who knew how quick Butch was?

There wasn't really any choice. He took a few backward steps and crouched a little, ready to sprint. But then he saw something to his left that gave him another idea. He turned and ran back down the bridge the way he'd come.

"Where are you going?" cried Butch. "I thought there was something important on the other side!" Donny heard the butcher's boots stomp down the bridge in pursuit.

"Oh no!" shouted Butch. He had guessed what Donny had in mind. "You can't be serious!"

A barge came down the river, full of souls. It looked the same as all the others, gaunt ferrymen at the front and the back, and souls packed in the middle. Donny raced along the bank, and he leaped toward the middle of the barge.

He knew it was ludicrous, but he shouted, "Excuse me!" as he was in the air. He came down with his feet on the deck but slammed into two of the dead. Ordinary people would have toppled over, but these were souls in the thrall of the ferrymen. They kept their feet planted on the deck while their upper bodies toppled over, nearly sideways, defying the laws of physics. Then they straightened up again, and Donny clutched their arms to keep himself upright.

"Sorry!" Donny told them breathlessly. The men he'd

jumped into were Asian. All of the dead on this barge were. When they saw him, they shouted at him in their native tongue. Donny didn't understand the words, but he sensed the fear and confusion in their cries.

He looked back and saw Butch on the shore, doubled over with his hands around his waist, hardly able to talk through his laughter. "Ha! Ha-ha! Nobody's ever tried that before! And they call *me* a madman!"

Donny gritted his teeth and started to push his way across. The dead were packed tight and rooted to the deck like trees, but he could grab their arms or shoulders and part them, stepping high to get past their legs.

He wondered if what he was doing would anger the ferrymen. The answer came in a terrible hissing sound. When he looked to the front, he saw one of those cloaked figures moving his way. When he looked to the back, he saw the other ferryman doing the same.

There was no need for those two to shove their way through the crowd. The souls before them stepped right or left to clear a path at the ferrymen's silent bidding. Donny was halfway across the barge, and he fought harder, shoving and shouldering the dead aside. He raised his voice, though he knew it meant nothing. "Coming through! Excuse me! Pardon me!"

Butch taunted him from the shore. "The ferrymen will get you! I wonder what they'll *dooooo*!"

Only a dozen souls stood between Donny and the side

of the barge. He fought madly, squeezing between their torsos. From the corner of his eye he saw the dead to his right step aside, and a ferryman appeared in the gap and reached for him. Donny slithered through another pair of souls and felt bony fingers brush his back, almost getting a grip. "Let me go!" he shouted. "I need to get to the shore! I'm with Angela Obscura!" He slid his arms between the last pair ahead and pushed them right and left. The side of the deck was right in front of him, and the other bank just beyond. He stepped onto the low rail and jumped.

A hand closed on his collar and yanked him back. He spun around, coming face-to-face with a ferryman. Inside the shadow of the cloak, there was a ghastly head. He looked away instantly, because it would have paralyzed him with fear if he'd gazed any longer. There was only the briefest impression of an ancient visage, hairless and infinitely wrinkled. Milky eyes quivered inside glistening red sockets. The lips had shriveled away to bare, broken gray teeth. The ferryman's other hand came up, pale and long-fingered, and clamped around Donny's neck.

Donny tried to speak, but the words were choked off. His eyes bugged. He raised his hand, trying to tell the ferryman to stop and listen. The grip loosened, and Donny saw those ghastly eyes focused on the palm of his hand, where Angela had imprinted her symbol.

The ferryman stared for a moment. Then he spoke with a slow, chilling voice. *"Don't. Do. That. Again."* He hurled

Donny backward, out of the boat and onto the far shore.

Donny landed on his heels and tumbled onto his back. His head hit the ground next, and he fully expected to crack his skull on stone, but the springy black moss growing there cushioned his fall. He rolled one more time, his legs flying over his head, and came to rest on his stomach.

"Thank you!" he shouted, giddy with relief, but he only got another hiss from the ferrymen in reply. Butch gaped on the other side of the river. He was no longer amused. Donny fought the impulse to taunt him back. Butch was dangerous enough without further provocation.

Donny turned and ran, grateful for the distance he'd put between himself and the butcher. He wondered why Butch was on the bridge to begin with. Butch had seemed surprised to see him, because his attention was focused elsewhere. He was looking toward the council dome.

The highest point of the bridge. *That would be a good place to watch something happen, wouldn't it?* Donny thought.

His lungs burned again, but even so, he ran faster.

CHAPTER 31

He made it to the dome at last, with so much pain in his lungs that he stopped at the bottom of the stairs, unable for a moment to take another step. His breath came out in a ragged wheeze, and he felt the metallic taste of blood in the back of his throat.

Chariots were lined up at the bottom of the hill, the runner imps at rest beside them. Up ahead, in the arches between the columns that supported the dome, massive guard imps stood, armed with brutal weapons. Donny's approach had caught their attention, and they turned their enormous heads to watch him.

A sound came from above as something struck the top of the dome. It bounced along the rounded roof until it pinged off and skipped down the steps a few yards to his right. Donny furrowed his brow as he stared at the object. It was a fragment of rock. He looked straight up just in time to see the clouds part again for a moment.

Before, he had glimpsed a line of white-hot light. Now it looked like a wiry circle of fire that almost surrounded the stalactite, directly above.

Go! Donny screamed to himself. He climbed the steps with his hands as well as his feet, too exhausted to run. One of the arches was unoccupied, but Donny didn't head for that one. He went to where Echo stood.

"Echo!" he said, barely able to gasp out the words. "It's me, Donny!"

Echo leaned forward. "Donny?"

"Get Angela! I have to warn her!"

"Warn?"

Donny gathered his strength, took a deep breath, and shouted as loud as he was able. "Angela! Everybody! Get out of there!"

The council members had been talking inside, but the chatter fell silent. Every guard stared. Echo looked uncertain, but still he unshouldered his weapon and held it sideways across his body to block the opening. "Angela," Echo boomed, much louder than Donny could manage.

It felt like broken glass was stuck inside his throat, but Donny shouted again. "Get out of there! You'll all be killed!"

Something in a dark red robe appeared over Echo's shoulder. Donny looked up, ready to tell Angela more, but the being who looked down on him was not what he expected. It was a demonic face covered in purple-red scales with fierce eyes, elfish ears, and pointed fins sweeping back across the skull like a tiara. It was both terrifying and beautiful, the way a tiger or cobra could be. And at the same time, there was something strangely familiar in those features.

Out of that reptilian mouth came Angela's furious voice. "Donny, have you lost your mind?"

At any other time he would have been too astounded to respond, but there was no time to be dumbstruck. He pointed straight up. "The roof is coming down on you!"

She squinted at him. "Try making sense."

"The clouds are hiding it!" Donny panted out the words. "They weren't released by accident. It's covering up what the shreeks are doing! And the fire that eats through rock was stolen, right? This is why—they're cutting through the rock up there! And that's why Sooth was killed!"

Her scaly head rocked back. "Sooth is dead?"

"Yes, they killed him because he knew what was coming! His riddle wasn't a riddle—it was a prediction! *After the light comes the fall!*"

Angela turned back and looked at the council members inside the dome. "Havoc isn't here," she muttered to herself.

"Well, now you know why." Donny jabbed his finger straight up again. "Angela, just *look*!"

"Excuse me, Echo," Angela said as she squeezed past the massive imp. She gave Donny a doubtful glance, then craned her neck to peer at the clouds.

"Keep looking, please," Donny begged. Drops of perspiration swarmed his face. Torturous, agonizing seconds passed. And then Angela didn't need to see anything, because a sound rumbled down from above. It was unmistakably ominous: a thunderous crack as something colossal broke. The entire stalactite began to descend. It looked like slow motion at first, but only because of the size of the object, and its distance above.

Angela sprang back to the dome. "Everybody, run! You'll be crushed!" She shoved Echo as she passed, and the huge imp tumbled down the steps, nearly taking Donny with him.

Donny glanced up again to see the dagger of stone, as big as an ocean liner, accelerating toward them. "Angela, get out of there!" he screamed. She had vanished into the building. He heard her shouting and saw archdemons and guards running. He took a step toward the dome, but realized it was death to wait another moment before turning. Even his momentary pause might have sealed his own fate. The atmosphere seemed to change as pressure built from above. He turned to run, and then Angela was beside him. She swept him up with an arm around his waist. They covered three steps in one of her strides as a monstrous shadow fell across the dome, and the loudest sound Donny had ever heard assaulted his ears.

It was an explosion and an earthquake all at once. The ground splintered, and rocks flew like popcorn. The stone below was suddenly a trampoline, and Angela and Donny were hurled into the air. Donny landed on his shoulder and rolled, knocked from Angela's arms. As he tumbled, he saw that the point of the stalactite had utterly demolished the dome and its steps. Chunks rained down and slammed into the ground all around them.

Donny rolled to a stop and looked back again. Not far away, one of the other guard imps raised an elbow helplessly as a house-size rock fell on him—he was gone in an instant under tons of stone. Something massive still loomed, and Donny saw what was left of the stalactite, at least half of it, waver in the air and start to tip.

In their direction.

This time Angela threw him across her shoulder, bent at the waist. Donny was able to lift his head and watch the race between her and the broken column of stone that was about to crush them like ants under a boot. She didn't run straight from the falling rock—they could never have made it that way. She angled right, shockingly fast, as Donny flopped like a rag doll. The stone hit the ground so close, he felt like he could have touched it. The sheer mass of it blocked everything else from sight.

The impact sent them flying again, but Angela was

ready for it this time. She landed at a crazed angle but somehow stayed on her feet long enough to run three, four, five more long strides before she lost her balance. They spilled across the ground. The remainder of the stalactite disintegrated. Chunks rumbled past them, and one might have crushed Donny in its path if Angela hadn't grabbed his ankle and hauled him aside.

The sounds of stone cracking and rolling seemed to last another full minute. The noise rebounded off the walls of the cavern. Donny rolled onto his back and sat up, staring at the mountainous pile of rubble they had barely escaped. The air was choked with dust, and he coughed some more. His arms were covered with bloody scrapes.

He saw Angela beside him, scrambling to her feet. "Echo!" she shouted, her hands cupped around her mouth. "Echo, where are you!"

"Echo," boomed the reply. A beastly shape hobbled out of the dust. Angela embraced the imp, barely getting her scaly arms halfway around. Then she turned to Donny. Her eyes were red-rimmed, her lizard lips pressed tightly together. She put her hands on his shoulders. "How did you know?"

"I . . . I just guessed. I had a feeling," Donny said. It was hard to look at her this way. He gritted his teeth and averted his eyes.

"Oh yeah. Sorry," Angela said. She reached into a deep

pocket of the robe and pulled out her bracelet. As soon as she clasped it around her wrist, the skin above the wrist began to change. The lizard scales smoothed and turned to the color of flesh. But the hand itself remained the same below the bracelet. Donny remembered the single glove she always wore.

As the change swept over her, Angela lost inches in height. The robe loosened around her body. Donny looked at her face in time to see the transformation sweep up her neck. The features softened, the sharp points and fins retracted into her skin, and suddenly it was the Angela he knew again. But this time the hair that sprouted and spilled past her shoulders was so blond, it was almost white. That was another mystery solved, he realized, remembering how her hair had already changed from black to auburn.

"So, that was the other me," she said with a shrug. "Too scary?"

"I didn't expect it, that's all."

"Those of us who can change take our demon form during council," she said. She exhaled heavily. "And speaking of the council, I need to make sure everyone got out."

"Angela," Donny said as she turned to head toward the wreckage. She looked at him. "Why wasn't Havoc in there with the rest of you?" he asked.

Her jaw slid from side to side. "I guess we'll ask when we see him."

Donny pointed back at the river. "Butch was standing

on the top of the bridge. I think he was there to watch."

Her nostrils flared. "If Havoc did this, he was trying to wipe out the whole council. I think he failed, for the most part. But I need to know. Echo, take Donny home and keep him safe." She turned and hopped nimbly up the piles of stone.

"I want to help," Donny called after her.

"Nope!" she shouted back.

"Safe," thundered Echo from a mouth the size of a garbage can. He took Donny by the arm and led him away.

CHAPTER 32

Hours passed. Donny sat in the big room by the front door of Angela's home. He read Dr. Seuss books to Tizzy to keep them both distracted until she fell asleep beside him on the sofa.

Once she was dozing, an awful vision played over and over inside his head. He kept thinking about that poor guard imp crushed under the stone. Who else didn't survive the disaster? If he'd gotten there a little sooner, he could have saved them all.

Finally the front door opened, and Angela walked in, exhausted and grim. Tizzy woke in an instant. She ran to Angela and hugged her.

"I'm fine," Angela said. She picked Tizzy up, and Tizzy wrapped her legs around Angela's waist, gripping her like a koala.

"Your new hair is nice," Tizzy said into Angela's shoulder.

"Thank you, sweetness." Angela plopped onto the sofa, and Tizzy curled up on her lap. "Where's Nanny?"

"Echo carried her away because she tried to bite Donny," Tizzy said.

"*Whoops.* Last thing Nanny heard, I was pretty mad at you," Angela told Donny.

"That's okay," Donny said. "But how did it go?" He wasn't sure he really wanted the answer.

Angela patted his knee with a fist. "The first thing I should tell you, Cricket, is that the council is very grateful. You saved most of them."

Donny bit his bottom lip. "Most?"

She answered quietly. "Most. We lost three council members and four guards."

Donny winced, and his head sagged back. "I'm sorry. I wish I'd been faster."

"Don't say that. What you did was amazing. Really."

He closed his eyes. "Were those your friends?"

"Sort of. *Friends* isn't the right word. We argue a lot on the council. One of them I liked very much, though."

The words pierced Donny's heart. "I'm so sorry. I wish . . ." His mouth twisted, and he couldn't talk anymore.

Angela clutched his knee. "Stop that. I won't allow it. We owe you a lot, Donny. If it wasn't for you, Havoc would be the only council member left. He'd have the pit back in flames by morning, and invite the Merciless up for milk and brownies."

Donny sniffed to keep his nose from running. "What will happen to Havoc?"

"I hate Havoc," said Tizzy.

"Me too, dollface," Angela said. She looked at Donny. "That remains to be seen, Cricket. He turned up a little while after you left, acting perfectly shocked and grief-stricken. It was a good show; I'll give him credit for that. I was ready to lock him up on the spot, but there was a disagreement among the rest of the council about whether we could assume he was truly guilty. They want to have an inquiry."

"You should ask him why Butch was on the bridge," Donny said.

Angela laughed. "Maybe you can ask him. The inquiry begins tomorrow, and you're going to testify."

Donny gaped. "I'm going to *what?*"

"It's weird how your hearing comes and goes. You have to testify. You're the only one who saw it coming. I don't know if they'll believe you, since they don't put much stock in what mortals have to say. But you have to try."

CHAPTER 33

Angela drove the chariot over the tall bridge where Donny had encountered Butch. Ahead was the enormous heap of rubble where the council dome once stood. Her crimson robe waved like a pennant behind them. Arglbrgl leaned over the side of the chariot, drool spooling off his flapping tongue.

"Why do they want to meet there?" Donny asked. "Nothing's left."

"This is an inquiry into what happened," she replied, "and the evidence will be all around us. Now, don't be nervous. They'll call you up, ask some questions, and then dismiss you. Nobody will hurt you, although someone might try to intimidate you."

Great, thought Donny. "Who are they?"

"On the council? Infernal beings, of course. Archdemons

from the eldest families. Some of them can look human, like me, but we'll all be in demon form when we meet. That's traditional for council. You want names? The head of council is Formido. He's the one with a head that looks like a nautilus shell. I'm on the council, as is Havoc—Havoc Arcanus, if you want the whole name. Umbrosus, Afflictio, and Tristitia are dead, somewhere under all that rock. That leaves Gravis, Caligo, Fumo, Morsa, Torto, and Devoro. Oh yeah, and Oblivium. I always forget about Oblivium."

There was another chariot ahead of them, and others arrived from different directions, carrying more red-robed figures and their guards. They rode as far as they could go, until the heaps of shattered stone blocked the road. The council members who had already arrived climbed the new mountain of rubble and headed for a spot where a tall, imposing figure waited, perched on a stone. Even from this distance, Donny saw the monstrous whorl of his skull. It had to be Formido, leader of the council.

They stepped down from their chariot. Angela tugged off the glove she always wore, revealing the reptilian scales beneath. The pointed fingernails looked like they could punch a hole in a can. She touched the gold bracelet on her wrist but then paused to look at Donny. "You ready for this?"

"Sure, no problem," Donny told her, and then he held his breath and clenched his hands.

She winked and pulled the band off. The transformation began in an instant. Row by row, the diamond-shaped scales swept up her arm, until the effect was hidden by the sleeve of the robe. Her torso stretched. She grew taller before his eyes. A look of pain or pleasure—it was hard to tell which—came across her face, and she arched her neck as the scales swarmed up like thousands of falling dominoes. Sounds came from her body, like bones creaking and soda fizzing. Her chin and cheekbones sharpened. Her brow jutted. Her ears stretched and grew points. Spiked fins rose from her scalp, running over the top and back of her skull. She reached up and gathered her newly blond hair in one hand, just in time for every strand to release from her scalp. She held out her arm and let the locks fall to the ground. It was as easy as shedding a wig.

The eyes were still her eyes, though they blazed a little brighter, a flickering candlelight in the center. Donny finally let out a breath when she looked at him. "This doesn't bother you?" she asked. She gestured to her face with her pointy fingers.

The first time he saw it, her demon form was a shock. This time he was ready. It was still terrifying but at the same time transfixing. "It's still you," he said. "You look good either way," he added.

She punched him softly on the shoulder, careful to curl her fingers and keep those wicked nails from raking his flesh. "Flattery. Always a good strategy." She looked up at the mound of broken rock. "I'll join the others now. We'll summon you when it's your turn. Wait here until then. Arglbrgl, keep an eye on Donny. If Butch shows up and gives you trouble, give a shout. You understand?"

"GRRRGRRGL."

"Wait," Donny said. "Is Havoc up there?"

She nodded. "Right, you wouldn't recognize him in this form. See Formido, sitting higher than everyone else? That's Havoc, closer to him." Donny saw who Angela meant—a slender figure with four horns on his face: two at the top, jutting back, and two at the jaw, jutting dangerously forward. He looked away as Havoc gazed in their direction.

Angela ruffled Donny's hair. "Don't mind him. See you soon." She headed up to join the others. Like a mountain goat, she hopped from boulder to boulder and finally took a seat far from Havoc Arcanus. Donny found his own rock to sit on. Arglbrgl spent the time circling him, sniffing the air and peering in every direction, now and then puffing himself up for no apparent reason.

Before long, the rest of the surviving council members arrived and climbed to where the others sat with their robes spread wide, crimson splashes across the dull gray stones.

Donny watched as the meeting began. Now that they were convened in the open instead of under the dome, he could marvel at their strange appearances. Their skins were silky, gnarled, beaded, or plated. Sails, spines, horns, plates, and spikes jutted from foreheads, temples, and jaws, and one had what looked like a pair of beetle mandibles that grew from his chin like a beard. They were beautiful but grotesque, and fascinating to behold, so the time passed quickly until he saw Angela stand. She pointed directly at him, and waved for him to join them.

CHAPTER 34

Donny clambered awkwardly up the mess of stone. He had to use his hands and feet to climb, and occasionally gathered himself for a treacherous leap across a gap. All eyes of the council were on him as he approached, and he felt his heart thump and his nerves jangle.

It seemed like an hour passed before he stood by Angela's side. The faces that stared down were already intimidating, but a few of the archdemons seemed irritated by how long it had taken him to climb up, or perhaps by the mere presence of a mortal. Havoc's eyes were narrowed to slits, and his lip curled on one side of his mouth. Formido was more frightening up close—as burly as a gorilla, with scales almost as red as his crimson robes. Heat came off him in waves and distorted the air around him so he looked like a highway mirage.

"This is Donny Taylor of the mortal realm," Angela said to the others. "A witness to this terrible crime."

"Or accident," Formido thundered.

"There was no crime!" Havoc shouted. He sprang to his feet and flung his arms wide. "And no accident, either. Can't you see what this was? A sign from below! It is the will of Lucifer himself. His return is upon us! This is our last chance to redeem ourselves and restore the Pit of Fire!"

"Get a grip, you fraudulent buffoon," said Angela.

Formido raised a thick clawed hand. "Hold your tongue, Obscura. And you as well, Arcanus. This isn't the place for your bickering." Donny's head sank between his shoulders as Formido turned his way. Like Angela, like all of the archdemons, he had that flicker of candle flame in the middle of each eye. "You. Mortal boy. Tell us what you know."

Donny looked at Angela, who smiled and nodded. He had to clear his throat twice and swallow before he eked out his first words. "I . . . I just got a bad feeling." Once he started, it was easier. He told them how he'd suspected the truth behind Sooth's final riddle, and the other clues: the theft of the fire, the return of the shreeks who might have carried the fire up to the stalactite, and the release of the clouds that would hide it all from sight. He talked about his glimpse of the burning rock, his race to warn Angela, and how the Jolly Butcher had stood on the bridge with a perfect view of the disaster.

When he finished, the council members exchanged glances and leaned toward one another to whisper. "Is that everything you have to say?" Formido asked.

"Yes, sir," Donny replied.

"Mortals have such vivid imaginations," Havoc said. It was easy to spot his allies among the group, because they chuckled at his remark.

"Most of us would be dead if it weren't for his 'imagination,'" Angela retorted. "Everyone except you, of course, Havoc. You were conveniently late for the meeting. Even your friends on the council must be pondering that coincidence."

"Fortune favoring the true believer," Havoc shot back. "Where you see conspiracy, I recognize omens."

"Be silent, both of you," Formido growled. He looked at Donny and pointed back in the direction he'd come. "We are done with you for now, mortal. Be gone."

Donny was tempted to say, *You're welcome*, but Formido and the others were simply too intimidating. Instead he said, "Yes, sir," and headed back down the pile of rocks.

When Donny reached the place where Arglbrgl and the chariot were waiting, he found Zig-Zag there as well.

"How did you fare?" Zig asked.

"Okay, I guess," Donny said. He heard voices rise in anger, and glanced back up at the mountain of rubble. "Angela and Havoc really hate each other, don't they?"

"GRGRBRGRGL."

"They hold opposite beliefs, and so they clash," said Zag. "But, remember, Havoc is only doing what he believes is right, and there are many who agree."

"What *does* Havoc believe?" Donny asked.

"Nonsense is what he believes," said Zig. "Ancient superstition."

Zag pinched the bridge of his nose. "Zig, would you kindly let me speak to the boy without interruption? Just this once? You owe me this. Remember, I dozed while you showed him those abominable Caverns of Woe."

Zig puffed air from his cheeks. "Very well."

Zag put a hand on Donny's shoulder. "You know about the being who once ruled this underworld, do you not?"

"You mean Lucifer," Donny said.

"Yes. That is the one. The founder. To Havoc and the other believers, our purpose was defined by him long ago. By extinguishing the pit, we defied the founder's will."

"I understand that. But Lucifer is gone," Donny said. "Angela says he may even be dead."

"The founder vanished a century ago—that much is true. But if you ask me, he is too powerful to die. The Merciless believe he merely sleeps, or bides his time, and will return one day. A hundred years is nothing to a being so old. What if he is testing us to see if we would stay true in his absence? When he returns, the believers say, and he sees what we have done, the vengeance he will wreak on the blasphemers will far exceed the torture inflicted on the dead.

"To Havoc, *that* is the truth. To him, the reformers have lost faith and turned their backs on the founder. Havoc wants to save himself from Lucifer's wrath, but he also means to save the rest of us too. That is why he will go to any lengths to see the pit restored and the dead cast back into the flames."

Zig sniffed and shook his head. "Donny, do you see why I call this superstitious nonsense? This is not faith. It's blind adherence to an outdated belief. Havoc and his ilk would have us frozen in time, unable to change, denied the chance to make the underworld a better place. Who can honestly believe that the Pit of Fire, with its mindless suffering and torment, is a better and wiser punishment than the Caverns of Woe? And what does it say about us that we would revel in that torture?"

"But the pit is the reason we exist," said Zag.

"*We* are the reason we exist!" snapped Zig. "We were given minds so we could always seek a better way!"

"Zag, are you a believer?" asked Donny. "Do you agree with Havoc?"

Zag frowned and looked up at the council members arranged on the broken stones, still debating. "I do. In my heart I think the pit should be restored. But I also believe in the rule of law. The council still votes that the caverns shall be used instead of the pit, and I will abide by that

ruling, even while I hope it someday may be overturned."
He looked at Zig. "And yet I have to wonder," Zag said.
"What is to become of me, a believer bound to one who
does not believe? When judgment comes, how can one be
punished and not the other?"

CHAPTER 35

Angela returned to her home hours after Donny had gotten back, announcing her arrival with a violent slam of the front door. She was back in human form, this time with red hair fiery enough to match her temper.

Donny was playing Chutes and Ladders with Tizzy, secretly cheating on her behalf to keep the game close. Before he could ask Angela how it had gone, she spoke. "Bunch of bozos."

"What happened?"

"Nothing. And nothing will." She sank into the chair beside the table where they played. "Without more compelling evidence, I doubt they'll do anything about Havoc. Looks like he'll get away with it."

"Is the inquiry over?" Donny asked.

"Hardly," Angela said. She folded her arms and twisted

her mouth. "But the rest will happen without me."

Donny furrowed his brow. "How come?"

"Formido says I'm too biased. Of course, I might have given that impression when I punched Havoc in the face."

Tizzy had been concentrating on the game, but her head popped up. "You punched him in the face?"

Angela leaned down and held Tizzy's chin between her thumb and forefinger. "Yes, I did, and I'm a terrible role model. People mustn't go punching people, young lady. Unless one person is me and the other is Havoc."

Donny thumped his fist on the arm of the chair. "You really can't take part in the inquiry?"

"Nope," she said. "Formido asked me to stay out. I'm thinking I should take a little break from Sulfur."

"Oh," Donny said. He slumped in his seat.

"Get out of Dodge for a while. Clear my head."

"Right," he said, slumping a little more.

"I know just what we should do," Angela said.

The word *we* improved Donny's posture. "What's that?"

"Well, those on the council who aren't complete morons are very grateful to you for saving their lives. They'd like to see you rewarded. Even I want to see you rewarded, despite your boneheaded stunt at my apartment. And I think I know how to do it."

Donny looked at her, unable to imagine what she had in mind.

"There *was* something you wanted me to do for you," she hinted, with a little smile.

"There was?"

She backhanded his shoulder. "You *forgot*? It seemed pretty important at the time!"

He shook his head and raised his palms.

"Silly Cricket. I'm going to scare your father straight, just like you asked. Go pack some stuff; we might be gone for a couple days."

CHAPTER 36

They arrived at the same Midtown basement room in New York, but the jigsaw-puzzle man wasn't so startled this time.

"Look at you: you've got it half put together again," Angela told him. The man grinned back uncomfortably.

Out on the street, Angela made a call. Donny listened to her side of the conversation, not sure who she was speaking to or why.

"Hello. It's me. . . . Yes, of course I know what time it is. Sorry, were you in your jammies? Yes, I agree. That was unfortunate. . . . Right . . . Uh-huh . . . Are you done complaining? Your message said you wanted to meet. . . . By the lions maybe? Swell. It won't take long. . . . Half an hour okay? Sounds good. Thank you, darling."

She hung up and tucked the phone into her bag. "I'm sure

you're wondering," she said to Donny. "That was a Foo."

"A Foo?"

"F-O-O. Friend of Obscura. One of the people who helps me out with topside stuff. He doesn't like to say much on the phone, so we always choose a place to meet. It makes me feel like a spy. I adore it. Now follow me."

"Where are we going?"

"Didn't you hear me? By the lions."

"I thought you couldn't go near zoos."

"Wrong lions. We're going to the library."

"Oooh," Donny said. He understood exactly. "Right."

A pair of marble lions rested on pedestals on either side of the broad steps in front of the New York Public Library. Donny and Angela sat on the steps and waited for her friend to appear. Angela reclined with her elbows on the step above and gazed over her shoulder at the porticoes at the front of the library.

Donny cleared his throat and asked a question that was on his mind. "Hey, Angela?"

"Yes, dear?"

He paused, hoping he wouldn't offend her. "Which one is the real you? This one or the other one?"

She arched one of her expressive eyebrows. "You mean my demon form? They're both me. And if you want to be my friend, you have to appreciate me in every way. At my best and my beast."

Angela's attention was diverted by a man walking toward them down Fifth Avenue. His hair was mostly white, and he looked about sixty years old. He appeared to have dressed quickly, wearing wrinkled slacks, a sweater, and loafers with no socks, but he still looked like the sort of man who played a high-powered lawyer on TV. He had a messenger bag slung over his shoulder. They stood to greet him.

"Good evening, Miss Obscura," he said.

"Howard," she replied. He was tall, and he had to duck his head for her to kiss his cheek.

Howard looked at Donny. "This must be the young man who caused all the fuss the other night."

Angela put her arm around Donny and gave him a playful hug. "That's the little rascal right here! But all is forgiven."

"Hmmm," Howard said. He didn't sound like he agreed. "Well, it happened, and that's that. Obviously, you won't be going back to that apartment. But it's fine; the tracks are covered. Any investigation into who owns it will hit a dead end. Also, I've got a friend in the police department, and he'll let me know if there's anything we have to worry about. But it doesn't look like your pretty face will end up on wanted posters."

"Silver lining," Angela replied.

"We got lucky, honestly," Howard said. "The world is changing quickly, Angela. It's harder to keep secrets.

Cameras are everywhere. If you don't want to be revealed, you have to be more careful."

"You betcha."

Howard took a phone from the messenger bag. "New phone. Sounds like you need at least one."

Angela looked sideways at Donny, who rolled his eyes. "We might," she said, taking the phone.

Howard noticed their exchange of glances and shook his head. "Anyway, we'll wait six months and then set up a new apartment in another part of town. Would the Upper West Side be satisfactory?"

Angela tipped her head and put a finger beside her chin. "On the park?"

Howard sighed. "Why not? It's only money."

"That's the spirit," Angela said, pumping her fist. "Well, splendid to see you, Howard."

"Hold on. One more thing," Howard said. He glanced at Donny again. "Your friend here. Donald Taylor. Yes, young man, don't look so surprised. I know who you are, thanks to the police reports. And I did some homework on you." He turned to Angela. "This boy is a missing person, Miss Obscura. He has a father who is desperate to find him."

Angela's face reddened. She pulled Donny closer. "Howard. Trust me, you don't know the whole story. Donny's with me now." Donny sucked in a deep breath when he heard those words.

"Is that right?" Howard said. He looked Donny in the eyes.

Donny nodded. "Yes, sir. I can't go home."

Howard glanced from Angela to Donny and back again. "That's your business, I suppose. But if you want to avoid trouble, Miss Obscura, stay out of New York for a good long while. And under no circumstances should you two go to Brooklyn."

Angela grinned and clapped Donny on the shoulder. "Come on, Howard. You think we're crazy?"

CHAPTER 37

Donny stared at the tall narrow Brooklyn brownstone where he had lived. "So," said Angela. "That's the homestead, huh? Nice place."

"Yeah," said Donny. They were on the other side of the street, hidden in the shadows under a small tree. Donny looked up and down the block, as nervous as a bird. If he was ever recognized, it would happen here. Fortunately, it was one o'clock in the morning, and the neighborhood was empty. Still, he flipped up the hood of his sweatshirt to conceal his face better.

"You look a tad nervous," Angela told him.

"Because I am," he replied. "Howard was right. I'm a missing kid, and this was my street. I don't want anyone to see me. And the police might be looking."

"Well, at least my hair is different. Maybe we should've put a fake mustache on you."

"I'm twelve years old; I wouldn't have a mustache. Sometimes I think you don't understand people."

She waved her hand. "Fiddlesticks."

The street was quiet, but his father was awake. Donny wasn't surprised to see the light on at the second-floor window. His father was often up until two a.m. and had never needed much sleep.

Angela looked the building up and down. "What do you suppose is the best way in?"

"I don't know—maybe through the front door?" Donny said. He took his house key out of his pocket and held it up for her.

"You're taking all the challenge out of it." She grabbed the key.

Donny looked at her black dress, full of lace and fringe. It was a few sizes too big for her, and he realized why. She had room to transform. "So you're going to show him . . . the other way that you look?"

"You said you wanted to scare him," she replied with a grin. "Didn't you?"

"Yes," Donny said. He pressed his hands together and tried to squeeze the tremors out of them. "Scare him really good. Make him be a better person. You can do that, right?"

"I can try," she said. "I have to admit, I had misgivings, but now I think this'll be all kinds of fun."

"Listen, you have to be careful. I think he has a gun in there. Actually, I know he does." Donny thought back to that awful night, the conversation he was never meant to hear, and the sight of his father on the stairs, gun in hand.

"Pshaw," Angela said. She waved the thought away. "Look at me. I'm adorable. No way he shoots me when he first sees me. And after that, he'll be too freaked out to breathe, never mind pull a trigger." She pointed at the curtained window. "So he's up there now?"

Donny nodded. "Yeah. Unless he hears you coming."

"Oh, he will," she said. "Watch the downstairs window. I'll put on a show. See you soon." She slipped off her shoes and started to cross the street barefoot.

"Wait," Donny said. She looked back. Donny took a deep breath. "Can you ask him something for me?"

She angled her head. "Now you want me to take a survey?"

"No. Just . . . just ask him what happened to my mother."

"What happened to your *mother*?" she said. "Wait, do you think he—"

Donny shook his head. "I don't know. I can't believe he would do that. But . . . she disappeared, you know. So, maybe you could ask him."

"Cricket. I want to help you out here, but you're really adding to the degree of difficulty."

"I know. You don't have to. But if you can—"

"We'll see," she said, and turned and trotted across the street.

Donny watched, barely able to breathe, as she ran up the steps to the front door. She put the key into the lock and opened the door, with no effort to be quiet. Donny heard her voice from across the street. "Hello? Benny Taylor? Are you here?"

"What the heck are you doing?" Donny muttered. He saw a new light come on, the one at the top of the steps inside the house. Angela's shape was silhouetted in the doorway. Donny's heart leaped as he heard his father's voice from inside, faintly. "Who are you? How'd you get in here? Don't move!"

Angela put her hands up, shoulder high. "Relax, Benny. We need to talk." She stepped inside despite the warning, and closed the door behind her.

Donny pressed his knuckles into his mouth, fully expecting to hear a gunshot ring out. Seconds passed, but they felt like eons. He stepped forward, out of the shadows, and fought the urge to cross the street. But he wanted to hear. He needed to see.

A muffled shout came from inside the house. Donny took another step forward. Then the curtain across the living room windows was torn away and flung aside. He saw the two of them inside in the dimly lit room. Angela was in her scaly demonic form, terrible and fierce, radiating menace and heat. The black dress looked absurd on her

246

monstrous body. She had a hand around his father's throat, while both his hands were wrapped around her wrist in a futile attempt to break her grip. His eyes looked ready to explode, and his mouth was frozen in a soundless scream. He kicked at her and thrashed but could not get away. She pulled him closer and turned his face toward the window.

Donny took a step back, afraid to be seen, but his father showed no signs of noticing him. Still, he grabbed his hood on both sides and pulled it even closer around his face.

His father squeezed his eyes shut. He looked like he expected to have his throat torn open, but Angela had only turned his head so she could talk into his ear. He answered her, his eyes closed and his mouth contorted with fear. It went back and forth that way, and then something she said made his father's eyes spring open. He mouthed the word *no!* and summoned the courage to look at her. He shook his head and said more, looking almost angry. Angela tossed her head back. She laughed and rattled her tongue. Then she cradled his head in both hands and drew him within an inch of her face, nose to nose. She spoke again, smiling under a fierce brow. When she stopped, Donny's father nodded—whether on his own, or because her hands forced him to nod, Donny wasn't sure.

It wasn't over yet. Angela had one trick left. Donny sensed it, even from outside the building, and he clasped his hands atop his head, heartsick for his father.

In the room where he and his father used to play video games and watch movies, Angela unleashed a beam of fear with all her furious energy. She took her hands off Donny's father, but he was paralyzed on the spot, unable to move until his legs went liquid and he thumped to his knees. His body trembled, and his face contorted until he looked like a frightened chimpanzee, all clenched teeth and manic eyes.

Angela pointed first at him, and then straight down at a place below the floor. She spoke one more time. When she was done, Benny Taylor's eyes rolled up in their sockets, and he toppled over sideways, dropping behind the windowsill.

Angela stared at where he had fallen. Then she looked out the window at Donny and gave him two hearty thumbs-ups. She reached into the purse still slung over her shoulder, took out the gold band, and slipped it over her wrist. Instantly, she began to change. She shrunk to her usual size, the scales turning to flesh, the claws on her hand softening into nails. This time when the change was done, her hair had come back a dark wavy brown and far longer than before, tumbling nearly to her waist.

She stepped out of sight and opened the front door, pulling her glove onto the hand that never changed.

Donny stood, rooted to the spot. "Is he still alive?" he asked quietly.

"Oh, sure," she said brightly. "He just passed out. And

he might need to change his pants when he wakes up. But I think it went pretty well, don't you? Come on, suddenly I'm craving a cappuccino."

"I don't know if we can get one around here this time of night."

"We're not getting it around here."

They went to Italy.

CHAPTER 38

Donny could only shake his head at how quickly it had happened. They traveled by fire from New York to Sulfur, and then from Sulfur to Florence. Before long they basked in the morning sun at a sidewalk café in one of the world's most beautiful cities.

"I have to admit, scaring your father half to death was way more entertaining than I expected," Angela said.

A woman came to serve them. She must have heard Angela speaking, because she smiled and addressed them in English, but with a wonderful Italian accent. "Welcome. What can I get for you?"

"I'd adore a cappuccino," Angela said. "You have gelato?"

"Yes, we do, signorina."

"Pistachio for me. How about you, Donny?"

Donny's head still reeled from the sudden journey to

the other side of the world and from watching his father terrified into unconsciousness. Food was the last thing he wanted to think about. "Sure," he said anyway. "Pistachio."

"This is my brother," Angela told the server. "He's fatally ill, so please treat him kindly and give him a really big scoop."

The server's smile crumpled. "You poor boy, I am so sorry."

"No, don't be," Donny said. He glared at Angela. "I'm not fatally ill. I'm perfectly healthy."

"He's in denial," Angela said, shaking her head. "Typical in these cases. He hasn't come to terms with his fatal illness yet."

"There is no fatal illness. I'm not even her brother."

"Calm yourself, Cricket. You know the doctor said you shouldn't get overly excited."

Donny huffed and looked at the server. "You know who's dead? My doctor, that's who's dead. He told me that himself." The server took a little step back.

"Oh, bring us the gelato already," Angela said. She waved the server away.

"Why do you have to do that?" Donny asked quietly.

"Just feeling mischievous, that's all," she said. Her newly brown hair was so abundant that it spilled over her shoulders and across her eyes. She brought a length of it up for inspection. "Wow, that's a lot of hair."

Donny shook his head and slumped in his seat. "You

know that what happened back in Brooklyn was painful for me, right?"

She laced her fingers together and leaned forward, grinning. "You're welcome."

"Right. Thank you. I asked you to do that to my dad, so definitely, thanks a lot. I guess I shouldn't have watched."

"Mmm-hmmm," Angela said. She took her phone from her bag and looked at it while Donny sat back, still numb. The cappuccino and gelatos came, and the server retreated the moment she'd set them down. Donny sat quietly and dissected his gelato with a spoon.

Angela put the phone away and took a sip of her steaming drink. "Oh, I almost forgot," she said over the rim. "I found out about your mother."

Donny shot up straight in his seat. *"What?"*

"I said—"

"I heard what you said! How could you not have told me already?"

"You were busy being ungrateful." She took another sip, then set the cup gently onto the saucer while Donny waited and nearly burst out of his skin.

"Well?" he finally said, trying not to shout. He had a white-knuckled grip on the table's edge.

"It went like this," she said. She leaned forward and waggled her shoulders. "I'm giving your dad the full boat, just scaring the absolute snot out of him. And in the middle of it, I say, 'What happened to your *wife*, Benny Taylor?'

His mouth is flapping open and shut, but he's not making much in the way of noise, so I throttled down a little. And he finally gets some words out, and he says, 'I d-d-didn't hurt her! Sh-sh-she just left; she wanted to leave me!' And I laughed at him, and I said, 'Leave without her baby boy? What kind of mother does that?' And he finally spits it out, he says, 'I told her I'd never let her take Donny. I'd find her no matter where she went, that nobody was taking my son away from me! And she was afraid, she knew I could be dangerous, so she ran away and left Donny behind, and I never saw her again, I swear!'" Angela grinned at Donny, but the smile faded when she saw the expression that had come over him.

Donny felt like a knife had scraped him empty on the inside. He shrank in his seat with his chin on his chest. His throat was a knot. His shoulders hitched.

Angela reached out and took his hands. "Oh, Cricket. I'm such an idiot sometimes." She stood up, circled the table, pulled a chair up next to him, and put her arm around his shoulders. She cradled his chin with her other hand and pushed his face into her wild mane of hair and kissed his ear. "I'm so sorry. Your mom was afraid, that's all. And your dad loved you, right? Couldn't stand to lose you? That's a plus, right? Even though he's kind of homicidal. Oh golly, I think I'm making it worse."

Donny's face crumpled completely, and he groaned

and sobbed. She let it go on for a while, and then whispered into his ear. "Tell me the truth. Can I be a little insensitive at times?"

And just like that it was funny. The tears didn't stop, but a weird bubbly laughter flowed with them, and Angela giggled with him as they rocked from side to side.

CHAPTER 39

The great cathedral of Florence, the Basilica di Santa Maria del Fiore, was just around the corner. Angela insisted on seeing it. It was a short walk from the café to the Piazza del Duomo, and then there it was: the soaring bell tower with its intricate bands of pink, green, and white marble, and the amazing dome. "The things you people dream up," Angela said as she gazed.

The piazza was full of tourists, but the wait for the cathedral wasn't bad. "Were you here before?" Angela asked when they'd walked inside.

"Yeah. My dad and I walked all the way up," Donny said. He pointed at the inner side of the dome.

"So you saw the frescoes up close?"

Donny nodded. The vast work of art, which filled the underside of the entire dome, was so high above the floor that it was hard to see from where he stood now. But he remembered it clearly from when he and his father had climbed that winding, claustrophobic staircase to get a better look. It was called *The Last Judgment*. Up high among heavenly clouds there were prophets, angels, and saints. At the bottom humans were cast into Hell, with grisly images full of torture and suffering at the hands of vicious demons.

"The infernal stuff is a little over the top," Angela said. "But they got the spirit right."

Donny stared at the highest point, his neck craned back. "You think there's still a chance for my dad?"

"To do what?"

He looked at the tourists milling about and dropped his voice. "To go to a better place."

Angela looked at him doubtfully. "Like what, Oregon?"

"You know what I mean," Donny said. He pointed at the peak of the dome. "Heaven. You call Sulfur the infernal realm. You call Earth the mortal realm. I mean the heavenly realm."

"If there is one," she said with a shrug.

Donny needed a moment to regroup from that remark. "What are you talking about? There must be a heavenly realm."

"'Must be?' What kind of logic is that?"

Donny stared with his mouth agape. He couldn't believe the turn the conversation had taken. "Well, it only makes sense. If there's a hell, then there's a heaven."

She chuckled. "If you say so."

"Don't you say so?"

"I've been to two places, Cricket. The mortal realm and the infernal realm. Never seen the third."

"That doesn't mean it isn't there!"

"Doesn't mean it *is*, either."

"But the souls that move on from Sulfur, after they've done their time——where else would they go?"

"Who knows? That's the best mystery of them all! Ever hear of reincarnation? Maybe that's the next stop. Step back in the queue and get born again in the mortal realm as a person, pig, or paramecium. Sulfur might be one big recycling center. Round and round we go," she said, twirling a finger.

"Wait, is that what really happens?"

"Don't be silly. I'm trying to tell you: I have no idea what happens. Heaven sounds fabulous. I'm all for it. But believe whatever you want."

Donny waved his hand, palm out. "Hold on, what about all the souls that never go to Sulfur? The people who don't get punished?"

"What about them?"

"They must go somewhere else."

"Not necessarily."

It was getting hard to keep his voice down. "Yes, necessarily!"

"Achieving goodness might be the end. Once you've done that, you might just . . . poof, dissipate." She waggled her fingers.

"What's the point of that?"

"Why does there have to be a point?"

"People should be rewarded for being good; they shouldn't just turn into nothing."

"You sound like a trained seal: you want a fish just for balancing a ball on your nose."

"What? No, I don't. The good souls have to go somewhere."

"Fine, they go somewhere."

"And that might be heaven."

"Or it might be a nudist camp. What the heck do we know? We don't get to see it."

"That doesn't mean it isn't there!"

"And now this conversation has lapped itself," Angela said. "Let's take a walk."

They strolled through the Piazza della Signoria, the breath-taking stone-paved square at the heart of Florence. It was remarkable to see the effect that Angela had in a busy place. Men constantly stole glances at her, and the bolder ones tried to catch her attention with smiles. It was more than her looks, Donny realized, or that spectacular blizzard of brunette hair she currently sported. It was the way she carried herself, and the air of mischief she projected.

An old man on a squeaky bike pedaled past, looked over his shoulder at Angela, and called out, *"Bella ragazza!"*

Angela waved with her fingers. "Thank you, random Italian man."

With its Renaissance palaces and towers and marble statues on display, all many centuries old, the piazza was a fresh air museum. The towering replica of the *David* stood outside the fortresslike Palazzo Vecchio. Not far from there, Perseus held the severed head of Medusa.

Donny heard someone gasp behind him. It was an elderly woman, staring at them. She had a bag of groceries, but it slipped from her grip, and she bit the back of her hand as it spilled onto the ground. The other hand rose up, shaking, and pointed at Angela. *"Mostro!"* she croaked. *"Infernale!"*

"Aw, shoot," Angela said. People around them stopped to look at the commotion. She grabbed Donny by the arm. "We gotta scram." They walked briskly across the piazza with Angela's boots clacking on the stone. A flock of pigeons ahead burst into panicked flight when she came near, which prompted a nasty scowl from Angela. Donny glanced behind them, but the woman wasn't following them. She simply stared and crossed herself over and over.

They turned a corner, and Angela finally stopped and leaned against a wall. She looked back toward the piazza, her bottom lip jutting.

"What just happened?" Donny asked. He noticed that

Angela was red-faced, and her eyes gleamed.

"Remember what I told you? Some people get freaked out when they get near me. That lady was one of the really sensitive ones. A big-time canary. But kind of a drama queen, don't you think?"

Donny nodded. Angela crossed her arms and puffed air from her cheeks. "Cricket, the only thing that'll improve my mood now is more food. At least for that, we're in the right country."

Angela leaned back from the table at the restaurant, wearing a sleepy smile. "Best meal ever," she said.

Donny twirled the last of his pasta around his fork. "Yeah."

"I don't want to go home yet," she said.

Donny had thought about something while they ate. He put his fork down and cleared his throat. "Can we go to another city, but back in the US?"

She stared back. "We *could*. But why? There's a place here where we can stay."

"I had an idea, that's all. Where can we go? Besides New York."

"You name it. Boston, Miami, New Orleans, Chicago, Denver, Los Angeles, San Francisco . . ."

"San Francisco is perfect," Donny said. He had spent a week there with his father the year before, and gotten to know the city pretty well.

Angela leaned forward with her chin on her hand. "You gonna tell me why?"

"As soon as I'm sure it's going to work," he said. It was his turn to have a secret.

CHAPTER 40

At four o'clock in the morning Angela rented a suite at a hotel in San Francisco, handing stacks of cash to the bedazzled clerk at the front desk.

"Sweet," Donny said when he walked into the suite. It occupied the whole end of the top floor, and it looked like a place the president might stay if he were in town. "It has a pool table, for crying out loud."

"I'm pooped," Angela said. "See you whenever. Don't be surprised if I sleep for a loooong time." She went into the biggest bedroom and shut the door.

Donny had a choice of two other bedrooms, and he chose the one with a view of the old prison island of Alcatraz, and off in the distance, the Golden Gate Bridge. He sat on the bed, tugged his shoes off, and flopped onto his back. He only meant to rest for a minute and then brush his teeth, but he was asleep before he knew what hit him, and didn't wake until nearly noon the next day.

He felt woozy and disoriented after the sudden shifts from time zone to time zone. Also, his mouth was pasty and disgusting. After he brushed, showered, and changed into the clothes he'd packed, he went into the living area of the suite. Angela's door was still closed. He found paper and pen and left a note on the counter for her, then took the elevator to the lobby. The doorman outside pointed him toward what he was looking for.

An hour later he got back to the suite and found Angela gorging on an enormous room service breakfast. She could pack away an astonishing volume of food.

"What are you up to, Cricket? You're so mysterious."

Donny bounced in place and rubbed his hands together. "Okay, they're going to do it. I can't believe how perfect our timing was. This is so cool."

Angela arched an eyebrow. "Who is going to do what?"

"You have to trust me," Donny said. "Um. But you didn't give me money this time. We need five hundred dollars."

"Five hundred! Not that I care about the money, but what exactly is it for?"

"Don't worry, you're going to like it! Stop eating, let's go already."

Donny pulled her along the sidewalk by the wrist, leading the way for the first time he could recall. "Almost there.

Just get the money ready." He tugged her past a white brick building, and turned into the narrow driveway that led to its back entrance and a small parking lot with an EMPLOYEES ONLY sign. A door swung open, and a young man dressed in green surgical scrubs peered out. "There you are," he said to Donny. "Whoa," he said when he spotted Angela.

"Give him the money," Donny told her. Angela looked quizzically at the young man, who grinned back with his eyebrows riding high. "Are you in need of medical care, Cricket?" she asked Donny.

Donny smiled and shook his head. "It's not a hospital. Not a *people* hospital anyway." Angela pulled out a wad of hundred-dollar bills and counted out five as the young man stared, wide-eyed. Donny grabbed the cash and stuffed it into the man's hand.

"I'm Billy," the man said. "Come on." Billy went into the building and held the door open for them to enter. As Angela went by, he looked her over from head to toe and back again. Angela gasped when she saw the decor in the hallway. The carpet was a pattern of animal paws. Posters lined the walls: the anatomies of cats, rabbits, and dogs.

Billy opened the door to a brightly lit room with a white-tiled floor and medical instruments all around. A woman standing at a high silver table looked back over her shoulder as Donny and Angela stepped inside. "You weren't kidding," the woman said. Billy showed her the five hundred-dollar bills, and she sighed. "This is so bizarre.

All right, then. Five minutes, though. And be gentle." She stepped to the side, and Angela's hand clamped over her mouth when she saw what was on the table.

A dog lay sleeping with its chest gently rising and falling. It was a golden retriever, plump with abundant fur. There was a plastic tube in its mouth, secured with elastics to its snout, and it stared blankly into space.

Angela's eyes were shining. Her jaw trembled. "What . . . Why is that thing in its mouth?"

The vet smiled. "Don't worry. That tube is how we get the anesthetic into her, so she sleeps through the procedure. It's normal for the eyes to be open too. But we keep them moist for her. So—you wanted to pet her?"

Angela's wobbly hand reached out. "Can I really . . . ?"

"That's why you're here, right?" Billy said.

"Really, truly?" Her mouth hung open. She slowly moved her hand toward the dog but then stopped with it suspended inches above.

"Go ahead," Donny urged.

Billy nodded toward Donny. "This little guy told me you're afraid of animals, but you thought you might be able to pet one this way?"

Angela looked sideways at Donny. "Something like that," she said. Her voice quaked. She closed her eyes and lowered her hand. When it touched the dog's side, she gasped again, long and deep. Tears rolled down like an avalanche, soaking her cheeks. "So *warm*. So *soft*." She ran her fingertips across the body. When she reached the cool, moist nose, she laughed, and a wide grin stayed plastered across her face. She leaned in and sniffed, and stared into one of the brown eyes. Then she turned to the vet. "Do you think I could pick her up?"

The woman looked at Billy. "I don't think——"

"Another thousand," Angela said. She pulled a stack of bills from her bag and thrust it at Billy. "Or whatever this is."

"As I was saying, I don't think that would do any harm," the woman said. "Just be really careful with the tubing." She helped ease the dog into Angela's arms. Angela cuddled the dog against her chest and whispered in her ears. Then she gently set her down on the table again.

"Wait a minute," Angela cried. "Is this animal sick? Is she going to die?"

"No, she's just getting fixed," said the vet.

Angela's nostrils flared. Donny held his breath. "You'd *better* fix it, whatever's wrong with her," she said.

The vet shot Billy a nervous look that seemed to say, *Why did you bring this lunatic in here?* "I mean, she's getting spayed," the vet said. "So she doesn't have puppies."

Angela's eyes boggled and her mouth opened wide. Before she could speak, Donny leaned close to her ear. "That's a *good* thing, Angela. There are too many unwanted puppies in the world."

"Exactly," said the vet.

Angela puffed air out her nose and seemed to relax.

She stroked the dog's fur over and over until the vet finally said, "We really have to start now. It's been more than five minutes."

Angela ran her hand from head to tail one more time, and then kissed the dog above one eye. She took a deep breath, stepped back, and pointed at the vet. "Fine. But you'd better be careful. And you too, mister. If I find out anything happened to this dog—"

"We should go," Donny said. He hooked Angela's elbow and turned her to the door.

"I'll be watching you," Angela threatened over her shoulder.

Donny noted, with a little satisfaction, that Billy averted his eyes instead of watching Angela leave. The young man's romantic aspirations had been put down, even if the dog would be all right.

Donny and Angela stepped outside into the parking lot. When the door was closed, she grabbed him by the shirt, lifted him off the ground, and pushed him against the wall with his toes barely touching the ground.

"What?" Donny cried.

"Why did you do that?" she said through her teeth. She looked like she'd lost her mind.

"Why? Because you did that thing for my father, and I wanted to thank you. And you were sad, after that lady in Florence called you those names."

"You made me lose *control*," Angela said. "Weeping in front of those idiots."

"I thought you'd be happy. You always wanted to pet—"

"Yes!" Angela shouted, and she yanked Donny off the wall and into a hug. "I've always wanted that. Always, more than anything. Thank you. Thank you." She sobbed, and nearly crushed him with her arms, and bawled and babbled into his ear. "Thankyou-thankyou-thankyou-thankyou-thankyou."

Donny didn't understand how she could be so strong and so soft at the same time.

CHAPTER 41

They returned to Sulfur the next day. Donny handed Grunyon a bag filled with dark bottles of vanilla extract, and Grunyon guzzled a pair on the spot. "You'll make yourself sick," Angela told him.

They returned to Pillar Obscura, and Tizzy squealed when she saw the Batman T-shirt Donny had bought her. He had a rubber ball for Arglbrgl and a pair of San Francisco Giants baseball hats for Zig-Zag. "Take him to a double header," Angela cracked when she saw them.

Two days passed uneventfully. Angela waited for news about the inquiry. She paced restlessly about the place until she couldn't take any more. "I'm going to find out what's happening," she said.

"Careful," Donny told her.

"Don't worry about me. I have touched a dog. I can die happy now."

Donny didn't see her for the rest of the day.

The next morning Donny sat with Tizzy in the diner, having breakfast. Echo and Arglbrgl had been instructed to keep them safe, in case Havoc tried anything else, and so the two imps waited for them outside. Echo tossed the rubber ball that Donny had brought, and Arglbrgl ran to fetch it over and over.

The bell on the door jingled, and Donny looked over to see Angela walk in. Her hair was as black as the first time Donny had met her, but the shortest yet. Tizzy ran over and hugged her.

"Hello, Sweetums," Angela said.

"Get you anything, honey?" called Cookie from behind the counter.

"A pot of tea will do," Angela replied. "Oh, and an omelet with everything you got."

Donny smiled at her when she sat in the booth. Tizzy piled in after and dug into her breakfast again.

"What happened with the inquiry?" asked Donny. "Do you think Havoc will be punished?"

"I have no idea. They made me leave almost as soon as I got there," Angela said.

"They wouldn't even let you watch?"

Her face reddened. "Well . . . I might have started

shouting at Havoc. That probably didn't help. After they booted me, I went topside for a while, just to calm down and check my messages." She took her phone out of her bag and held it up for Donny to see. "You'll find this interesting," she said. There was a message to Angela on the screen. "I got a note from Howard," she said. "It's about your father."

Donny gripped the edge of the table. "What does it say?"

"I asked him to see what your good old dad has been up to since the big scare," Angela said. "Howard writes, 'Regarding Benjamin Taylor, father of Donald Taylor: he is somewhat of a mystery man. There is no good indication of how he makes his living. A few days ago he was devoting all his time to the search for his missing son.' That's you, Cricket!"

"I know," Donny said.

Angela returned to the note. "'An abrupt change seems to have come over him. He is currently in the process of selling many of his worldly possessions, and has made inquiries about putting his extremely valuable brownstone up for sale. He has also begun making substantial donations to charitable organizations in the city, in addition to volunteering at neighborhood soup kitchens and homeless shelters. He is in fact a model of selfless and generous behavior. One might almost think that an intense experience has prompted Mr. Taylor to reevaluate his life. I would hope that you, Miss Obscura, were not involved in this, given our last conversation, and our many other talks about maintaining a low profile.'"

Angela smirked. "Oh, Howard, such a killjoy." She put the phone away. "I love how he calls you Donald. Maybe I should call you Donald. It's formal, but at the same time it calls to mind a certain pantless duck. No, you're a Donny. Or a Cricket. I'll just call you Donald if I'm mad at you."

Donny sank into his seat again, a smile spread wide on his face. He felt as warm as the teapot that Cookie set on the table in front of Angela. "Wow. You did it, Angela. You really did it."

She leaned back and clasped her hands behind her head. "Did you doubt me for a second?"

The real answer was yes. Donny thought his father might wake up after fainting and figure he'd just had a nightmare, or a hallucination. He never dreamed that the transformation could be so fast and complete. It seemed too much to hope for. "I just hope it lasts," he said.

"Oh, I think it will," she replied with a sly smile.

Something in her voice made Donny wonder. "Angela, what exactly did you say to him? It must have been good, whatever it was."

"Oh, nothing much," Angela said. She poured herself a steaming cup of tea.

"Really, I'd like to know," Donny said.

"Maybe you don't," she said, taking a sip. She didn't seem to mind that it was boiling hot.

"Actually, I do."

Tizzy stopped chewing her scrambled eggs and looked from Donny to Angela. Angela returned Donny's gaze.

"You know what?" she said. "I forgot exactly what I said."

"No, you didn't," Donny shot back.

"Yes, I did."

"Angela, I think you do remember, but you don't want to tell me."

She set the teacup down and put her hands up. "Whoa. Now you're calling me a liar? Easy with the accusations, Colonel Slanders."

"I didn't call you a liar. I just—"

"I can't remember, Donald. Deal with it."

CHAPTER 42

They left the diner and walked back toward Angela's pillar. Along the way they passed the broken column where Sooth used to squat. A gnarled, potbellied imp who Donny had never seen before emerged from the rubble and stood before them. "Obscura," he croaked. He was tiny, barely two feet tall. Blunt spikes jutted from his elbows.

Angela looked down at the creature. "Do I know you?"

"A clue," the imp said. He pointed at the rubble. "Who killed Sooth. A clue. In there."

Angela stiffened, and stared at the jumble of stone. "You know who killed Sooth?"

The gnarled imp shook his head and pointed again. "A clue. Who killed Sooth. In there."

Donny saw her jaw slide back and forth as she considered this news. "Arglbrgl," she finally said.

"ARGLBRGL?"

"Take Tizzy and Donny home. Make sure they're safe."

"I want to stay," Donny said.

Angela looked at him sideways.

"Please," Donny said.

"Fine," she replied. "Arglbrgl, take Tizzy home."

"GRBRGL."

"No!" shouted Tizzy. But Arglbrgl took her by the hand and led her away.

"Echo, you stay with me and Donny."

"Stay."

Angela nodded at the imp. "Okay. Show us."

The imp plunged into the rubble, using hands and feet to climb over the chunks of marble. They followed him over the piles, out of sight of the street. The imp was nimble, Angela moved like a panther, and Echo was surprisingly agile given his bulk. Donny tried to keep up but quickly fell behind.

"In there," the gnarled imp said. He waved for Angela to follow. "Who killed Sooth." They disappeared over another heap of stone. Donny tried to move faster but stumbled and fell, bruising his knee. He had to wait a minute for the pain to subside before he could limp on.

When he finally made it to the top of the heap, he looked over and saw the other three descending into a pit. It looked as if there had been a circular cellar down there. The ceiling had caved in, and there was no exit aside from the narrow stairs that curved along the edge. At the bottom of the pit Donny saw a small pile of belongings. There was a bloody cloth, a wooden box, and what looked like a butcher's knife.

Donny frowned. His heartbeat quickened, and it wasn't just from the exertion. Something felt wrong about all of this. The evidence at the bottom of the cellar seemed too obvious. It might as well have had a fishhook stuck through it.

He looked around them, to see if some enemy might be hidden among the stones. There were a thousand corners and crevices. The remains of the building were visible all around—some smashed furniture, and ceramic pipes that must have carried water through the structure at some point. One large pipe was directly across from him, and its jagged broken end stuck out over the edge of the pit.

He stared at the pipe. It looked like the barrel of a gun.

Angela was at the bottom of the pit, along with the gnarled imp and Echo. She suddenly seemed to realize that Donny wasn't with her, because her head snapped up. When she saw him, she relaxed and waved. "Keep a lookout," she said.

Donny didn't wave back. He said, "I don't like this."

Angela didn't seem to hear him. She picked the knife up with her gloved hand, between her thumb and a finger. Then she tapped the wooden box with a toe. "What's in there?" he heard her ask.

"A clue," said the imp, his head bobbing.

"Maybe you shouldn't open that," Donny called down, and then a noise caught his attention. It sounded like something heavy had shifted on the other side of the pit. He stared in that direction, trying to see what might have caused it. Then came a scraping sound.

"Something's happening up here," he called out.

The scraping sound came again, louder this time. Then came a dull roar, and suddenly the pipe was filled with orange light. A river of liquid flames gushed out and poured into the pit.

"Angela!" he screamed. He caught one final glimpse of her as the liquid flames filled the space between them. The last he saw was her looking up as the fire rained down.

Donny pressed his knuckles into his temples and screamed her name over and over. Everything the flames touched, they burned, even the stone around the edge of the cellar, which melted like wax. The fire finally burned through the pipe itself, and chunks of it rained into the cellar. Donny fell to his hands and knees as waves of heat flowed up from the depths, rippling his clothes and hair. He still tried to scream her name, but it had turned into a mangled, heartsick croak.

He didn't know if it was in his head or real, but he could have sworn he heard a burst of hysterical laughter from the other side of the pit, quickly suppressed.

Choking and sobbing, he peered down again. Whatever

form of fire this was—the flames of destruction or annihilation or some new distillation—it was hungry and destructive. The liquid flame had stopped flowing and was pooled at the bottom. Finally it burned away and revealed the terrible truth. Donny saw the huge, lifeless, blackened bulk of Echo, a creature born to dwell in fire, but not strong enough to withstand this terrible flame. He looked around the edges of the cellar, hoping to see a door, a tunnel, a hiding place, anything. But there was no escape from that pit. Of Angela and the gnarled imp, there was nothing left at all.

CHAPTER 43

Donny bent over, his forehead touching the ground, his hands clasped behind his head. He rocked back and forth.

Finally he lifted his head and stared out through the blur of his own tears. Someone was there. It was an imp he'd never seen before, broad and muscular, only a few strides away, ready to grab him.

Donny's hand closed on a brick-size chunk of marble. He got to his knees and hurled it at the imp with a hoarse but savage cry. It hit the imp in the chest, but that only caused the imp to stagger back for a moment before he advanced again. Donny turned to run, only to find another wicked-looking imp right behind him.

He darted to the left to dodge the second imp, but powerful hands seized him from behind and pulled him off the ground. Donny kicked behind him with his heels, striking the imp in the legs over and over again, to no effect. A hand clapped over Donny's mouth, and then liquid splashed over his face. The world dimmed, and his vision darkened at the edges, shrinking to a tiny circle and winking out.

CHAPTER 44

Donny woke slowly. He became aware of a rumbling sound, and a motion that rocked him from side to side. *I'm in a chariot,* he thought. He opened his eyes, but it was dark, and when he felt his own warm breath rebounding on his face, he knew he'd been wrapped inside a cloth, bundled tight.

He wriggled his hand near his face, pushed the rough fabric aside, and was able to look out. The stony ground went by in a blur. Ahead he saw the mound of rock Havoc called home, smoldering like a tiny volcano. When he twisted his neck around, he saw the imp driving the chariot. He recognized that brute. It was the thorn-faced imp who served as Havoc's bodyguard.

A face appeared above his, inches away. It was Butch, with his thick waxed mustache, murderous eyes, and grin of a madman. "Look who's up!" the Jolly Butcher cried.

The chariot rolled to a stop. Butch hopped down while the thorn-faced imp lifted Donny, still wrapped in cloth but with his head partly out.

"Help!" Donny screamed.

"Yes, help! Somebody help!" Butch shouted. He put a finger across Donny's lips, but pulled it back when Donny tried to bite it. "Might as well hush!" Butch told him. "Nobody comes around here but us."

He walked to the iron-banded door that guarded Havoc's lair and unlocked it, and then came back. The thorn-faced imp tossed Donny over Butch's shoulder. Donny shouted some more and looked for anyone who might help. The only other figures he glimpsed were two more nasty imps atop Havoc's volcanic mound, serving as guards and lookouts.

"I hope you like it in here," Butch said as they went inside. "You may never leave."

Donny went numb. He'd spent all the energy he had left on his cries for help. Butch pulled the door shut behind them and locked it again from the inside.

The place was a fortress, hacked from pockmarked volcanic rock. Butch carried him deep inside, past other rooms. One on the left looked like the dining hall of some Victorian mansion, with a long table, elegant chairs, and a candelabrum as a centerpiece. On the right there was something like a study, with old hand-lettered texts on a broad desk. Other doors were closed. Donny was carried past them all and into a vast hollow space in the center of the cone. There Butch dropped him to the ground and tugged hard at the cloth so that Donny tumbled roughly out onto the floor. Butch grabbed him by the armpits and pulled him to his feet, where Donny wobbled unsteadily, still dizzy from whatever potion had knocked him out.

Donny rolled his head left and right and looked at the nightmare he'd been trapped inside. It was like the belly of a volcano past its prime, and it was filled with objects that made it feel like a cross between a laboratory and a torture chamber.

There were niches carved from the walls and covered with bars. Only the mummified remains of infernal creatures, and maybe a human being or two, remained inside. Weapons of all sorts were mounted on the stone walls. The machinery scattered everywhere looked familiar somehow, and Donny remembered where he'd seen the like before: at the refinery. There were thick pipes embedded in the ground, connected to thinner horizontal pipes that ended in spigots. Smoke leaked from the pipes and from cracks in the floor. In the center of the chamber, a spout of flame danced from a deep, glowing crevice, big enough for a car to disappear inside. High overhead, Donny saw an opening in the cone. That space had been secured with a grid of iron bars.

Butch whistled merrily and shoved him in the chest

with two hands. Donny stumbled into a chair that struck him in the back of his knees, causing him to fall into the seat. There were iron cuffs on the arms of the chair, and Butch clapped them down over Donny's wrists. Then Butch patted Donny on the head and stepped aside.

Donny heard footsteps behind him. Havoc appeared in his human form, dressed like someone out of a Shakespearean play, wearing buckled shoes, black leggings, and a ruffled white shirt with billowing sleeves. He carried a stool that he then set down in front of Donny.

Havoc reached for Donny's hand and turned it palm up. With the hint of a smirk, he traced Angela's mark with a warm fingernail. "Property of Angela Obscura. Do you miss her already? Were you very fond of her?"

Donny didn't want to give him the satisfaction of answering the question. "What do you even want with me?" he asked quietly.

"Not much," Havoc said. "Just a chat before we say good-bye."

"You killed Angela," Donny said quietly. "And Echo. And that other imp—he helped you, and you killed him, too."

"Yes. That other imp—what was his name, Butch?"

"Marbo," said the Jolly Butcher. "What a fine job he did!"

Havoc nodded. "A worthy imp who believed in our cause. Marbo thought his job was to bring Angela to the pit and show her that evidence. He was not smart enough to lie, so it was better that he did not know what was going to happen."

Donny squeezed his eyes shut and tried not to picture that moment. "You're horrible."

"Sacred duty sometimes requires sacrifice," Havoc said. He crossed one leg over the other and clasped his hands on top of his knee. "Throughout all history, mortal and infernal, horrible things have been done in the pursuit of noble goals. What nation are you from, boy? Surely, your country has waged its share of battles and dropped its share of bombs. And why? For your *beliefs*.

"You call this act horrible because you were Angela's possession. You were under her spell, and so you embraced her point of view. But others who see more clearly disagree. To those who think like me, Hell must be returned to its righteous state, at any price."

"Not that. You shouldn't have done that," Donny said.

"Thousands died in the war between the Merciless and these reformers, on both sides. I lost my parents to that senseless conflict. The home where my ancestors dwelled for millennia was destroyed, along with too many other magnificent buildings. Compared to that, Angela's death is insignificant."

"No, it isn't," Donny whispered.

"Poor boy," Havoc said. He patted Donny's knee. "Don't think me a monster. I understand your feelings.

Angela was a charming and clever creature—I can't deny that. But she had to go. For the good of Sulfur. The trouble with Angela was that she was so obscenely persuasive. She could talk the council into anything. Putting out the Pit of Fire—such an abomination. We discarded thousands of years of tradition in the name of what? Some misguided mercy? Well, soon the council will meet again, without Angela's interference. And there will be a motion to return to the old ways. We will make peace with the Merciless, beyond the barricade. And then I know, in my heart, Lucifer will come back to us."

Donny tried to talk, but could barely move his lips. The words came out soft and jumbled.

"What was that?" Havoc said. He turned an ear to Donny's mouth. "What did you say?"

Donny took a breath, gathered his strength, and spoke louder. "You won't win. There are still more on Angela's side. In the council."

Havoc leaned back and grinned. "You really don't understand how these things work, do you? Politics and alliances? Angela held that coalition together with the force of her personality. I can name two council members who will change their minds about the pit tomorrow without Angela there to keep them convinced. I can assure you, it won't be long until the dead are back in flames. As it was always meant to be, forever and ever."

Donny raised his face and finally looked Havoc in the

eyes. "When they learn that Angela's gone, they'll know it was you."

Havoc leaned back and clasped his hands behind his head. "Will they? They might suspect, but there won't be any proof. It's important to cover one's tracks in these situations. To leave no one behind to tell their tales. You understand that, don't you?"

Donny knew exactly what Havoc meant, and it sent a chill up his spine. Havoc's smile flattened into a straight tight line. "I'm very upset with you, testifying before the council the way you did."

"It was true, though. You destroyed the dome."

Havoc put a hand beside his mouth and whispered like a stage actor. "Do you know what the trouble with secret plots is? You don't get to talk about them, even when they work, because nobody is supposed to know. But you and I can talk now, can't we? Because you're not going to tell anyone else. Will he Butch?"

"I don't see how!" Butch said, from somewhere behind Donny.

"I had helpers, obviously," Havoc said. "The shreeks who carried the fire to the ceiling. My spies in the refinery. Others who believe in the cause. The destruction of the dome was a fine plan. It was a grand gesture, a sign of destiny. If most of the council members were slain, there was a good chance that those who took their places would be of a better mind. When that failed, removing Angela from the picture seemed like the next best thing."

While Havoc was talking, Butch had begun pacing around the chamber, mumbling to himself. Now he appeared over Havoc's shoulder.

"Can I have him now?" Butch said.

"In a moment," Havoc replied over his shoulder. Then he turned to peer at Donny again. "I promised Butch he could have you. After all he's done for me recently, he deserves a reward." Donny shut his eyes and ground his teeth together. He heard Butch clap his hands and give a swinish squeal of glee.

Donny's head jerked as Havoc gripped him around the jaw and stared into his eyes. "Tell me something. Are you frightened, little mortal?" He waited for a response, but Donny gave him nothing.

"Hmm," Havoc said. He tugged up his leggings on one side, and Donny saw a battered band of gold around his ankle. It looked like Angela's bracelet, with the same sort of marking.

There was a clasp on the band. Havoc undid the clasp and set the band aside. Donny knew what would happen, but he still barely kept himself from screaming. Starting from the ankle, Havoc's skin transformed. Flesh became scales, layered like shingles. Havoc stood tall, holding his arms out. His shape altered beneath his clothes, and fabric ripped at the seams. Donny saw the transformation reach his hands, beyond the sleeves, deepening in color and turning to snakeskin. A sound like bones crunching came from his face and his jaw. A pair of horns sprouted on his temples, pointed back, and a second pair grew forth from his jaw.

"How about now?" he said to Donny. A three-pointed tongue stuck from his mouth and rattled in the air an inch from Donny's face. "Are you frightened now?"

CHAPTER 45

Havoc looked over his shoulder at the Jolly Butcher. "Butch, bring me the jar, will you? You know the jar I mean."

Butch giggled and skipped away on his errand.

Havoc waved a hand at the room around him. "This was once a refinery, until the flames thinned out," he said. "But I kept a small operation here, and produced special varieties for my own entertainment."

Butch returned with a jar made of black glass, stopped with cork and wax, and handed it to Havoc. Donny saw flames trapped inside the jar. They slithered and writhed like octopus tentacles. "Have you ever felt the truest fire, Donny? The Flames of Torment? Did Angela include that in your education?"

Donny stared at the jar and shook his head. He felt

prickly beads of sweat spring up along his hairline.

Havoc propped the jar on one hand and used the other to peel the wax away from the edge of the cork. "It's a miracle, this stuff. Able to produce the most exquisite agony without the slightest damage. The dead could bathe in it forever, and the pain would never lessen." He pulled the cork from the jar. Havoc put his fingers near the edge, and the flames seemed to sense the movement. They struck like cobras and curled around his hand. "Of course, it has little effect on infernal folk. To me it's as pleasant as a warm bath. No, it's the mortals who suffer from the Flames of Torment. The dead ones . . . and also the living."

Donny pressed his lips together to keep them from trembling.

"Before Butch puts an end to you, I think you should experience the flames," Havoc said. "You can't appreciate them until you do! Are you ready?"

Donny shook his head. "No."

Havoc brought the jar down to where Donny's hand was clamped on the arm of the chair. Donny made a fist, but Havoc uncurled it easily, and held the fingers out. He brought the jar toward Donny's fingers, and when they were mere inches away the flames snapped forward and latched on.

Donny's head rocked back. His legs jolted and kicked madly. It felt like a bolt of lightning had struck him in the hand, surged through his nervous system, and lit up his brain. He clamped his teeth together, trapping a scream inside his mouth, and rolled his head from side to side. Pain was the only thing that existed, the purest agony he'd ever known.

Havoc pulled the jar back, and the pain vanished instantly. Donny trembled, all his muscles turned to jelly, and moaned softly.

"Open your eyes and look at your hand," Havoc said. Donny shook his head. With his thumb and a finger, Havoc pried open one of Donny's eyelids. "Come on, mortal. Take a look. I know what you're thinking: You are sure the flesh has been burnt away. But behold! You are unscarred!"

Donny looked. It was true. His hand was almost a blur because it shook so hard, and he saw it through tears, but the flesh was undamaged. He stared, horrified, at the jar in Havoc's hands. The flames still groped for his fingers, hungry for flesh.

"See?" Havoc said. "I could do that to you for a year, and nothing would burn. Shall we try again?"

Donny turned his head away, unable to bear the thought of another second of that agony. How right Angela was, to put a stop to it. He rocked from side to side in the chair, trying to break away, but the clamps on his arms held firm.

A voice called from above. "GRGRBRGRRR!" Donny looked up. Arglbrgl was there, peering through the grate that covered the opening of the cone. His bristles were up. He spat with fury and tugged at the grate.

Havoc sniffed. "Isn't that Angela's imp? Butch, go tell the guards to dispose of him. And remind them to keep their eyes open!"

As Butch trotted away, his eerie high-pitched giggle rolled off the walls of the corridor.

"Hello there!" Havoc called up to Arglbrgl. "Would you like to come in? Wait right there—I'll send my friends to fetch you!"

"GRRBRRGRR!"

"Arglbrgl, don't!" Donny shouted. "Run!"

Odd sounds came from the hall where Butch had disappeared. First the groan of ancient hinges as Butch opened the door. And then a shout, abruptly silenced. Next came a series of thumps as an irregular object rolled out of the dark corridor and into the red light of the central chamber. It tumbled across the stone floor until it thumped against Donny's legs and rocked to a stop.

Donny sucked in a sharp breath when he saw what it was. The head of the Jolly Butcher stared up. Mist flooded from his neck. With a strenuous effort of his jaw, Butch managed to rotate his head enough to look Havoc in the eye.

"Er, Havoc?" said Butch.

Havoc didn't answer—he just glared down the hall from which the head had just been bowled.

"You'll never believe who I just saw," Butch's head said.

"What are you babbling about?" Havoc spoke to Butch, but his gaze was locked on that dim corridor.

Butch cackled so hard, his eyes squeezed shut. He sounded more unhinged than ever. "Oh! Of course! I should have thought of it sooner!"

Havoc didn't respond. He backed toward the wall behind him, still watching the corridor.

"Angela's guard, Echo—that imp with the giant mouth," Butch said through his laughter. "I just remembered what his old job was, in the pit!"

Havoc's lips pulled back and bared sharp teeth. Against the wall stood a long trident with three barbed points. He wrapped his free hand around it, and kept the jar of flames in the other.

"Echo used to swallow the dead whole then spit them out. So now I'm thinking, just before the fire hit Angela—"

"Shut up, you idiot," Havoc snarled.

Donny heard steps from that passageway, scraping across the stone. His heart thumped so fast, he thought it might burst. A shape appeared from the shadows and stepped awkwardly into the hall.

It was the rest of Butch, a body without the head, dressed in the bloody butcher's apron and striped shirt. The arms reached out and groped blindly at the air. Mist wafted from the top of the neck, just above his red bow tie. It gave him the look of a snuffed candle.

"Over here!" Butch called out, and the body dropped to its hands and knees and crawled toward the head.

Donny glared down at Butch's face. "*You* dropped the

fire on Angela," Donny said. "And you killed Sooth, too, didn't you?"

Butch snorted, suppressing another laugh, and winked at Donny. The body was almost there, reaching for its head. Donny clamped his teeth together, drew his leg back, and, with a furious grunt, kicked the head as hard as he could. The sound of Butch's laughter rose and fell as the head tumbled across the floor.

Donny hadn't aimed it, but the head rolled all the way to the deep, flame-spouting crevice in the center of the chamber. With its last revolution, it teetered on the edge, like a golf ball over the hole. Butch felt himself tipping over, and his eyes bulged, but he went on laughing as he dropped over the edge and into the flames. The laughter faded into nothing as he plummeted to depths unknown. The rest of his body crawled on hands and knees all the way to the crevice and followed the head down. The last Donny saw of Butch was his legs kicking as they slipped from sight.

A second figure stepped out of the corridor. Havoc gasped and dropped the jar. It shattered on the floor, and the fire spilled out.

"Hello, Cricket," Angela said. She was in her serpent form, terrifying and beautiful, dressed in leather armor with a silver breastplate. There was a sword in a scabbard by her side.

Donny tried to speak, but with his breath hitching, all he managed was "Hi."

"Havoc. You look surprised," Angela said.

Havoc took the trident in both hands. "I am."

"I finally got to see your place," Angela said, glancing around. "It's cozy." She put a hand on the hilt of her sword.

Donny saw something bright move near his feet, and his joy evaporated for a moment. The flames that spilled from the shattered jar had composed themselves into a liquid spidery shape. They crawled toward him and reached out hungrily. He lifted his feet off the ground and put his heels on the seat.

Angela drew her sword out of its scabbard. It was enveloped in white-hot flame, and it filled the room with flickering light.

Havoc sneered. "Didn't know you had one of those."

"Family heirloom," she said. "For special occasions."

Havoc tightened his grip on the trident. "Shall we?"

"Maybe we should," Angela said. She stepped closer. "Echo is dead because of you. You plotted to destroy the council. And you tried to kill me."

"I haven't finished trying," Havoc said.

Angela swept the sword through the air. It left a trail of flame in its wake. "You're such a card," she said. "You almost had the council convinced, you know. But here's the truth. There were no omens. There were no signs of Lucifer's return. There was just a murderous, misguided fanatic." She took a step forward and leveled the sword at Havoc.

His mouth bent into a sneer. "I did what had to be done." He thrust the trident forward, meaning to swat the sword aside, but Angela swirled the sword, evading the points, and leveled it once more.

"You did it, all right," she replied. "And that's why nobody would blame me for letting the fire out of you." She lowered the sword, stepped back, and relaxed. "But I'd rather see what the council wants with you, once they find out what you've done."

Havoc bent at the knees, ready to spring. "Perhaps they never will find out."

"You're going to hate the next part," Angela said. She called over her shoulder. "Come in, everyone."

Red-robed figures filed into the room and gathered behind Angela, staring furiously at Havoc. They were the surviving members of the council.

"Havoc Arcanus," rumbled Formido, looming above them all. "You and I believe in the same cause. But your methods cannot be abided."

"See, Havoc? Even your allies are disgusted," Angela said. "Now put your silly weapon down. You know I'm stronger. You can't hurt me."

Havoc's eyes bugged, and his mouth curled in a sneer. "I know how to hurt you," he said. He brought the trident over one shoulder and threw it like a spear, straight at Donny.

Donny threw himself back, but moved only inches as he struck the back of the chair. There was no way to avoid

297

the three-pointed weapon as it flew toward his chest. A white-hot light flashed before his eyes as he heard a harsh clang of metal on metal and felt a sharp pain.

Angela's flaming sword had swept down, catching the trident between two of its prongs. The longest point had pierced Donny's skin, but not terribly deep. The trident clattered to the ground.

Havoc turned and headed for the wall, where other weapons were mounted. But with shocking speed, the red-robed figures swarmed past Donny. They pounced on Havoc and lifted him off the ground. He was carried out of the chamber, held by his arms and legs as he thrashed and shouted terrible threats. Lucifer would return. The Merciless would seize control. The pit would be reignited. They would all be annihilated. Finally Havoc saw Angela and twisted himself around to shout at her. "And you, Obscura! You and your friends! You will suffer most of all!"

Angela gave him a mock salute. "Go smite yourself."

Once they were gone, Havoc's threats echoing into silence, Angela and Donny were left alone. She walked to where he sat. The flames were still crawling up the leg of the chair, reaching for Donny's foot. She peeled them off and tossed them into the crevice.

"You're hurt," she said. She looked at the red stain that surrounded the torn fabric on Donny's shirt.

"I don't think it's too bad."

"We'll take you to the doctor though." She put a warm hand on his cheek.

Donny trembled, this time from relief instead of terror. "Echo really saved you?"

She nodded. "My darling Echo. I barely knew what was happening. He just stuffed me into his mouth when the flames hit."

"I'm glad you're alive," Donny said.

"You should be. I'm your best friend, aren't I? Say that I am, or I'll leave you here to rot. Say it right now."

"You're my best friend."

"Swell. Now let's get these manacles off and go see Doctor Stupid."

CHAPTER 46

Angela was away for much of the next few days, dealing with further inquiries into Havoc's treachery. She came home each evening after visiting the mortal realm for takeout food, and told Donny what was happening: Havoc refused to reveal who had helped him plot the destruction of the council; more guards had been assigned to the barricade that kept the Merciless trapped inside the Depths; and discussions were ongoing about who would replace Havoc and those who had been slain on the council.

Donny was fine with the slow pace. He needed it to recover from his ordeal in Havoc's lair, and especially from his exposure to the Flames of Torment. Sometimes he woke up thrashing and screaming in his bed, his mind filled with a vivid, almost physical memory of the pain. During the day it was good to pass the time with Tizzy.

They played games, and he read her old Batman comics.

A week later he was woken by Angela in the middle of the night.

Donny blinked and dug grit from his eyes. "What's going on?"

"It's your dad," she said.

Donny sprang up, electrified. "My dad?"

"He's here."

"*Here?* What do you mean here? If he's here, that means—"

Angela nodded. "Sorry, Cricket. Get dressed and meet me downstairs."

Donny ran down the stairs a minute later, still pulling his shirt over his head. "How did you know?"

"Howard got a message to me."

Donny's brain felt numb, his thoughts muddled. "Then . . . what? Where is he now? In the caverns?"

She shook her head. "Not yet. We managed to find him and take him aside. Come on. I have a chariot waiting."

The chariot clattered through the dim Sulfur night, only a few wisps of the fiery clouds lighting their way. Donny stood beside Angela as they rode, and she kept an arm around his shoulder.

"What happened to him?" he asked.

"I don't know exactly. Howard didn't give me a lot of detail."

"Was it an accident? Was he sick?"

She looked at him, bit her bottom lip, and shook her head.

They rode another mile in silence.

"How am I doing?" she asked.

"What do you mean?"

"I'm trying to be sad on your behalf and comfort you. Is it working? Am I a good friend?"

Donny didn't think he was capable of a smile just then. But he was. "Yeah. You're doing swell."

From a half mile away, Donny recognized his father outside the mouth of the Caverns of Woe: tall, athletic, and like a movie star in his fine Italian suit. Zig-Zag was with him. Donny's father heard the chariot coming, and his face transformed when he saw Donny. He sprinted over to meet them as the chariot rolled to a stop, glancing for a moment at the remarkable long-legged runner who had pulled the vehicle.

"Donny," his father cried. He dropped to his knees and wrapped his arms around his son. "It's true—they do have you! Did they hurt you? I tried to be good. I tried to save you."

"Save *me*?" Donny said. He looked at Angela, who just shrugged back. "I don't need saving. Angela, what did you tell him? Dad, what did she tell you?"

His father glanced at Angela, and then his eyes returned to her for a longer look. He seemed confused at first, and then his jaw dropped and he sucked in a great breath of air. He lurched to his feet. "It's *her!*" he said.

"Nice to be remembered," Angela said.

"It's all right, Dad," Donny said.

"I wouldn't go that far," Angela sniped. Donny frowned at her, and then he reached out and took his father's cold, waxy hand.

Benny tried to push Donny behind him. "She's a demon, Donny. A monster."

"Yeah, I know," Donny said. He squirmed back in front. "And she's a major pain sometimes too. But, Dad, you have to tell me: What did she say when she went to our house?"

Benny looked at her, and back at Donny, blinking madly. "She . . . she said that you were here. In Hell. She said that they had you, and that you were burning, in the flames. She told me if I didn't change my ways . . . if I wasn't a good man . . . that you'd suffer until the end of time."

Donny looked at Angela, his head wagging. "Well, that was a lie."

Angela pinched a finger and thumb close together, almost touching, and mouthed the words, *Small one.*

"Why'd you do that?" Donny asked her.

"Hey, you asked me to make him go straight." She folded her arms. "That seemed like a surefire way get it done. I figured he might care more about what happens

303

to you than what happens to him. Isn't that what human parents do?"

Benny held Donny by the shoulders. His voice fell to a whisper. "What? Donny, what? I don't understand."

"I'm not in any danger, Dad. I wasn't in the flames. But . . . well, that's Angela over there. You saw what she is. I thought maybe she could scare you into being good."

Donny felt his father's arms tremble. "You sent her to me?"

Donny nodded. "I was right outside the house, Dad. I watched it happen. I wanted her to warn you, so you didn't end up here."

Benny let go of Donny. He looked from Angela to Donny and back again, trying to absorb what he'd been told. Finally he breathed deeply and lowered his head. "I see. I get it. Thank you for trying. I . . . I did my best, Donny. After she came, I was better. I was as good as I could be."

"I heard what you did, Dad. I know you tried."

Benny kneeled in front of Donny. "I did it for you. When I thought they were making you suffer . . . Donny, you know I care about you more than anything, right?"

Donny couldn't talk. His eyes were burning. He sniffed, mashed his lips together, and nodded.

Benny hugged him again, for a long while, and then he stood and looked at Angela.

"So, we didn't expect you so soon," she said. "What happened?"

Benny thought about that for a moment, and his eyes widened. He gritted his teeth and put a hand on the back of his head, probing. Then he looked closely at his palm and fingers but didn't seem to find anything. He shivered a little from a terrible memory. "You get into business with the wrong people, sometimes they don't want you to get out."

"Ah," Angela said, nodding. "Well, don't worry. Whoever punched your ticket is probably not too far behind you."

Benny sighed. "Now what happens?"

"The judgment. The punishment," she told him.

"Will it be bad?"

"Won't be a picnic."

Donny watched as his father tried to come to terms with his fate. Benny stood straight, took a deep breath, and tugged the bottom of his jacket. He looked at Donny and smiled weakly. "I tried to change at the end. I know it wasn't for long. But I was a different guy, no question about it. It's funny, you can actually do a lot of good in a small amount of time. Will that make any difference?"

"It might, actually," Angela said. "But . . ."

"Too little, too late?"

She twirled a finger at the fiery, cavernous world around them. "Apparently."

"Angela, wait," Donny said. "Can't my dad help out around here? You have the doctor, and the chef. They're not in the caverns."

"Firstly, we don't really have a need for a hit man," Angela said. Benny started to object, and then closed his mouth. "Secondly, both the doctor and the chef were in the caverns for years before we took them out. And remember, they only delay the inevitable by—"

"Hey," Benny said. "Donny. It's okay. Whatever's coming, I earned it. I chose that life. Now I'm going to pay for it."

Donny tugged at Angela's arm. "But . . . can I visit him?"

"Donny," Benny said. Donny knew that tone of voice. It was the one his father used when he was at his most serious. It usually preceded a lecture about paying attention at school or dressing neatly or doing his chores.

"Donny, this is it. I tried to make it right, but it was too late. I get it. You have to get it too. You learn from this, you hear me? I did so many things wrong in my life. I kept it a secret because I never wanted you to find out about it. That should have told me something right there, I guess. But I liked the money. I liked the thrills that came with it. All that was a mistake. Most of my life was a mistake. But I did at least one good thing: I brought you into this world, Donny. You're better than I am in every way. Who knows? Maybe that'll work in my favor." He looked at Angela. "A few years off my sentence, maybe?"

She shrugged. "It's like bowling. I don't know how they keep score."

Benny took Donny by the shoulders. "Be good, Donny. I know I don't even have to tell you that, but I felt like saying it anyway." He kissed Donny on the forehead and smiled at him one more time. Then he looked sideways at Angela. "What do I do now?"

Angela gestured toward the Caverns of Woe. "Walk inside. Keep walking until someone comes to you. Then it'll just . . . *happen*."

Benny gulped and squeezed the knot of his tie. "Uh. What'll happen?"

"You'll spend an awfully long time reflecting on your wrongs. That's about all I can tell you."

Benny nodded. He gave Angela a long appraising stare. "So, you're watching out for my son now?"

"We're watching out for each other," she replied.

"Not sure how I feel about that."

"Well, you're not exactly calling the shots these days, are you?"

Benny pointed at Donny but spoke to her. "You just take good care of my boy." He lowered his head for a moment, mumbled something to himself, and then looked at Donny one more time. Donny stepped toward him, but Benny raised a hand to stop him. He turned and walked into the cavern. The mist started to obscure him. Donny watched his father's silhouette slowing, holding his hands out to find his way as the mist thickened.

Benny looked to his right and stopped. Another shape

appeared, dim and thin, rising from the heavy mist that was pooled around his knees. It took him by the hand and led him deeper into the caverns, and then Donny's father passed from sight.

Angela and Donny stood for a while in silence. He reached for her hand.

"Angela?"

"Yes, dear?" she said, giving his hand a squeeze.

"Can we go home now?"

THINGS HAVEN'T COOLED DOWN FOR DONNY AND
ANGELA. READ AN EXCERPT FROM BOOK 2:

DOWN IN FLAMES

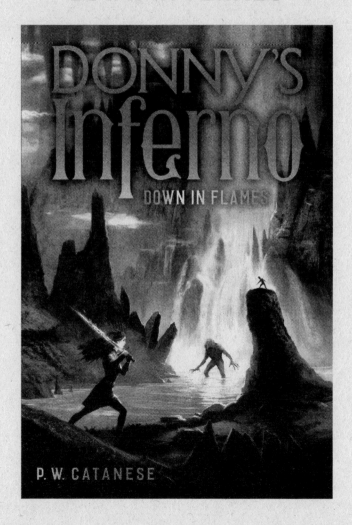

CHAPTER 1

What if you were hit by a train?" asked Donny. "Could you survive that?"

Angela Obscura, beast of the underworld, traveler to the mortal realm, member of the Infernal Council, and friend of Donny Taylor, popped another cheese curd into her mouth and chewed it while considering the question. "You mean," she said after a gulp, "hit and bounced off, or run over and scraped underneath?"

"Both," Donny said. "I mean, either."

"Bounced off, I'd probably be okay. Run over, not so much. I'm not completely impervious, you know. If an infernal being's wounds are bad enough, all the heat and steam leaks out. Then you're gone, good-bye."

Donny nodded and grabbed another curd. "But fire doesn't hurt you, right?"

"Don't talk with your mouth full," she scolded, one of

her own cheeks puffed with food. "And no, I thought that was obvious. I'm fireproof, right down to the hair."

"Oh yeah, that makes sense," Donny said. Angela's hair, which returned in a different length and color every time she switched from her monstrous to human forms, was currently long, auburn, and abundant with curls. She'd also been remade with a cinnamon sprinkle of freckles across the bridge of her nose.

Donny pointed with a curd. "What if you were electrocuted?"

"This one time, when electricity was kind of new, I didn't know about the no-appliances-near-the-bathtub thing, and I got a pretty good shock. It would have killed you, but I was fine."

"How about hit by lightning?"

"Happened once, when I climbed a tree for a better look at a storm. Apparently you're not supposed to do that, either. That hurt like crazy, and I'm pretty sure I saw my skeleton for a second."

"Wow." Donny thought for a while. "What if you fell a long way, like out of an airplane?"

She brushed her hands with a napkin and dropped it onto her empty plate. "Donny Taylor, are you trying to figure out how to kill me?"

He laughed. "No. It's just . . . It's just cool. I'm curious."

"No doubt you are," she said. "So, the verdict on cheese curds?"

"Pretty great," he said. They were sitting at a sidewalk table under a blue umbrella on a street in Milwaukee. Across the street and a block over, he could see where the Milwaukee River flowed toward Lake Michigan, barely a mile away. Back in Brooklyn or Manhattan, where he'd spent his first twelve years, the streets would have been bustling with crowds and crackling with the weird, grimy energy of that frantic metropolis. This town was sleepy in comparison and sparsely peopled, but perfectly pleasant, especially on a crisp fall day.

Speaking of pretty great, he thought to himself, looking at his friend across the table. A person might possibly think Angela Obscura was anywhere from fifteen to nineteen, but they would *certainly* think that she was beautiful in a way that was different from all the other beautiful people. The truth was that she was approximately one hundred and fifty years old, and wasn't human at all. Angela's left hand, currently clad in an elbow-length red glove, was always covered with reptilian scales. There was an ancient gold bracelet on that wrist, and if she were to take it off, the rest of her body would quickly transform.

Just a few months before, Angela had saved Donny from a fiery death. In return, he'd promised to assist her on her missions in the mortal world. That was the deal, anyway. Most of the time it felt like she just dragged him along because she wanted the company.

"Not a bad little town, eh?" she said. "It all smells like bratwurst and beer, don't ya know?"

Donny laughed. "Kind of."

"And, golly, look at all the sandy-haired, earnest Midwesterners. Bless their hearts." She put a fist to her mouth and burped. "Well, I guess we should go. Now that my craving for cheese curds has been vanquished." She pushed her chair back and stood up.

"We didn't pay for the food," Donny said.

She reached into her handbag, pulled out a hundred-dollar bill, and looked questioningly at Donny. "That'll cover it, right?"

"With, like, an eighty-dollar tip," Donny observed. But Angela was already on the move and five paces away. Donny anchored the bill to the table with a saltshaker, grabbed the empty backpack Angela had given him, and followed.

Before Donny could catch up, a car slowed beside her. It was filled with guys who looked like college students. The driver, a brawny blond quarterback type, put his elbow out the window and patted his horn so that it gave a little squeak. He grinned at Angela. "Hey, girl. You're pretty sweet, you know that?"

Angela gave him a sideways glance and rolled her eyes.

"C'mon—don't be that way," the driver said. "Why can't you be friendly? Hey! I'm talking to you!" He kept the car rolling at the same pace that Angela was walking. His friends inside the car laughed.

Donny kept a few paces back. Part of him was twitchy and nervous, but part of him wondered how this would play out. This guy had no idea what he was dealing with.

"Hey, how about a smile, girl? I bet you have a pretty smile."

Angela stopped. She pivoted on her feet, turning to face the car. The driver slowed to a stop and grinned at her. Inside the car, the friends nudged one another and stared.

Angela's mouth spread into a broad, toothy smile, but Donny recognized a fiery look in her eyes. *Uh-oh,* he thought. She stepped off the sidewalk, right next to the car. Before the driver could say another word, she put two hands on his side-view mirror, tugged, and snapped it off. There were wires inside, and she pulled it sharply back to break them free. Then she turned the mirror to herself, looked into it, and announced: "Look, I'm smiling now!"

The driver stared back, his mouth open. His friends burst into laughter, and the one behind the driver reached forward and slapped him on the shoulder.

Angela tossed the mirror through the window and onto the driver's lap. "Now you can use that to take a good look at yourself." She blew him a kiss and walked away.

Donny heard the clunk of the car being thrown into park. The driver's door swung open and the driver shot out, the broken mirror in one hand. "Hey!" he shouted.

Angela turned, and Donny took two steps to the side. He knew from the look on her face that she was about to hit the driver with a telepathic beam of sheer terror, and he didn't want to be anywhere in the line of fire. Even from where he stood, he felt the tiny hairs on his arms tingling. The driver opened his mouth again, almost certainly to bark something truly unpleasant, but instead of speaking, he moaned with fear as his eyes bugged from his face. Inside the car, his friends sensed it too. Donny heard their manic, high-pitched shrieks: "Get back in the car! Let's get out of here!"

The driver staggered backward, stumbling over the curb. The mirror slipped from his hand and clattered onto the pavement. He fumbled his way back into the car, tugging the door shut behind him. The tires squealed, spitting blue smoke, and the car accelerated away, driving straight through a red light. Cars that were crossing the intersection slammed on their brakes to avoid a collision. The driver's bad day got even worse, because a police car appeared from around the corner, firing up its siren and flashing its lights.

Angela rolled her shoulders and cracked her knuckles as Donny jogged up beside her. "You really need to be careful," he said. "I mean, that guy was a jerk, but he could have hurt someone just now."

She giggled. "What do you suppose he'll tell the officer?"

"That there's a crazy girl down the street with gorilla muscles," Donny said. "We shouldn't attract police attention, you know."

"Why not?"

"Because I'm still a missing kid. Remember?"

"Oh, ha-ha, yeah," Angela said. "Well, we only came for the curds. And something almost as good. Come on— it'll be dark soon. Time to get to the marina."

CHAPTER 2

Long after sunset, they waited in the shadows of the building beside the marina. The slips were filled with sailing ships, cabin cruisers, and other powerboats. The water was calm, protected inside a long stone seawall. Beyond that barrier, the vast waters of Lake Michigan glittered with fractured light under a crescent moon.

Nobody was in sight, though a few of the boats had lights on, as if the owners might be spending the night inside.

"Are you sure this is safe?" Donny asked.

"Courage, Cricket," she replied. She pointed to one of the biggest of the boats, an expensive-looking cabin cruiser. "That's the one." It was as big as a small house, nearly three stories high with a tower perched on top. A floodlight was trained on its stern. Donny read the name in curving letters above the waterline: BEAN COUNTER.

"*Bean Counter*," Angela said, and snorted. "He should've

just called it *Embezzler*. Come on—let's check it out." With a final look left and right, she walked casually out from the shadows and onto the dock.

"Hey," Donny whispered. "Security cameras? Witnesses? Hello?"

"Land's sakes, you worry too much. Just walk like you belong here. Who'd be suspicious of an adorable girl and her little brother?"

Donny frowned at that characterization as he sped up to her side. Something about her referring to him as her brother, even as a cover story, irked him in a way he couldn't quite define. "Nobody says 'land's sakes' anymore," he grumbled. His heartbeat accelerated as she hopped onto the boat. He jumped on after her and followed her to the open deck on the stern. She headed straight for the door that led inside.

"Not even locked," she said, swinging it open. "Thought for sure I'd have to rip it off the hinges."

Donny was going to mention that an unlocked door didn't seem like a good sign, but it was too late. She had already slipped inside. He followed her into the dark interior.

"Must be a light switch in here somewhere," she said. He heard her hand slide along the wall until she found the switch and flicked it up.

Donny was about to remark on how luxurious and roomy the boat was, until a more important detail became apparent. Someone had been here and made a mess of the place. Cushions had been pulled off the furniture and sliced open. Cabinet doors had been flung wide. Panels on the walls and floor had been torn out, exposing the spaces behind and below.

"Aw, for crying out loud," Angela said, putting her fists on her hips. "Well, he warned us about this."

Before Donny could ask who had warned them or what the warning was about, a narrow door opened and a man stepped out. It was bad enough that someone had caught them, but even worse, the man had a gun in his hand.

"Who are you?" he said, nearly growling the words. He didn't look like the violent type—he looked more like a businessman, with thinning close-cropped hair and glasses. He was dressed in a black turtleneck shirt and dark pants.

"Eww, were you in the bathroom?" Angela asked, wrinkling her nose. She edged sideways until she'd put herself between Donny and the man with the gun.

"What? Yes, but—never mind that!" the man snapped.

"You're Francis, aren't you?" Angela said. "Walter said you might get here first."

"Walter s-said . . ." the man sputtered, and then recovered. "What do you mean? Walter's dead! How do you know my name?"

Francis was using the gun to gesture, pointing it at Angela and Donny to emphasize his words. Angela put her hands over her face, and her knees began to tremble. "Please, mister, don't hurt us," she whined. "We're just a couple of kids. You're scaring me with that gun!" Donny didn't find the display convincing, but Francis lowered the gun for a moment, looking bewildered.

Angela must have been peeking between her fingers. Her arm was a blur as it shot out and snatched the gun. Francis stared at his empty hand as if a magic trick had been performed.

"So you didn't find it?" she said, holding the gun the way someone might hold a rotting banana.

Francis raised his hands halfway, unsure if he should be surrendering. "Find what? I wasn't looking for anything."

Angela shook her head with disdain as she looked at the trashed interior of the boat. Then she rushed at him, using the palm of her hand to shove him into the tiny bathroom. "Get back in there, Francis," she said with a final push that sent him staggering into the far wall. She tugged the door closed. "And flush it, you pig!"

She handed the gun to Donny. "Shoot him if he comes out," she said loudly.

Donny shook his head and whispered back angrily. "I'm not shooting anyone! I hate guns!" He laid the gun on the kitchen counter.

Angela jabbed her thumb at the bathroom door. "*He* doesn't know that!" From the other side of the door, they heard a flush, and Angela clapped a hand across her mouth to stifle a laugh. The laugh turned into a snort, and she kept chuckling as she opened the freezer door in the galley and pulled out what appeared to be a frozen fish wrapped in aluminum foil.

"Fish? That's what we came here for?" Donny asked.

Angela smirked and tore the foil open. Inside were stacks of hundred-dollar bills arranged in the shape of a fish. She reached into the freezer and pulled out five more just like it.

Donny nodded, finally understanding. This was how Angela got her endless supply of cash. A man named Walter, the owner of the boat, had died and, like the evil soul he was, ended up in the underworld, which was currently known to its denizens as Sulfur. The dead were encouraged to reveal any hidden money they'd stashed away—and Walter had hidden these bills here before he'd died.

Angela twirled her finger, gesturing for Donny to turn around. She shoved the bundles of foil-wrapped money into the empty backpack that Donny had worn all day. "You should have checked the freezer, Francis!" she shouted at the door. "The money you two stole was wrapped in foil, just like Walter said!"

"Are you *serious*?" came the muffled reply. "In the *freezer*? I looked everywhere! Wait, how did you know about the money? Who are you anyway?"

"I'm a hundred-and-fifty-year-old archdemon of the

underworld, and my little buddy is the runaway son of a hit man." She grinned at Donny, who shook his head grimly at her.

"Oh yeah? You think that's funny? Well, you know where you can go, miss!"

Angela guffawed. "Yeah, look me up when you get there."

On the way off the boat, she took the gun from Donny and tossed it into the lake.

"So this is where the money comes from, huh?" he said as they left the marina and walked along a footpath in the park nearby. "People hide it like this?"

"Sometimes it's in banks or safe-deposit boxes, and we have people who are good at retrieving it," she answered. "I don't usually go after the cash myself, but this one looked like fun. Plus, I had a craving for cheese curds."

"So that guy Francis, and Walter—they stole the money from some company?"

"Uh-huh. Embezzled it."

"Shouldn't we give the money back to the company instead of keeping it?"

She gave his shoulder a gentle push. "You're hilarious."

"That wasn't a joke."

"Chortle," she replied.

CHAPTER 3

They caught a cab a few blocks from the marina. A ten-minute drive brought them to a stately home built with cream-colored brick, in a well-to-do neighborhood only a few blocks from the lake. A grandmotherly woman answered the doorbell, opening the door a crack. She nodded when she saw Angela. "Leaving already?"

"Yes, but we had a splendid time," Angela replied.

The woman opened the door wide. "Can I make you some tea?"

"Aren't you a darling?" Angela said as they stepped inside. "But no, thanks, we should be getting back. Don't mind us—we know the way."

She and Donny went through a door in the main hallway that led down an old set of creaky stairs. In the basement was a tall fireplace, empty except for pipes running across the bottom. When Angela turned the knob of a timer that was set into the wall, fire burst forth from the pipes. Donny caught a whiff of propane.

Angela cupped her hands beside her mouth and whispered into the flames. A moment later a space appeared inside the wall of fire, covered by a thin sheet of ash. The dark space expanded until it was wide enough to step through. Angela poked her finger into the ash, and the sheet crumbled into tiny flakes. On the other side, Donny saw the familiar passage carved from stone, and the strange little demon named Porta who controlled the fire-portal on the other side.

They stepped through the hole in the fire, leaving the mortal realm and entering the infernal world of Sulfur.

CHAPTER 4

Donny used to feel like he was losing his mind when he stepped into the underworld. But lately he was start-ing to believe that a person could get used to almost anything. They left the fire-portal behind and walked down the curving tunnel. As usual there was a hint of rotten-egg smell in the air. Next was the ominous door guarded by a tall, cordial monster in a suit of armor. Then came the short walk through another passage that ended with the mind-blowing vista of a vast, cavernous world with mile-high ceilings propped up by titanic pillars.

Clouds made of luminous vapor billowed overhead, bathing everything in reddish-golden light. There were towns and cities at the feet of some of the pillars, with architecture ranging from crude to exquisite and ancient to modern, some in pristine condition and some in ruins from the great war that had happened decades before. The rest was a strange, twisted wilderness with vast stretches of undulating stone, fissures and craters, eerie formations of rock, and forests of dark mushrooms and ferns. A river slithered through the midst of it all, glittering under the burning clouds. On it, Donny saw one of the ferries, crowded with the souls of the newly arrived dead.

But the most significant feature amid all this strangeness, more vast than any earthly canyon, was the Pit of Fire. Once the great pit had been filled with torturous flame and the howling, suffering dead, but since the reform, it had been extinguished and now only steamed with lingering heat. These days the dead were ferried to the vast Caverns of Woe instead, where they spent years spellbound, trapped in dreams woven from their own misdeeds. That fate was hard to bear, but not as cruel as the flames, of course. And, unlike the flames, a soul that entered the Caverns of Woe could someday be released and allowed to move on. It might take decades or centuries or even millennia, but redemption was possible.

Donny stared at the bizarre world in all its strange grandeur. It was fearsome. It was unimaginable. It was terrible.

It was home.

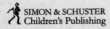

Well, what do we have here? Someone who likes to peek at the end of the book to see how things turn out? Or even worse, some bookstore browser who thinks it's perfectly acceptable to jump to the last page without the decency to make a purchase?

Obscura here. I never understood people like you. And I'm not at all happy to have caught you in the act. But I knew it was coming. Turn around. I'm right behind you.

Not really, obviously. Although wouldn't it be hilarious if I were? Criminy, is it so hard to read the pages in the order they were written? Shall we begin your life with the funeral?

For those of you reading this after digesting the story, the way it was intended—kudos. To the rest of you: I'll be waiting for *you* at the end, you fiends.

Seriously,

A. O.